The Lochmore Legacy

*One Scottish castle. Four breathtaking
romances through the ages.*

The bitter feud between the Lochmore and
the McCrieff clans is the stuff of legend. And
Lochmore Castle has been witness to it all.

The battles, the betrayals, the weddings,
the wild passions.

But with the arrival of a new owner to Lochmore,
the secrets buried deep in the castle are about to
be revealed through four romances, as we fall back
in time through the Victorian, Regency, Tudor and
Medieval eras...

Discover more in

His Convenient Highland Wedding
by Janice Preston

Unlaced by the Highland Duke
by Lara Temple

A Runaway Bride for the Highlander
by Elisabeth Hobbes

Secrets of a Highland Warrior
by Nicole Locke

Author Note

What can be said about a marriage of convenience except it's never convenient? This is true for Rory and Ailsa, as well. After all, they are from enemy clans, and every time they talk, they argue.

Then circumstances change, and marry they must. Then everything changes on their wedding night for they are now a combination of their clans, and they have to do a bit more than talk.

So what happens after? Well, there are still those circumstances that forced them to wed, and there are still those reasons why they argue. Just because they get tangled in Ailsa's laces doesn't mean all is resolved... In fact, matters go from bad to worse.

As I went on Ailsa and Rory's passionate journey, I wondered how they could possibly find their happily-ever-after. They surprised me, and I hope they surprise you, too.

NICOLE LOCKE

—

Secrets of a Highland Warrior

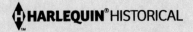

Special thanks and acknowledgment are given to Nicole Locke for her contribution to The Lochmore Legacy series.

Special thanks and acknowledgment are given to Janice Preston for her contribution to the epilogue of *Secrets of a Highland Warrior* in The Lochmore Legacy series.

ISBN-13: 978-1-335-63524-2

Secrets of a Highland Warrior

Copyright © 2019 by Harlequin Books S.A.

Recycling programs for this product may not exist in your area.

Printed in U.S.A.

www.Harlequin.com

Nicole Locke discovered her first romance novels in her grandmother's closet, where they were secretly hidden. Convinced that books that were hidden must be better than those that weren't, Nicole greedily read them. It was only natural for her to start writing them—but now not so secretly.

Books by Nicole Locke

Harlequin Historical

The Lochmore Legacy
Secrets of a Highland Warrior

Lovers and Legends
The Knight's Broken Promise
Her Enemy Highlander
The Highland Laird's Bride
In Debt to the Enemy Lord
The Knight's Scarred Maiden
Her Christmas Knight
Reclaimed by the Knight

Visit the Author Profile page at Harlequin.com.

Traveling through romantic dialogue and dense Scottish mists. Careening over passionate scenes and rocky Highland paths. Forging on ahead in character conflicts to a Highland castle (or two), this book is dedicated to Elisabeth Hobbes, Janice Preston and Lara Temple, who are brilliant writers and even better friends. Thank you!

Chapter One

Spring 1293

'I don't like this.' Rory surveyed the landscape surrounding him and his men. Tall branches bending slightly in the spring breeze, birds calling softly, the stream mere horse-lengths in front of them, rushing past carrying winter's melting ice.

Around them was nothing else but rolling fields and a wide sparse treeline that had been manned and maintained to remain that way since before he was born. Enough trees for game, but not enough for enemies to hide behind.

Not that there should be enemies while they stood on Lochmore land, but across that stream…

'Perhaps they are waiting over that ridge.' Paiden sidled his horse alongside his and whispered low.

Rory didn't turn his attention to the other men. They had maintained their position and were far enough behind to not hear the words that Paiden inevitably desired to share. Of the same age, if different temperament, Paiden had been at his side for as long as he had memory.

Paiden had been talking for that long as well and Rory was used to his friend's humour even in the direst circumstances. Now, on this mildest of mornings, the circumstances weren't dire, but they weren't safe either. His men, well back from the stream few ventured near, didn't need to hear words to comprehend their predicament.

'How likely is it that a garrison of McCrieffs and their horses are crouching behind a hill no taller than a couple of rabbits could breach?'

'Oh, as likely as toothless Joan is capable of eating overcooked venison.'

Not likely at all. There was no one to greet him and his men this fine spring day. Twenty of them in all here, one hundred more waiting at the castle should he make the agreed signal. Twenty was enough of a force for the expected confrontation, but not enough to provoke a first strike. If the McCrieffs wanted a fight, then there were enough to defend the Lochmore claim. If they wanted to negotiate, the numbers weren't so intimidating that the possibility was there as well.

Months had gone into the planning of this day. A fortnight spent on discussing the number of men, the weaponry, the day and the hour. Rory was prepared for every likely scenario when it came to this day. The nothingness they faced wasn't any scenario at all.

Which was why they stayed on the Lochmore side of the stream. Across the water was the beginning of McCrieff land. Or what was McCrieff land. It was now his by royal decree.

After his clan supported the crowning of John Balliol last November, the English King Edward had granted the Lochmores part of the McCrieff lands. The ones that bordered along the stream that for years had separated the two clans. The two enemies.

The stream had been a firm divide between the clans and a well-welcomed one. *Owning* the land, however, gave the Lochmores even more pleasure. To take by any means something precious from the McCrieffs was worth any price paid.

But months had passed since Edward's decree. During that time the McCrieffs ignored Edward's law and the Lochmore Chief's messages.

So it came down to this day, to this hour to fight, to battle. Except all that was before him was the rising of the morning sun and the blades of plentiful grass the horses fed from.

Certainly, the beauty of the land was enough to please any Highlander, but the landscape wasn't what he intended or expected to see right now.

The granting of this land wasn't at the McCrieffs' consent. In fact, this very land had been bitterly fought over for years. Everything between them had been fought over for years.

Also, being Highlanders, it wasn't expected that the McCrieffs would agree to an English king's decree. After all, what right did he have over a Highlander's lands?

However, since it was convenient at this moment for Lochmore's Chief, Rory's father, to accept, he did. But with no word from the McCrieffs, it seemed they didn't accept the terms.

Now, with no one here, it didn't seem like anything at all.

'It's a trap,' Paiden said.

'Truly, that ridge wouldn't be able to hide one horse and we'd hear them if they laid in wait. Where would they lay a trap?'

Rory looked behind at his men waiting for command. They were as restless as the mounts beneath them. They expected to let out a war cry today. Indeed, they'd feasted and bedded in celebration the night before in case today was their last.

If they returned now, it would be without gaining the honour of such celebration. If he returned to his father emptyhanded with no resolution or information, today might indeed be his last. His father wouldn't allow such ambiguity. McCrieffs present or not, Rory's only choice was to confront.

'I'm crossing,' Rory said. When Paiden pulled his horse only slightly more ahead, Rory stopped. 'The others didn't move.'

'That's because you didn't give the signal to move.'

'Exactly, so what are you doing?'

'You can give the men commands all that you want, but I'll still be by your side.'

'When I'm Chief—'

'You can give me orders and I won't cross you in front of others, but until then… Forget it.'

When he was Chief. Not yet. Not without his father's death and an elder's approval. But Rory hadn't been concerned for approval because of this honour today of leading his men to confront the McCrieffs. To demand why they ignored a king's decree and a clan's chief.

For months, the firm conclusion as to why the Mc-Crieffs had ignored the decree and messages was that they contested the claim. So in the last message the Lochmores had arranged this day. To meet and agree or if not, to fight. The McCrieffs made no reply, but that, too, wasn't a concern. For no Highlander would be so cowardly as to ignore a challenge and the last missive was a challenge.

Thus, because he was the only son, the only child of the Lochmore Chief, he wore the best armour his clan owned and wore a sword he'd sharpened himself. The McCrieffs had all to gain with his death and they would not claim it. This was to be his day to prove himself to his father, to his clan. To himself. It was all to be his. His to battle, wrest and claim.

If no blood was to be found on this side of the water, he'd simply ride forward to find it. The hatred between the Lochmores and McCrieffs was too deep for there not to be some argument this day. Some trophy to be won so when he did face his father again, Finley would give his proud approval. Rory would never give up until he finally obtained it.

'If I can't rid myself of you…' Rory sighed with exaggeration '…then the others will want to ride as well.' With his arm raised, he drew a large circle in the air. Whatever might come, this land was his to ensure this day and ensure it he must. For once, he'd be the Lochmore his father wanted him to be.

Chapter Two

Ailsa set the bowl of bone broth and bread on the table and raised the cup of tisane to the thin lips of the Chief of Clan McCrieff. Only a few drops did he take this morning, only a few more throughout last night. The tisane was important for the pain, the beef-broth mixture crucial to retain his strength.

But this last fortnight both had been increasingly difficult for him to swallow. It was that which was telling of the sickness overwhelming him more than the grey pallor of his skin and his laboured breath. His body was slowly wasting away. His ice-blue eyes, however, were sharp as ever and steady on her.

If his eyes could speak, Ailsa knew the barrage of hate would be fierce. Though he was losing his strength day by day, he hadn't lost his opinions.

The fact he didn't speak now meant he was saving his strength...for what she didn't know. She never could understand their Chief who was and had always been filled with rage and suspicion.

Even towards her, their only healer. She glanced up

to find his eyes piercing her the entire time he drank the tisane. Mistrust. As if her long sleepless nights and tireless searching for calming herbs weren't because she was there to help, but to harm him.

She would never, could never, do so. It went against everything she was. It was also a sin. God's law should have been enough to appease Hamish McCrieff that she would do her duty to him. But she suspected Hamish had committed so many sins he didn't see the breaking of one as much of a deterrent.

Blasphemous thoughts. This man was Chief of the Clan and deserved respect and loyalty. But everything about him made fear climb like poisonous vines under her skin.

Standing and setting down the cup, Ailsa nodded towards Mary, one of the most faithful of servants, who stood as well, and they adjusted the bedding so Hamish was made more comfortable. She didn't know what ailed him, but she'd seen it before. The decline was slow, the body consumed on the inside until there was nothing left. All that could be done was to ease the pain and ensure a longer sleep until he died.

A quick death would be more merciful and she had heard of men doing so to their brethren on the battlefields. But for her it was too kind for this man, who wasn't worth risking her soul for. There was many a day when she wanted to. Something she went to confessional with often. Weeks of confessionals now. The seasons were changing and still McCrieff lingered, leaving the clan in a vulnerable state.

It was no relief when Hamish's gaze shifted over her shoulder. No relief at all since his accusing stare was aimed entirely at the only other person in the room. Her father, Frederick, who months ago had been elected to be heir apparent to the Chief. To become, in effect, Tanist. Further because Hamish was so ill it was also agreed that her father would be privy to any and all decisions that Hamish would decree. Most significantly, Frederick could suggest and, in certain circumstances, make decisions of his own that would be equally revered by the council. Unusual, but Hamish was dying and her father was a greatly respected warrior, with a bloodline linked to chiefs in the past. The decree was unanimous, including that of Hamish himself. However, Alisa always felt Hamish had given it unwillingly.

Her father must have felt the same way as well. And whether it was because of loyalty to the Chief who he had served under for years or to keep the peace among the Clan, Frederick still consulted with Hamish. In front of the clan, it kept the peace. Only she knew what a toll it took on her father and it was no surprise that, after he gained her attention, he left the room.

As quietly as possible, Alisa stepped away from the bed and let Mary continue with the rest of the routine. Months of working together, they no longer had to discuss the Chief's care…they only had to endure it.

The room next to the chamber was empty save for her father and Alisa closed the door behind her. He let out a breath.

'He eats less every day,' Ailsa said.

'But drinks your tisane more. Is this because of the pain?'

Hamish hid his pain from her; Ailsa suspected, because he didn't want her father to know. But at night, when Hannah or Mary took over, when he tried to sleep, he cried out. For a man of Hamish's stature to do so meant the pain was horrific.

Ailsa nodded. 'The pain is expected at this stage. For now he seems aware, but it will increase and he will be less... He may not even know who he is.'

Frederick exhaled. 'The others will not care.'

'Others?'

Her father raised his finger to his lips and shook his head once.

Ailsa tightened her jaw and kept her words to herself. If Hamish's health was in further decline, more decisions would be made by her father. The issue, of course, was even at the height of Hamish's power, her father never saw eye to eye with their Chief. In the past, there were arguments, but to keep the loyalties strong, her father always yielded to the clan Chief...as he should.

Since Hamish didn't have the strength for all decision making, the clan would lean more on her father, whether Hamish wanted it or not.

There should be no *others* when it came to the rule of McCrieffs. Everyone should be behind her father, who was a fair man. The Tanist vote and shared ruling was unanimous. It was rare and, to keep McCrieffs strong, to everyone outside the clan it was unknown, but that didn't mean it wasn't the right course for her clan. Hamish couldn't be expected to rule as he once had. However, Hamish had lived long and had spread his venom deep. There were rumours that others were loyal to only him. It incensed her. Her father had every right by blood and sword to rule the McCrieffs and rule them justly. Yet, as long as Hamish lived, Hamish still kept his power and her father was forced to keep the balance.

And she was forced to keep Hamish alive. When Hamish died, her father would face adversity no other McCrieff had ever faced before: To mend a divided Clan. Her father was a warrior, not a negotiator.

However, Hamish's decreasing strength could change the stalemate—

The outside door burst open and both swung their gaze towards the messenger who bent over his knees to catch his breath. 'Lochmores are here,' he panted.

Ailsa's entire body seized. Their enemy was on their land. How could this have happened without her father being at the forefront of the fight? 'Father, what is—?'

Frederick kept his gaze on the young man before him. 'How far?'

'Just outside the village.'

'Again!' Ailsa gasped and Frederick laid a hand on her arm.

The Lochmores were on McCrieff land. It was too soon since the last time. The bodies were still raw in the graves and they were here this soon again? Never!

Lochmores attacking again and this time their clan was divided. They were weak. Is that why they struck? While she'd been tending a dying man, already her clan were dying defending their land.

Ailsa wrenched her arm free of her father's restraint. 'They've never returned this soon before. Why now?'

'And the people?' Frederick asked the messenger.

'Holding steady.'

For how long? As Tanist and warrior her father would

want to be part of that battle. As Clan healer it would be her duty to attend those in need. 'My pouches are full and ready, I need to only go to my room.'

'No,' her father commanded. His expression was not one she'd seen before. The warrior, the father and leader were there, but a flash of something else exposed itself to her. A look she'd never seen before and it took her aback. That vulnerability was of a man facing something far stronger than himself.

'Whatever happens here today, stay hidden until I say otherwise.'

'Stay hidden while people die?' The last time there had been an attack was mere months ago and he'd let her tend the injured. Two McCrieffs had died. The time before that, she'd been a mere child. Too young to comprehend what she saw, but old enough to remember her friend, Magnus, charging towards the oncoming Lochmores. Too small to make a difference and far too inconsequential to be seen. The horse's hooves cut his life down immediately. 'You can't expect me to sit still. I can't!'

'There will be no deaths today, not by my hand or decree. If it was my will, all would be spared. Except...'

'Except?' She seemed only to think and speak in questions now. Stupid. Ineffectual. Useless. Even her emotions were weak. She knew that all too well. Magnus had been all smiles and then violently nothing but blood and crushed bone. The Lochmores were no longer just some clan hated by the McCrieffs. *She* hated them, too. But then... Ailsa shook her thoughts away. There should be no *but then*... 'There are no exceptions! If the Lochmores are here, then I am needed.'

'You have twenty years, my Ailsa, my daughter, and I'm a selfish man—if I could keep you for longer I would.'

'I'll stay safe. I have and can again.'

'*I'll* keep you safe…until I can't any more.'

'Father?' Did he mean to sacrifice himself? No. To sacrifice himself was one matter, but he was Tanist and he'd be sacrificing his clan, his life, the life of his ancestors.

'Stay hidden, Ailsa, until I call for you. That is my only wish and desire as a father, but if that won't do this time, I order you to. Do you understand?'

An order. Aware the messenger was rapt with every gesture and word, Ailsa held still. She would question her father, but never the clan's leader. When she nodded, her father swept out of the room with the messenger following.

Exhaling the breath she held, Ailsa thought only a moment about what she would do. Quietly, she stepped into Hamish's room. He was mostly awake, so she waved Mary over to her to whisper what was happening. Told her to stay with Hamish and care for him. Mary glanced at Hamish, but agreed.

With that done, Ailsa left the room. She'd keep her silence in front of others, but to stay hidden wasn't an order she'd obey from her Tanist or her father. Their enemy was on McCrieff land. Blood had or would be spilled. A true healer was neither daughter nor clan member. She would heal.

The battle armour Rory wore weighed heavily on him as he travelled further on to McCrieff territory.

Paiden rode by his side, watching his back, and the rest of the men stayed evenly spaced behind them.

They were as silent as a troop of Highland warriors could be. Only he, because of his armour, made sounds unlike the others. The sound and the burden chafed the further they travelled on McCrieff land. Rory rolled his shoulders, but it gave no relief in the tightness of his gambeson over his tunic, nor did it ease the weight of the chainmail of his hauberk. None of the others wore armour. Their shields and swords were enough for any true Highland battle.

An hour, maybe two, travelling like this and he felt as tense as a burdened deer being hunted. A weighted deer was a slow one.

What he wouldn't give for flinging both shield and sword in the air and crying out for war. This hiding game of the McCrieffs wore thin. Mere months ago, when Edward granted McCrieff land to Lochmores there'd been a clash of swords. Small, significant... unsanctioned. The border of their land was always patrolled. Some Lochmores, gloating over what they perceived as a victory, had raced over to McCrieff land. It was a small battle unknown until too late by their Chief and the men had been well punished. More so since blood was shed. Two McCrieffs had died and one Lochmore.

That had been nothing more or less than it'd been for generations until this very moment. His sword arm ached with the need to swing. To feel the rough reverberation of metal against metal. Instead, they rode through empty fields until they saw the village surrounding the motte and bailey with a centre keep.

Even from this distance, Rory could see the weakness of the McCrieffs' half-stone and half-timber defence. It was encircled by a partial wall at its lowest point, but nothing a bit of fire and a medium-sized battalion could not destroy.

McCrieff's castle was, mostly, as his father remembered and recalled to him. Had they made no improvements since then? His own land was surrounded by water, but even they fortified their walls. The McCrieffs had not prospered like his own clan.

Riding slowly, they approached the village, which wasn't empty, but full of wide-eyed silent residents. So much silence, which weighed heavier than his armour. Ominous. Foreboding. Not one resident moved. It was as if they feared one flick of a wrist would erupt in bloodshed. Rory slowed his horse even more and quieted the breaths through his lungs.

There was always a moment of stillness before a battle, but he felt none of the menacing tenuousness now. He craved to fight, but with soldiers who also craved to draw their swords. Not villagers and children. Not with domesticity that chafed more than the unusual circumstance he found himself in. Only the animals didn't seem to understand that the unnatural stillness wasn't to be broken.

So they rode through gaggles of squawking hens and through small herds of sheep. Always Rory observed every detail of the residents, buildings and houses. He might not feel the hatred of enemies, but he knew there were those who hated him. Anything he missed could be his death or the demise of his men. He didn't want either, but he wouldn't accept the latter at all.

They had prepared for battle. Instead, they walked through the McCrieffs' village as if this was no more than a neighbourly visit. Except the silence. This was the indication that all was not welcoming. Good, he wanted to fight. Why weren't they fighting?

Damn the coward, McCrieff. Hamish's reputation was as a duplicitous ruler, but rumour was he faced you as he lied. This nothingness was something else and unwanted. How could he prove to his clan, to his Chief, his father, that he, too, would be worthy of power if at this moment he was denied proving himself?

On through the silent village until the wide open gates. Here, Rory stopped and Paiden pulled his horse alongside his once again.

'I don't like this,' Paiden said.

'Now you show caution?' Rory said.

'I wanted to turn away at the stream, but you wouldn't let me,' Paiden gave a fake wobble to his voice. 'But I'll agree if you turn back now.'

Deep on McCrieff land and it wasn't safe for any of them. The questions kept mounting. 'Why bother? If it's a trap, we're in it and it matters not if I go through that gate or not.'

Paiden gave a grim chuckle. 'I think it matters very much. About what that is, is up to you.'

It was a trap Rory knew he must purposefully step foot into. He was already a dead man simply riding to this point. If he rode past the gate, he'd be in the Great Courtyard surrounded by McCrieff warriors who could easily strike him with arrows. Armour or not. Enough arrows and any protection would eventually fail.

However, he was also a dead man if he stood outside

the gates, so it was possible they intended to take him prisoner, but the McCrieff Chief wasn't that clever. So what else could it be? Did they intend to lay out a feast for him and his men and tell tales by the fire?

He'd rather kill the entire clan than sit at their table. If his father discovered he'd done so, he'd lose all honour.

'Stay here,' Rory said.

Paiden snorted, but he held his mount still as Rory approached the gate and assessed each gatekeeper. They gave no indication of their intentions to his presence. Their bodies tense, but no weapon in either hand. Of course, there was no welcoming greeting on their lips either. Just more of that unnatural stillness like the villagers.

So he passed through the gate on well-worn dirt beneath smaller buildings in different states of disrepair.

Once through to the other side, Rory could see two men above, but from the angle of the gate and the high walls, he knew there were hidden places where numerous men could walk the wall, aim their bow and arrow over the slats and pull the killing shot.

Just past the walls' shadow and Rory spotted a lone man descending the keep's steps. There were many steps, tightly terraced, yet he took them one at a time. He spotted no limp or deformity in the Scotsman. No, the McCrieff took the steps slowly and deliberately to waste time.

Another scan of his surroundings and Rory waited while the stranger strode towards them. He appeared the same age as his father, but that was the only certainty he could be Chief of Clan McCrieff.

He was tall, thick, his shoulders wide. Lochmore's

Chief was a scholar—this man led troops, fought in battles and had shed much blood. His father had said Hamish was large, but everything else didn't fit. This man didn't look as if he spoke to councils and negotiated.

A flash of movement at the top of the stairs and Rory glanced towards the new threat. It was a woman half in the shadows of the doorway, her white gown giving a shape and size to her. She appeared younger than the man striding towards him now.

None of her features were clear. But her unbound hair was a riveting flaming red. She could be across the moors in the furthest field and he'd see her.

He felt…he felt as if he knew her.

Disconcerted, Rory dismounted and took in the courtyard. As expected, the ramparts were full of men, arrows locked though the bows were not taut. Around the wall he saw more men standing. No swords drawn, but their stances were wide—they were ready to charge—and the man who had descended the stairs now stood in front of him.

'You are not Lochmore's Chief.'

'You are not the McCrieffs',' Rory guessed.

The man gave a regal nod, but didn't divulge any further information. So be it. Rory purposefully looked around them. 'Is that why we face each other freely in this courtyard?'

'You stand freely because I will it.'

'You could not will it, if I did not freely stand here.'

The old warrior tilted his head, assessing Rory as a man, as a soldier, as an opponent. He'd been given the same look all his life from his own father. This time, however, there was humour in eyes framed by wrinkles and the slight curve lifted the harsh corners of his lips.

This McCrieff, warrior or not, wanted to smile at Rory's words. Was the man humoured by his own words or was the joke finally on him?

'I've come to address the King's decree.' Rory got to the point.

'You intend to claim part of the McCrieff lands.'

Rory pulled out the royal scroll, certain the McCrieffs had received a copy as well. 'They were no longer yours the moment Edward signed this parchment.'

The warrior didn't glance at the seal. 'Don't want yours. Got one of our own.'

'Then—'

'I'll ignore both.'

'Where is your Chief?'

The man remained quiet, but he turned his gaze to men along the sides. Men who kept their weapons lowered, but who walked slowly towards them.

'Are you or the Chief ignoring our missives as well?' Months of preparation. Hours of manoeuvring and counselling for every circumstance. But there wasn't a circumstance here. The sun was well risen, the day was warm, the armour was heavy and getting hot, and nothing…nothing was occurring. He wanted this done with and to return home. 'Are you conceding the lands are ours without a fight?'

'I'll concede those lands will remain as they are, Rory, son of Finley and *only* heir.'

Rory didn't let his gaze stray from the man in front of him, but he was acutely aware of the bowmen at the top of the gates and the men on the ground. Aware of the woman trying to hide in the door's shadows and failing. She wore white, her hair like a bright flame, her hand now rested on her stomach as if she was holding herself in.

He knew how she felt. A trap he had stepped in and one that was unavoidable. He could take on one, maybe two of the men before him, but not all. 'You know who I am and yet…' Rory let the sentence drop, hoping the man in front of him would complete it.

The warrior shrugged. 'Time would be better spent eating and drinking, no?'

'You prepared a feast for our arrival?'

'We knew you were coming. You wrote us a missive to that effect.' The man turned slightly and indicated for Rory to follow him to the keep. 'You haven't broken your fast yet?'

Rory ate nothing other than was necessary for strength this morning. Any more and he couldn't fight well. 'Lochmores have never eaten at a McCrieff table.'

'That is because you've never been invited before.'

This conversation was more along Paiden's gift for circuitous conversation. What he wouldn't give for his friend beside him to interpret. All Rory knew in this moment was if they wanted him dead, he'd be dead. Sparring with words wasn't his way, being direct was. 'Tell me what game this is and get on with it.'

'Do you like games?'

'I never played a game in my life.' He'd been honed to be a weapon by his father and, when he could think or act for himself, he'd kept to the regime. Once the arrow was shot, it had no choice but to continue where it was aimed.

'But this one you've entered into already. I know you see her.'

Anything of frustration in him left immediately and his focus remained locked on to the warrior before him. Older, but no less deadly. A worthy opponent by the way he held himself. Fearless since he had no weapon out in preparation to an attack.

His father was like this as well. But the man did keep his eyes on Rory their entire exchange. The woman, for she was the only woman visible in this courtyard, was still half-hidden. Yet this man knew she was there watching them.

'She's hiding from you.'

'Little escapes my observations.'

'Who are you?' Rory said.

'I'll introduce myself and my daughter when you've entered the McCrieffs' Hall, son of Lochmore.'

So be it. Rory turned to signal his men. A fatal mistake. A bite of steel against his side, a harsh grasp of one arm, then the other.

There was time to free himself, to fight, but Rory knew it would be brief. He could negotiate for his men better alive than dead. With a shove at the men holding him, he allowed the wrenching of his arms behind his back as he faced the McCrieff.

The warrior gave a knowing smile. 'I said you're invited, I didn't say as a guest.'

Chapter Three

Hurry, hurry, hurry. The mantra hurtled itself through Ailsa's thoughts faster than her feet carried her to the safety of her rooms.

Lochmores on McCrieff land. Arrows and swords drawn, shields low, but ready, and one armour-clad man riding freely into their courtyard.

Shocked, she had stood on the steps and gawked. He was…huge. Broad of shoulder, his arms twice as thick as any man's she'd ever seen. His horse was the largest, because he was the largest. All her life she'd been surrounded by warriors, fierce, protective. But there was no one like him…this stranger who rode through their gates as if he owned McCrieff Castle.

He'd worn no helmet, but the distance between them was not far and she had seen the glint of determination as he surveyed his surroundings. Everything about him screamed of dominance, of power, of ownership. He was a ruler and, like all rulers, he held himself as if he owned it all.

She had watched as he minutely adjusted the reins

of the great beast he rode, as he dismounted and strode towards her father. The sound of the chainmail slapping against leather, the crunch of pebbles under his feet, the way his brown hair brushed against his forehead when the wind picked up.

She had felt the way her fingers tingled as he swiped away the errant curl. And in that, she knew she hadn't only gawked because he was a Lochmore who held some power. She'd gawked because he was a man. And the shiver through her body had nothing to do with the slight wind at the time and all to do with the man whose searching eyes found her.

She reached the top of the stairs only to find the winding hallway to her chambers empty as well. Everyone was down below or in hiding. This part of the keep was her refuge and domain. But she didn't feel safe.

She hadn't felt safe downstairs hiding partially surrounded by thick walls and a great door. She had thought herself well hid and certainly well beyond the man's acknowledgement.

Yet, his eyes hadn't remained on her father, they had scanned his surroundings, finding the men with arrows and swords, finding...her. Her heart had skipped before it thudded strong in her chest as their gazes met. He'd been too far for her to discern his features with clarity, too far for her to hear the conversation they'd held properly.

It hadn't mattered. The distance hadn't taken away the impact of his gaze on her and it hadn't masked some of the words exchanged with her father.

Words, a name she never thought to hear. His name was Rory. *Rory.* A name that shouldn't hold significance to her except that the old healer had told her a fable. A mere story, but it was lodged as a fact firmly inside her thoughts and memories. She'd curse the healer for telling that story if it didn't risk her very soul blaspheming the dead.

Could he be the same Rory? Ailsa scoffed at herself for thinking that thought, rushed into her room and slammed the door. No one here. Good, for her knees trembled so badly she leaned against the door and forced them to lock before she slid to the floor in a useless puddle.

He couldn't be the same Rory, even if Rhona's story was true. Rory was a common enough name. And even if he was that baby, should it make a difference? No. Her friend Magnus was dead for ever. Just last winter two McCrieffs guarding the border had died when several Lochmores rushed across the border and engaged in a fight.

No a name shouldn't make a difference. The only difference between how McCrieffs treated Lochmores was when a Lochmore strode through the courtyard, her father had invited him in, and then…and then confiscated his weaponry.

As he should. Her father should have also marched him to the dungeon or beheaded him right then and there. Instead, there had been an invite for breaking fast and more words exchanged that she couldn't fully understand since most were lost with the distance between them.

Pushing herself away from the door, Ailsa hastily grabbed her shears she kept in her room and strategically folded them into the pleats of her belt and gown.

Her father might have confiscated Lochmore's weapons, but that didn't mean she couldn't have hers. If Lochmores were invited to dine at McCrieffs' table, she would be ready.

'Your Chief is bedridden and you are Tanist,' Rory said, repeating her father's words slowly.

He sounded stunned. Ailsa was stunned as well, but at least this fact she knew. Everything else was as much a surprise to her as it was to the man who sat on her father's left side while she sat at his right.

Her shears tucked into her belt, she had descended the stairs, a roaring in her ears as introductions were made. As the proximity to this Lochmore filled in the details the distance of the courtyard had not revealed.

His eyes were not the dark brown of earth, but held the light of a gem lit behind it. His size was formidable as she'd thought. Yet it wasn't that which made her eyes unerringly fall to him again and again. There was something about *him* that compelled her. It felt like a tincture of awe and wariness.

She shouldn't have felt either. Lochmores didn't deserve admiration, and as for wariness…her father had unarmed them all. They weren't out on the battlefield, but in the comfort of McCrieff Hall, eating and drinking food. Decent food, too. Not the usual fare. Her father had ordered a true feast for this occasion. Ailsa had never seen the Hall so full. There were three tables in the hall. Theirs, the smallest that sat no more than ten on one side, was perpendicular to the two larger tables. Lochmores kept to one side, their backs to the wall and they faced the inside, faced the McCrieffs.

She focused her thoughts on that. There might be no battlefield, but the men had sat as if there was. That was the cause of her wariness. Not this man who bore the name of Rory.

'The Chief is bedridden and has been for months,' Frederick replied.

'And you didn't think to notify us, though we sent letters regarding the King's demand?' Rory said.

'His illness has nothing to do with our lack of reply, Lochmore.'

'Then you are the one who ignored them so we could dine here. A letter to that effect would have been more agreeable. Or at least more comfortable for me, since I would have worn different clothing.'

'Your being comfortable doesn't concern me.'

'Nor my safety.'

'You're alive.'

'Without a weapon, so I wonder for how long.'

'Isn't it enough that you eat at our table?' Ailsa knew it was rude to talk around her father, but would not hold her tongue when it seemed the King made demands she knew nothing of. A serving tray laid out with vegetables and covered in a rosemary sauce was presented, giving her an opportunity to break the argument between the two men. 'Are these leeks not fine enough for you?'

Rory's gaze fell to her and she refused to look away. A full dining hall and her father between them and yet no one else existed. The tray lowered and broke their line of sight, but only for a moment. A moment more while his eyes remained on the tray and the leeks were laid upon his trencher.

Those few brief breaths allowed her to reflect on the

curl of his brown hair, the squareness of his jaw, the strong brow with eyebrows that slashed as if they had a purpose. He looked as if he had a purpose.

Then his gaze was on her again. 'The leeks look delicious,' he said, stabbing one with his knife, 'but are insufficient if I wanted to defend myself.'

What was happening here? 'Why do you need to defend yourself?'

His mouth quirked as if she told something amusing. 'We are enemies, are we not?'

Frustrated at her useless question and his fruitless answer, Ailsa searched the Hall for the truth.

She sat where she always sat with her father since Hamish no longer could sit at the same table, yet she didn't feel as if she was in the same chair, the same Hall or in the same place she'd always been.

This wasn't a battle and yet it felt as though it was. Deadly silence and watchful stares. Food was served, but no trenchers were shared. Every man had his own goblet. Where the extra spoons, food or goblets came from she didn't know. She also didn't know how her father arranged such elaborate plans without her knowing.

On a typical day, by now there would be banter, and arrangements made for tomorrow. Instead, a few of the McCrieffs farthest away from the Lochmores murmured heatedly, and one Lochmore closest to their table kept up a conversation no one engaged in.

This wasn't a typical meal and, no matter how much she observed everyone here, she knew there was more division in the room than that between Lochmore and McCrieff. Only she couldn't identify the 'others' her father had spoken of.

Only Rory and her father exchanged words and she'd never heard her father be so diplomatic or evasive before. They were enemies, but something else was amiss. She needed him to convey to her *why*.

'Is Hamish here?' Rory addressed her father.

'Upstairs,' Frederick said. 'It will be necessary for you to see him after we break the fast.'

'Necessary for what?' Ailsa demanded.

Frederick was turned away from her and Ailsa couldn't see her father's face, but she saw Rory's. Keen intelligence burned in his eyes and he must have seen her father's hesitation. She saw it in the slight tenseness of Frederick's shoulders before Rory answered.

'Necessary to discuss the King's granting McCrieff land to Lochmores.'

'Land!' Ailsa cried.

Rory glanced to Frederick before he pinned her with a dark gaze. 'Why else did you think I was invited to eat leeks with you?'

Ailsa pushed away from the table. The sharp scrape echoed in the Hall and earned her glances.

'Ailsa, please.' Her father turned to her, his eyes darting to others in case their conversation was overheard.

This. This was what had been plaguing the clan. Not her father's position or Hamish's illness. An English King decreed McCrieff land to Lochmores and they were here to collect.

Aware of Rory's eyes on her, she laid her hand on her father's arm. 'All of it?'

'Some,' her father whispered low. 'Along the water.'

Reeling, Ailsa gripped her father's arm. Her father had been acting strange for weeks. Nothing untoward for everything was kept to a routine that was sustained by the Chief before him. Hamish was still too cognisant to do otherwise. Months of her father attending council meetings, inspecting land, conversing with tenants. So much to do and more so since John Balliol was crowned King of Scots last November.

Many Highlanders believed he was nothing more than a vassal of the English King Edward. But some supported him more openly than others. The Lochmore clan was one of those…

It became clear to her. The Lochmore clan supported the English King and in doing so had been granted part of their lands.

Land that McCrieffs firmly maintained was theirs and which had been fought over time and time again. It was politically crucial land since it contained water and naturally separated the clans. For her, it was important because it fed McCrieffs and provided foliage she needed for remedies. She wanted to stand and wave her arms. To shout for them all to leave the land alone. To lose such an advantage was detrimental to her and the clan. Hamish, in his day, would never have agreed to such a granting.

Hamish would have called men to arms, he would have called for battle. He would never have let Lochmores on his land, let alone in the courtyard. But her father, whose loyalty she had never questioned before, practically invited them here and prepared a feast for them.

She couldn't cause a scene, but she would say what she needed to. 'You can't.'

'Ailsa,' Frederick said.

'Why can't he?' Rory said. 'If he is Tanist, with the agreement he has authority to do so. Even if he didn't, it is already done by King's decree and by mine.'

'That land is not yours,' Ailsa said.

Rory's eyes went to Fredericks. 'She didn't know. What is happening here, Tanist?'

She'd like to know as well. Since Balliol's claim, many secrets were being kept. Her father held private meetings, but so did Hamish. Her father acted as though he didn't notice these meetings and, though she asked, she wasn't privy to her father's secrets. But everything about their behaviours filled her with unease. She couldn't be the only one who observed their leaders' movements. The 'others' would have seen as well.

'You have to have some ideas,' Frederick said. At Rory's shrug, he added, 'You can't be a Lochmore and not want more,' Frederick continued, his voice low so that if people tried to listen, they would not hear. 'Especially, since it's about to be handed to you.'

The King hadn't decreed that *all* McCrieff land should be handed to the Lochmores, just the land against the border, so that couldn't be what his father was hinting at. Even confused, Ailsa felt relief. Until…

Until Rory's eyes locked with hers and she knew he understood a fraction of a moment before she did how Lochmores could gain more without a fight.

'All you need to do is marry my daughter.'

Chapter Four

'No!' Ailsa cried.

Lochmore made some sound she couldn't determine. Her father wasn't looking at her even though she had never raised her voice in her life. That didn't bode well especially when he stood to address the hall. His words were formal as he declared there were important matters to be discussed. No one stood to question or protest. It appeared that everyone had assumed as much. Fuming, wondering how she couldn't have known, Ailsa followed her father when he retired to the room in the back. She felt rather than saw Rory follow behind her.

It was a small room with several doors and she saw with some consternation there were also provisions on a table and several chairs. It was all previously laid out for comfort and for private discussions. Her father expected and planned well.

For her to marry a Lochmore.

She wanted to do more than raise her voice, she wanted to brandish her shears. Secrets. Her father had been acting odd for months. Why had she not suspected this? Or at least demanded answers to his behaviour. But how could she have guessed what questions to ask him?

She'd been telling herself he'd been worried about Hamish, about the clan's discontent. She never could have guessed this. But she should have suspected something because her father was never worried or alarmed.

She was the one who worried. Especially when her father ordered her to hide when the enemy clan arrived instead of providing her an escort as she tended her clan. She was the one who grew alarmed the moment her father brought her and Rory into this tiny room and gave her that wistful paternal look. The one that asked for forgiveness even before she knew there was something to forgive about.

This wasn't forgivable and she'd have words with her father. For now, she needed to make clear to the Lochmore her position in this matter. Yet when she met Rory's gaze, the emotions roiling in the depth shocked her anew. Surprise definitely, but something else she refused to believe. His consideration.

'Never!' The word felt inadequate to express her rejection, so she said the simple word with as much vehemence as she felt.

She knew she shocked her father. She had always been the sensible one. After all, her mother had died when her sisters were born. By then she'd already started helping the clan healer. Everything she'd done up to this point was for others. Now, it appeared her father thought she'd automatically sacrifice herself. Not this time.

'Ailsa, think about this.' Her father sat in one of the chairs and used the voice she'd heard thousands of times before. That of a father to his daughter. But if he was acting like a father, he wouldn't ask this.

'I am thinking about this. How could I not know that our land was given away? And it appears as if I'm the only McCrieff who doesn't know! Me, the healer, your daughter, who needs the marsh and soil. You know how important that land is!'

She planted there. Rhona, the old healer and the healer before that, planted there. There was need and tradition rooted in that dirt. It was dangerous, yes, since it was on the border, but it was the best place for certain necessary herbs.

'He can't have the land. They can't have the land!'

'A king decreed it.' Rory crossed his arms and leaned against a wall. Her father said nothing.

She tightened her lips before she could commit treason. Pointing at Rory, but addressing her father, she said, 'I want him gone.'

The Lochmore in question only said, 'No.'

She waited for an explanation—none came. All the while she felt everything, betrayal being foremost. She had been kept in the dark about the King's decree and McCrieffs' obligations to Lochmores. She certainly hadn't been told she had to marry.

'No?' Brandishing her shears, she strode over and pointed them at him. 'Did you know of this?'

'Ailsa! Put them away!' Frederick called out. She ignored him.

'What…this?' the Lochmore replied with barely a glance at the shears.

The marriage, the welcoming feast, the King's decree!

'Any part of it,' she bit out.

A muscle ticked in his jaw. 'Yes.'

So only the female was kept in the dark even though it was her life in play. 'Father, I ask for privacy.'

'This matter must stay secret, so here we remain until it's resolved,' Frederick said, leaning further in his chair.

Ordered about like property. Her father had never treated her as such. Shame washed hotly with the betrayal. Her father deigned to bargain her off to a Lochmore. A clan that was, even now, their enemy. All her life, she'd been told to run or hide from Lochmores should she should spy them. Now she was told to marry and bear his children.

There wasn't a redeeming factor to him. Lochmores knew nothing of McCrieff land, the way their hills sloped or how the sun hit the trees. He wasn't amused by the erratic guttering of the worn paths that wound around the back of the castle or dismayed by the leaking corner in the chapel's roof.

Even if he wasn't a Lochmore, he was a man she had never met. His age could have been anything. His countenance, his strength and personality could have been the vilest of all. But her father, who never gambled, never guessed on the weather, risked her happiness and that of their clan that Rory Lochmore would be suitable for her.

'Is this what you will decide with my sisters as well? Just sell them off to the best alliance?'

'Sisters?' Rory interjected.

Ailsa huffed. 'Two of them and too young for your plotting, Lochmore.'

'Ailsa!' her father reprimanded. 'Think it through.'

'I have and I want no part of this!'

Ailsa strode to the door where the noises flooded in. It appeared by their absence that conversation began. She could storm from here. Nothing would resolve and everyone would know. Let them. Her friend had been murdered by Lochmores. How could her father ask this of her?

Her hand was almost on the latch, when her father banged his hand against the table. It made her jump. It made her turn.

The pounding of a fist was a demanding sound and one she would have ignored, but she couldn't ignore the look in his eyes. Her father's eyes pleaded with her. Her father *never* pleaded.

Did he plead with his daughter who had lost her precious friend? If so, her answer would remain no. A political alliance? Countries were built and torn down. She was a healer, what did she care for alliances except that they often stopped—

Ah. A quick twist in her heart and her mind listened. Political alliance stopped war…stopped deaths from occurring.

What care did she have for Lochmores? None, even though Rhona tried to soften her with a story about a babe named Rory, who was born and lost. No! She wouldn't think of that tale now. And she wouldn't forgive Lochmores for Magnus's death.

As a healer she had an obligation to stop further deaths. Now wasn't the time to not care for others. Now wasn't the time to be selfish even if it was justified and in self-preservation. Though their numbers were great compared to the few Lochmores who travelled here today, if McCrieffs waged a battle only more Lochmores would arrive and these wouldn't allow their swords to be taken.

Allow. That moment when her father captured Lochmore, their men had been quick, but something about this warrior's manner... He'd allowed his capture...maybe even expected it the moment he stepped through the gates.

What did she know of this man, the only heir to the Lochmore's Chief? Formidable even now though he stood silently and watched the exchange between a daughter and her father.

This man; her husband? Never, but what wouldn't she do for her clan as daughter to the Tanist, as their healer? She would do anything. With utmost resolve she turned away from the door.

Rory regretted the small shocked sound he released when Frederick had made his declaration. Through all the challenges in his life, he thought himself better equipped to mask his emotions.

But this challenge, a Lochmore marrying a McCrieff, wasn't one he could ever have prepared for. It seemed Frederick's daughter felt the same.

She was one flick of the lock away from leaving the room before her father brought her back. From where he leaned against the wall, he couldn't see the looks exchanged. He couldn't determine why in the silence that followed she did listen to him and sat in a chair though the shears stayed available on her lap.

Anticipating that finally she would behave as other women, to bow to the orders of her father, to present mild and pleasing manners, he kept his gaze to her. Yet though she sat, her chin was raised, her fingers clasping the shears. No meekness at all and far too much defiance. He couldn't predict this woman's behaviour and thoughts.

But though she was tense and her brow was creased, she continued to sit. She was reasonably contemplating her father's words.

It was time to do so himself. If it was even true. 'You want me to marry your daughter?' Each word felt unreal.

Frederick exhaled. Part relief that his words were listened to, part something else…like grief or loss.

'Yes. Marry her. As she is my daughter, you would have influence on this clan.'

Influence, but not power. 'You would remain Tanist and inherit the rule of McCrieffs.'

'Of course,' Frederick replied. 'Further, there would be no guarantee that you would gain any more than that.'

A swift glance to the woman at his left revealed she was listening, but the tight grasp on the shears told him the cost of her remaining silent.

This was a woman who thought with her mind. She was beautiful and intelligent. Such a daughter would be prized and even an old swordsman would have hopes that his issue would do better than merely marrying a man from an enemy clan, even if that man was the Chief's son.

'You are saying, that even upon your death, I, as a Lochmore, may not be accepted by McCrieffs.'

'In truth,' Frederick said, 'it would be…beneficial for me to remain ruler of McCrieffs.'

'A bright future for me. Marrying a woman, who doesn't want to be married. To marry into a clan, who may never accept me. And all of this to inherit nothing more than what a king already granted me.' Rory crossed his arms, watched the play of emotions in Frederick's eyes until he saw what he needed to see. 'But that is not all you want.'

A fierce gleam in the warrior's eyes, before he hid it with a shrug. 'What I expect and what is possible, what *could* be, are two different matters.'

Could be. Rory was right. The generations of animosity were too long furrowed into the families of McCrieffs and Lochmores. Even if they married and had issue, the divide could be permanent.

Or it could be more. But if he didn't marry Ailsa, there would never be the chance of something more. A chance to combine the clans. He choked down that bit of hope which had no place in these negotiations.

'Not a generous offer. What makes you think I'll accept?' Rory said as evenly as possible. No tone of flippancy, no curiosity. Nothing to reveal his roiling emotions at the McCrieffs' leader suggesting a hope for his future or his descendants. 'I am a Lochmore, son of a chief, and will be Chief one day. I am a not a pawn to be moved at the whimsy of anyone.'

He'd underestimated the McCrieffs. Or maybe it was only this man, whom he needed to be more cautious with and whom he needed to warn. Rory had no intention of being underestimated.

Frederick rested his arms on the chair's rests. 'I never presumed that you were such a sort. If I did, I would not have made the offer of my precious daughter to you. Know this, Lochmore, she is very dear to me.'

At that the woman in the chair shifted and Rory's eyes were drawn to her again. No crease between her brows, no tenseness in her shoulders. She had decided. From her silence, and the fact she wasn't trying to leave, he could only presume she agreed with her father.

Rory allowed himself to look at the man not as an enemy, but as a father. To see the lines of age and care in his face. The strain around his eyes not because he faced a foe before him, but because he made himself truly vulnerable. He meant it. The old warrior meant to give his daughter to him.

'Dear or not, she is only a gift if I want her and I do not accept.'

Frederick stood then, his expression revealing he'd heard the insult.

Rory raised his hand. 'Do not tell me to think about it. I am not your son, nor part of this clan. In fact, Lochmores lose power and control by this marriage.'

'How?' Ailsa demanded. 'How do they lose?'

'The land,' Rory said. 'The King decreed the borderland to now be Lochmore land. If we marry, there will be a question whether the land belongs to the Lochmores or the McCrieffs. McCrieffs will no doubt still use it and how could I wage war against my wife's family?'

'You throw away much too quickly and without thought,' Frederick said. 'Think of the future.'

'I live in the present. Your daughter is only a prize if I should want her. Did you think her so fair that my head would turn for her? The ale so potent that it would muddle my thoughts? A king decreed the land already to be mine. What you offer gains me nothing. I do not need to bargain with you, I only came to claim what is Lochmores.'

'Then you are a fool just like the others,' Ailsa said.

The words were quiet and steady…almost reasonable sounding. However, if she were her father and said such words, he would have drawn his sword. If he had one.

Another almost reaction when he didn't want to reveal a single one. He consoled himself that the impulse was still there only because he was too close to the edge. A Lochmore marry a McCrieff?

He addressed Frederick. 'Give me time alone with your daughter.'

'There's no need for it. He said his piece,' Ailsa said.

'There is a need,' Rory said. 'I'm unarmed, unlike your daughter, and she could make a cry that would be heard by every man in the Hall should she need it.'

'Will this change your mind?' Frederick adjusted his sword.

Rory doubted it. But he'd been plagued all day with too many questions. And the nature of this woman was one question he would find the answers to. She agreed to it, but why? 'Perhaps.'

Frederick pointed. 'I'll go through that door. Very few people will see me, but I will not escape notice long so you will not have much time.'

Rory watched Ailsa, who played with the shears in her hands, but remained quiet until the door closed.

'What is it that you want, Lochmore?'

With her red hair and green eyes, she looked very much like something from tales told to him as a child.

A harpy, a sprite, a vengeful faery. But the rest of her wasn't from his childhood. The rest of her reminded him that he was very much a man and she was a full-grown woman. Her twirling the shears in front of her accentuated her breasts, tightened the fabric of her gown, so he could admire the dip of her waist and her generous hips.

She was petite, but then everyone was to him, yet she was generously made. Whereas some women might have a shine to their hair or a sparkle in the eyes, Ailsa's pale skin, moss-coloured eyes and sunrise hair overflowed with colour. Her body was ample, thick in areas where a man could grab and sink into her lusciousness.

Everything about her called to him. It was the reason he'd seen her across the courtyard. Enemies with weapons in their hands and just the mere glimpse of her arrested him.

Now that he had seen her this close, exchanged a handful of words, he couldn't shake the feeling of déjà vu. As if…he knew her already.

'You threatened me with shears,' he said ignoring her question and adjusting his large body in to one of the chairs. For an instant, he was distracted by the fact the chair was not too small for him. He stretched, liking the fact he could do so. At home, there were no chairs built for him and he didn't ask for them to be. In truth, he preferred to stand, but knew in this negotiation, his size would be to his detriment. He was here to find answers, not intimidate.

She shrugged. 'They were handy and you arrived on short notice.'

'They're sharp. You could do me harm.'

'I ensure their usability, that is all.'

'For gardening,' he guessed.

'Of sorts,' she said, tucking the shears in her belt and laying her hands in her lap. 'What are you here for?'

'To claim the land,' he said. 'What is it you do here, Ailsa, that you need shears?'

She sighed. 'I heal. I'm the healer...you seemed surprised.'

Not surprised, but somehow, oddly pleased. She was intelligent in more ways than one. 'Aren't healers old and wizened?'

'They don't start out that way. Rhona, my mentor, died two winters past. So I'm it now. Though my father...' She shook her head.

'Though your father?' he prompted.

Her eyes narrowed and he saw the spark of fire she held when she'd aimed her shears at his throat. 'I'm a healer, Lochmore, and that's all you need to know.'

'Though we are to marry?' he mocked.

Her frown increased and he found he didn't like it. When she talked of Rhona, even that little bit, something of the true Ailsa had emerged. It was that which he wanted to coax from her, even though he had no business here except to secure the McCrieff land. He certainly didn't need the complication of this woman or the Tanist's proposal.

'*If* we marry,' she said. 'Why are you here? The land is already yours since the King decreed it. Despite, if I understand correctly, our not answering your letters. You didn't have to come here and demand that we agree.'

'It is uncertain otherwise.'

'So you recognise the fact we could have fought you

for it despite what King Edward granted. That men could die.' She canted her head, the tension in her body easing a bit more. 'You care about that?'

There was much and little that he cared about. He tapped the chair's arm for a beat before he answered. 'If no blood needs to be shed, it would be foolish to insist on it.'

'And yet you don't agree to marry me in order to avoid the shedding of blood. You're a fool.'

'A fool?' he repeated.

'When there's so much to gain and you baulk, yes.'

'Men die every day for bits of land.'

'So saving your men isn't enough to marry me?'

'My men? I know the worth of Lochmore swords and do not expect any of our blood to be spilled.' Another tap on the chair's arms as he waited for her to reply. When she didn't he said, 'If you remember, you did not immediately agree.'

A moment of hesitation before she arched a brow. 'We are enemies, are we not?'

Something punched through him fast and hot when she repeated his words from earlier. He thought there wouldn't be a battle today, but perhaps he'd found a worthy one.

'Not good enough,' he said.

She sighed. 'We didn't answer your letters so obviously McCrieffs don't agree with the transfer. Marriage would help because if we marry, the transference of land would be done without bloodshed. I, unlike you, do care if blood is spilled. Whether you believe it or not, I care about any man, whether he be Lochmore or McCrieff. I am a healer.'

He leaned forward to rest his elbows on his knees. This brought them closer though she didn't acknowledge it…or realise it. But he did, he was a large man, and with little effort he could yank her off the chair and on to his lap.

Clenching his hands to prevent himself from doing just that, he shook the idea from his thoughts. His inexplicable desire for this woman, for this McCrieff, had no place here.

And yet…they talked of marriage, so how could he stop his thoughts straying? 'You would help heal Lochmore men. Are you now saying we are not enemies?'

'We are.' Ailsa stood and her gown gracefully fell around her, though her own movements were uneven as she secured her shears. 'We will always be.'

He agreed, but he was surprised by her answer. 'And yet—'

'I agreed to marry you?' she interrupted. 'Know this, Lochmore, I was told of the Great Feud as well as you. Our clans have the right to hate each other.'

Maybe here were the answers he sought. 'Such vehemence for such old history. There's more you're not telling me. You revealed your anger when you shouted at your father.'

She skirted around him and he felt the impatient brush of her gown against his legs. 'This history keeps occurring. Even now, I worry about what is happening in the Hall.'

He did, too, but he was more fascinated with watching her pace the small room.

'When did the King make the decree of McCrieff lands?' she asked.

Her father was a fool to have kept her in the dark. Her ire was justified. Maybe was even angry at herself for not realising that something was amiss. 'Last winter after Balliol was crowned.'

She didn't hide the flash of incredulous anger that crossed her fine features. 'That is why your men crossed the border to McCrieff land?'

He nodded.

'Were they celebrating?'

They had been. He'd never seen his father in a rage before, but he had been that day. The men thought a victory had been made. That the land, just because a king decreed it theirs, was theirs. His father had pointed out when it came to bordering land that had been fought over for centuries, nothing was that clear. 'They were punished.'

'Two McCrieffs died that day.'

'And you are the healer,' he said. She didn't act like Lochmore's healer with her gentle ways. Ailsa was fierce. She'd likely stab Death in the heart before it came to take her clansmen away. Anyone she truly cared for she'd most likely… Then a thought occurred to him. 'Or were you close to one of the McCrieffs?'

'I'm close to every McCrieff. I care for them all.'

Not a lover or a husband, then. Still, her pacing seemed to increase as he asked his questions. There was more here. As the son of the Chief, he, too, cared for his clan, but losing a clan member would be different from losing Paiden. If that had occurred, it would be a loss he would roar against until his dying day.

'Did you lose someone else?'

She suddenly hugged her body, her hands roughly rubbing her arms as if she was chilled. 'We should be talking about my father's proposal for us, not my childhood.'

'Your childhood?'

She made a sound of frustration, of anger. 'You don't deserve my secrets, but know that I have just cause for my reservations about this marriage,' she said. 'But even then, I ask you, can you not see the benefits?'

His body recognised the benefits. His desire couldn't avoid them. That red hair and rosy lips. Those blushing cheeks. Her fiery temper.

Even now when he was refusing such connection to her, his body conjured images. How he'd wrap the flames of her hair around his fist as he plundered those lips, as he coaxed her to her knees...

Hands suddenly greedy, he clasped them before she could tell what was truly in his thoughts. Her. She talked of past deaths and he could only think of her. Her father was foolish or maybe wise to leave them in this room together...alone. The small unadorned room only highlighted her worth and he kept noticing it.

'You don't want more deaths, Ailsa. I understand. But your father prevented McCrieff deaths when he confiscated our weapons,' he said. 'Of course, he could kill us. How would I know, since this is our first meeting?'

'As if you'd simply let him. You're wasting time, Lochmore.'

Until her father's return. Her father had made it all too easy for them to come to McCrieff land. Now he understood why.

Sighing, Ailsa continued, 'We know nothing of each other, but that matters not when it comes to our clans. If we marry, no one dies.'

'Perhaps today, or for the next sennight, but distrust and animosity between our clans runs too deep,' he stated.

'Marriage is permanent. The change would be permanent,' she said.

'One was tried before and failed. And we all know whose fault that was.' Legend had it that a woman who had promised to marry a McCrieff had married a Lochmore instead. True or not, it was also well known that the McCrieffs retaliated and relations deteriorated from there.

A slight frown. 'What is known and what is speculated does not matter. The fact is we can start anew.'

If she had experienced the deaths of people she cared for, how could she believe so naively? Frederick, the Tanist, proposed it, but he also said he would remain Tanist and that nothing was a guarantee. 'Did you not hear your father? This is not about starting anew. This is about preserving McCrieff power.'

'That's why you care,' she said. 'Not for lives, but for power.'

Power was everything. Lochmores were given McCrieff land because they held more power. For once, he'd like control of his life. With power, he could.

'Don't you care about it? You want to marry and, by doing so, you preserve the land you have regardless if the King says it is Lochmores. I could not wage battle against your family. Further, you also probably prevent King Edward from taking any more away.'

She opened her mouth, closed it abruptly.

'You didn't think that?'

'I told you why I want it. For lives, which appears to be nothing you care about.' She fingered the shears around her belt. 'It doesn't matter. In the end, the outcome is the same. Two people who have...position and influence in both clans marry.'

'You think I gain power by marrying you though your father said otherwise?'

'You certainly don't lose it. There would be no fight over the land by the border.'

'I'm Lochmore's Chief, I could marry anyone and gain other lands.'

'But none closer or convenient. And for that matter, none merely handed to you.'

Ailsa's beauty was one thing, her unexpected intelligence was another. Everything about her was unexpected. She was fair of face and body. Mere hours in her presence and he knew she had a fine mind as well. There would be no burden to marry her.

He wouldn't voice it, but there was a possibility to gain all the McCrieff lands. An achievement none of his clan would expect. All of this done without bloodshed, but there was a catch. There was always a catch when it came to the McCrieffs and the Tanist confessed it. He didn't intend to concede power. By doing so, Frederick projected to his clan that McCrieffs remained in power.

Where would that leave him? Waiting for the warrior's death, counting the years until he could wrest control...even if he could. However, it was inconceivable that Frederick would want that for his daughter's children. Maybe the old man had hope to combine the clans as well. Frederick, as a McCrieff, would be in a better position to know if that hope was possible.

So he married a McCrieff's daughter, which solved nothing now and only perhaps gained something in the future. Even with all this disclosure, and the almost certainty that Frederick would want a brighter future for his daughter, Rory still sensed a trap.

It was Frederick's movements before he left the room, a jitter to his leg, his sword hand opening and closing. The frequent glances to the door as if he expected it to burst open. His readiness to be on the other side of the door. He left giving the pretext of privacy, but was it possible he stood on the other side of the door to guard it?

For now Rory could hear muffled voices and the clinking of goblets. There was much talking and occasional shouts of merriment. Was he being merely suspicious?

The danger surrounding him hadn't been the travelling on McCrieff land, or the offering of marriage. The danger was something he couldn't see or understand. And for a moment, Rory wished for his sword so he could lay it firmly against Frederick's neck and demand the truth.

There were lies everywhere. That same instinct that told him something was wrong with his past told him something was wrong now. There was disclosure in this room, but something still felt amiss. Secrets, he saw them everywhere, he'd been trained at it since he was very young.

He knew, though he had never been told, he was not, and could not be, Chief Lochmore's son.

Though he emulated his parents, though he behaved and trained as the son of a chief should, something inside him warned that he didn't belong. And it was that which made him refuse the offer now. Not some trap or unknown future. Not some false sense of pride that he wasn't a pawn to game. They were all pawns and everything a trap. It was that frisson of something amiss that held him back.

'As the son of a chief, as an enforcer of King Edward's decree, I cannot accept this offer.'

'Why, because of this power?' she scoffed. 'Because you will not have any since my father will not concede his?'

Power. It was all about power. She might think he held off because of her father, but in fact, he held back because he had none. 'Power is everything.'

'So shortsighted! Today we could have some peace. Blood would not be spilled.'

Rory stood then. He was irritated that he could not tell the full truth because he knew these people weren't. Since that was the case, he'd continue to argue what was known. 'Shortsighted? A marriage isn't only for today, it's for the future. And your father's proposal curtails mine.'

Small room and a woman who should have looked insignificant against his size now that he stood, but she raised her chin defiantly and he saw nothing but her own stubborn strength and fire.

He had some of his own and his impatience with these people, with his own circumstances, roiled harder inside him. But when he took the steps necessary to be even closer to her, to now intimidate her, she held her ground. And he knew, absolutely knew, he lost some of his. Despite the facts and the glaring falsehoods, he wanted her.

'I have shears, Lochmore.'

'Call me Rory.'

A flicker of something across her stunning green eyes and the elegant lines of her neck moved when she swallowed. When he stood with her at the dining table, she had not shown this wariness. Was it the privacy of the room and the fact they were alone? Or was it because his asking her to call him by his name felt too personal?

'If we are to marry, you would need to say my name,' he said.

'But you said we would not marry?'

'Perhaps you persuaded me with your shears.'

Her eyes narrowed, and he couldn't help the curve to his lips. She didn't believe him. Good, she shouldn't.

He shouldn't marry her either and that had nothing to do with what they discussed. There was every chance he could leave today without marrying her and there would still be no bloodshed. Frederick could take him prisoner if he refused the proposal, but that would bring the entire Lochmore clan here, and, if Frederick cared for his daughter, he would not jeopardise her life.

Another scenario could be him leaving here and informing his father that he had ensured the border's safety. A partial untruth, but he'd bet his life that Frederick, meeting him and his men, wouldn't now fight over something that was almost...personal.

All the conjecture led to one conclusion: to marry Ailsa was superfluous.

A half-step more and her gown brushed his legs again. This time there was no movement from her to indicate her impatience or frustration. Her gown was still, like she was before him. Confusion, yes, he saw it in her eyes and the barely discernible way her body tensed. But there was something else now...an awareness that perhaps matched his own.

Could it be she felt as he did? After all, she had agreed to marry him. 'Perhaps you persuaded me, Ailsa, that the marriage is necessary to ensure no more bloodshed.'

'You don't believe that.'

He wanted privacy so he could gain some answers to this day. To understand or at least appreciate Frederick's bargaining his only child. Nothing was clear, except this moment. Right now.

There were falsehoods here, but Ailsa and her need to heal was not one of them. She actually...cared. How that was relevant or whether it should be, he didn't know. But something eased within him.

'You know, we could marry and our clans could still war. There's the probability it could make matters worse. What you want to prevent may come about by our joining.'

She exhaled roughly. 'I told you that our animosity runs deep. I understand that. I also know the land is already yours by a king's decree. Marrying me could solve nothing. And yet... I know that the way matters are between our clans is of no benefit either.

'I lost...' She canted her head and raised her hand. For one infinitesimal moment, he thought she'd lay it on his chest, right on his heart that suddenly beat uncontrollably.

Then the moment was gone. A stuttering of her fingers as if she realised what she was about to do before she lowered and clasped it before her. 'All I want is the possibility of something different.'

A possibility. Her words were another punch to his battered body. Everything here was a possibility. For her the lives saved. For him…power. Control. The chance for more for his clan and hers, for a family of his own, children. He'd have a wife who cared for others with a fierceness he didn't realise he'd wanted until he met her.

Impossible, these possibilities. All the more so for the other pressing reason he shouldn't marry her. They believed him to be the Chief's son and if it ever came to light that he wasn't, what then?

Yet, a possibility for a future he didn't dare dream of… Any warrior, any *man*, would lie and steal for that dream. Maybe he didn't have to go that far. In truth, he was at least named a Lochmore. His mother might have lain with another, but it must have been done in great secret given the truth had never been revealed in all these years. As a result, their marriage would still be a Lochmore marrying a McCrieff and maybe that was enough.

Unless the Tanist discovered the truth one day and took it as an insult. So many possible possibilities. But once something was done, it couldn't be undone. He was proof of that. Marriage and their children were permanent despite his fears of his past.

Thuds and roars from behind the door. They both froze, until goblets thumped on heavy oak tables and laughter rang out.

An offer of marriage.

Marriage. He returned his gaze to Ailsa, who gazed back unwaveringly at him. He admired her again. More so because he'd refused her and she'd replied with reason and pride.

Such fire within her veins and it called to his own. But it was a reminder as well. No matter his dreams or hopes, there was no talk of a happy marriage or children from her. She talked of preventing bloodshed, not peace. She cared, but she didn't say she cared for him. This wasn't personal for her and it shouldn't be for him.

And yet, if this was a trap, they had made the prize too dear not to reach for it. All he needed to do was agree and the possibility of more would be his. But the possibilities of a better future wasn't what pummelled through his chest and coursed hotly through his veins because his body didn't concern itself with property or power. His body believed Ailsa was the prize. Thus, she was his right not as a ruler, but as a man.

He'd take her.

'Say my name, Ailsa. Say it and that possibility you want will be so.'

She straightened, seemingly to brace herself. 'Rory.'

Victory and far sweeter than he had envisioned for this day. Two strides to the door, he flung it open to see Frederick on the other side with his sword out. At Rory's glance, Frederick sheathed it.

A moment of hesitation and a truth rang out. Frederick was guarding the door. But his expression showed something else. Gone was father and warrior, now he carried only the expression of a politician.

A wife who didn't care for him. A father-in-law that had an agenda he knew nothing about. Still, the possibility of more… 'I, as representative of Clan Lochmore, as son of Chief Lochmore, agree to this offer.'

Frederick's eyes switched to his daughter and held. Whatever he saw there, it was enough for him to say, 'As my daughter is witness, it is made in good faith.'

'That won't be good enough,' Rory said.

'Ah, yes, this calls for a formal announcement.'

Chapter Five

Frederick strode to the door leading to the Hall and opened it. Rory held back and looked at the woman who would soon be his wife. Her face was as implacable as her father's. She, too, was a warrior in her own right.

He didn't touch her, nor did he speak, but when she walked quietly up to him he approved. When they left this room, they would be side by side. The image of them both as one entity would be solidified, the words that needed pronouncement almost redundant.

Their entrance quieted the Hall. All his men were hale, hearty, Paiden's keen alertness showing though he lounged as if he was relaxed in his own home. He was up to something as usual.

Then Frederick was saying the words with the necessary reverence and Rory ensured his own gaze locked on to as many clansmen as possible in the cramped quarters. There was surprise by his own clansmen and by McCrieffs. There was also hostility and defiance, which meant Frederick had kept this secret not only from his daughter, but also from his own clansmen. The underlying sense of wrongness again clamoured inside Rory. It was one matter to surprise the Lochmores with an arranged marriage, but such an alliance would have, under normal circumstances, been discussed from every angle with the elders of a clan. Why would Frederick keep it secret from them?

A trap, but he obtained the prize. He and Ailsa's marriage had been announced to all and could not be undone. If he had to sleep with one eye open and keep a guard at his door, if he had to threaten every clansman from now until his death, he would ensure the future he wanted. Because now that hope he'd been trying to contain expanded inside him. He'd made this deal on his own, without his family's approval. Without his father's approval. He would argue that he did it for the clan, to secure the land. He knew the truth—he did it for himself.

When Frederick shoved his hand into the pouch around his waist and cupped dirt in his palm, Rory, without hesitation, accepted the transfer of it to his hand. The dirt was not mere dirt, but McCrieff soil.

More formalities would have to be done, more announcements and ceremonies. So many more customs to uphold, but this Tanist had the foresight to gather dirt to make the legal gesture of transferring McCrieff land to Lochmore. By accepting the dried clods, the transfer of land was complete and binding.

Wily warrior. Frederick had expected Rory to agree to his offer and had gathered the soil before the meeting. But what man wouldn't agree to it? He almost hadn't. He still shouldn't. Frederick had planned for his daughter to marry the Lochmore Chief's son, but Rory alone knew that Lochmore's blood did not flow in his veins and that should have been enough to stop him from marrying now.

Servants were bustling in with freshly filled flagons. Paiden swiped a flagon and a new goblet off the tray to extravagantly pour the contents of a deep rich wine.

His eyes held Rory's, a mixture of all their years of friendship. There was no confusion or surprise in Paiden's eyes. There was true admiration because Paiden understood the struggle Rory had to prove his worth to his father and to his clan. He'd been there all the years, had seen his disappointment and regrets.

He'd been by his side today and didn't flinch when Rory entered the courtyard. Paiden knew why Rory did it. The question would come later if his father and clan would approve the match. And Paiden, with a smirk just under the surface as he gave his congratulations, appeared to already relish the upcoming battles.

The rest of the men he'd brought today were divided in loyalty to him and his father, but Paiden would watch his back in the days and weeks to come.

So when Paiden finished his speech and gulped deep from his goblet, Rory raised his cup as well. But this moment wasn't only about Paiden or his clan, it was about the two people still standing by his side and Rory turned to his soon-to-be wife and her father. Frederick was still gazing at the crowd. Ailsa's gaze, however, was on him.

Steady. Sure. There was hesitancy, but no fear there. In private, she'd given an impassioned speech as to why they should marry and now, after the announcement, it seemed she had not changed her mind.

At that moment, he should have turned again to the crowd, to his clansmen, who were watching, but Ailsa's gaze did not turn away from him and he was loath to look away.

She seemed to be assessing him, watching him as steadily as he wanted to watch her. He could feel the pull of her in that moment, like a man aware that the sun rose and set, but unable to perceive moment by moment how the day changed from day to night.

Her hair might have been what caught his eye, but it was the emotion in her eyes that snared him. His eyes kept to hers and he didn't know when the assessment of each other turned from political to personal, but his body felt it. His soul felt it and he could do nothing to stop it.

And he felt himself being lost as he lifted his cup to his lips to acknowledge Paiden's words when her expression changed. Suddenly. Violently.

Still trapped in the flood of heat in his body, and the tenacious fixation of his thoughts, it took him far too long to register the moment a cry rang out in the Hall and there was a heavy thud. When he swung his gaze to the tables, his own goblet was knocked from his hands.

But the lost goblet didn't matter because the sound and cry wasn't of an oak bench tumbling over by the weight of people. It was Paiden, whose body was crumpled to the ground, and the wild circle of both his clansmen and McCrieffs already forming.

On instinct, Rory pounded to the nearest McCrieff, stealing his weapon. Then, with sword drawn, he stood at his friend's side.

* * *

It wasn't happening. Any of this. All of this. Ailsa couldn't comprehend what had happened before the Lochmore clansman collapsed to the ground, but the instant his goblet slipped from his grip and his pallor drew white, she did. Utterly and absolutely.

A Lochmore, the one with an easy smile, had swiped a flagon of wine and poured it before the servants finished their service. He'd been first to swallow and first to collapse.

Then chaos. Shouts. Violence erupted in that already strained room. She shoved Rory's goblet to the ground, her father's next as she yelled out to the crowd to not drink any. She didn't know if she was heard, but she'd done all she could for others, it was the man who fell who was her only concern now.

Rory was there standing over him. The sword he'd seized cut a wide vengeful swathe around him. The closest to him were the rest of the Lochmore clan. Her own clansmen were standing back, a few with weapons and more reaching for theirs.

McCrieffs and Lochmores in battle in her very home at her very hearth with children around them. She had to reason with them and quick. The collapsed man was prone, panting, his skin beginning to glisten.

Rotten food did not cause this. Poison did. Whatever was given to him was fast, and dangerous, and the small pouch around her waist held no roots to induce vomiting. There was only one way to help him now, but that meant she needed access to him. That meant she needed to argue with a madman.

Rory wasn't the reasoning giant she'd verbally

sparred with just moments before. He was a man, a beast. Thick of bone and looking not quite human. Not the man who had been watching her while her father proposed marriage. Nor the man who courteously escorted her to stand before their clans.

This man was feral and full of rage. She snapped her eyes away from him and surveyed the room. Her father was already issuing orders, demanding for his men to stand down. Half of the McCrieffs lowered their swords, but there were a few who kept theirs out and pointed. Those men did not follow her father's orders, something that alarmed her, but she had no time for that now.

The man dying on the ground had no time for swords or politics. She had no more moments to waste, but grabbed a servant and demanded boiling water and salt to be brought immediately. By the time it reached her it would have cooled enough to pour down the man's throat.

A few Lochmores had swords. She ignored them all and put herself between two Lochmores who stood shoulder to shoulder. 'Let me through!'

No one was listening to her. She shoved the nearest one, but he stayed firm. That man would die without her. 'Lochmore!'

Eyes flashed to hers. She'd seen animals caught in faulty traps that didn't kill. Everything about this man reminded her of a tortured animal.

'Never,' he vowed.

'He'll die.'

'You intended that, McCrieff. You invited us here. Lowered our guard with fake promises of peace. Fed us poison to destroy us.'

'Nothing is false here,' Frederick said. 'Our truce is true.'

'My friend at my feet proves your lies.'

The man groaned, clutching his stomach. She only had moments to spare him. She shoved herself forward and made it through the Lochmores, who were taken by surprise.

Rory lifted his sword and stared her straight in the eyes. The hairs on the back of her neck rose.

'You point a sword at a woman?' Frederick roared.

'I point at an enemy.'

Ailsa had enough. 'While you point that sword, he's dying. I'm not a woman or an enemy right now, Lochmore.' She indicated the pouch around her waist and spied the water bearer enter the room. 'I am a healer and his only chance.'

This was ridiculous. She'd been ordered around enough tonight. Keeping her eyes on him, she moved around the sword, knelt and froze again as she felt the prick of a sword at her neck. She ignored it. She didn't care, it wasn't what concerned her. Whether she lived or died was a matter of fear, whether this man lived or died was up to her.

Shoving with all her weight to move his body on to his side, she retorted, 'You can stab me all you want, but I will save this man.'

'You harm him further and I'll kill you.'

Save her from men who did not think! 'Kill me all you want, but help me now!' Another shove, but he was too heavy. Damn them all. Another shove. Why wouldn't they help?

A clatter of metal and Rory knelt at her side. 'What do you need?'

She'd ask him later what changed his mind. For now, she'd take his help. 'Turn him on his side, stick your fingers down his throat. We must rid him of the wine.'

There were complications when inducing vomiting, but those would have to wait. Rory shoved two fingers. It wasn't enough. Grabbing the warmed water and salt, she forced it down the man's throat. Waited, then pressed on his stomach.

Heaves of water, of wine, of food burst out. With a nod to Rory, she pressed again and he shoved his fingers deep. The man emptied his stomach again. Most of it was clear.

Pouring another goblet of hot water, she crushed and threw in mint and clove. Usually so careful with amounts, but now she went by instinct and haste. The man was losing consciousness.

'Pull him up!' she ordered Rory. 'Drink this,' she demanded and poured the contents down the man's throat. A moment of relief when he swallowed. After vomiting, she needed to be alert for dehydration.

It would only take moments to know if what she'd done had worked. She glanced at Rory, whose considerable body was cradled around his friend, the look in his eyes and countenance too vulnerable for the crowd around them, and she drew herself taller to shield him. When that wasn't enough, she gripped his arm tight until he looked at her and she showed him where to place his arms.

'What is his name?' she asked.

'Paiden,' he said and a wealth of information was in

that said name. This wasn't only a fellow comrade of Rory's, this was his very dear friend.

Ailsa's first fear was conquered, but there were more. Paiden not rousing being only one of them; Rory holding him and the men surrounding them was another. Here on the floor, her concentration on Paiden and Rory, she could believe there was no one else. But now...

'He needs a bed.'

Rory shoved his arms under his friend and stopped. 'Your gown.'

Ruined beyond any recognition. No matter, it wasn't her best and the chemise was still good. 'Cut it and secure it. I'll look at the contents later.'

He drew a blade, and the cloth fell from her body. It was done.

Swiping the ruined cloth and standing on shaking legs, she ignored the murmurs and tense glares assaulting her and faced her father. He stood alone, his body ready to fight as he faced the room and not her.

'Our guest needs a room,' she announced. Chin raised, she waited until Rory and another man lifted Paiden from the floor, nodded to Hannah who now held the water, then walked slowly out the side doors and away from the crowd.

Chapter Six

Hours in this room passed as he watched the morning turn to late afternoon. Hours hearing his friend's uneven breath, but nothing else. Even asleep Paiden usually talked, his limbs moving as though he was marching across Scotland.

Desperate to get some sleep, he'd been four years of age when he'd begged his mother to make Paiden sleep anywhere else but in his bed. It been a joke between them ever since. To see him still was unnatural.

As was being locked in a McCrieff bedroom with a healer sitting in the corner. The chair was giant with pillows and she pretended to be asleep. Her eyes were closed, her breath soft, but he felt her awake like him.

He'd been the one to lock the door after Frederick spouted words that justice would be done. Rory didn't listen to anything except the healer and another woman called Hannah who seemed too young to be of any use. For himself, there were two Lochmores on the other side in rotating patterns. They wouldn't be caught unawares again.

'I know you're awake,' he said.

A creak of the chair. 'I can't sleep.'

It was late, she needed to, he needed to, but though the castle was quiet, the tension permeated the very air they breathed.

'My men won't attack tonight,' he said. 'I ordered them not to.'

'For how long?' she said.

He wanted to growl. 'I could say the same for your clan. Your father took our weapons.'

'To keep the peace.'

'That didn't work did it? And here I am, tending my friend who may be dying.'

A louder creak of the chair as if she sat up properly, but he refused to turn around to confront her. He held on by a thread. He might have cocooned them in the room to help Paiden, but part of it was to protect everyone from him. There was a part of him that wanted to slaughter everyone in his path.

'I'm here, too,' she said quietly. 'I'm here for your clansman. For you.'

'Don't,' he snapped, but his words didn't hold the heat they'd had just a moment ago. They couldn't. She hadn't yelled back at him, but stated a fact. He didn't dare believe it was the truth. She wasn't here for Paiden, whom she had never met, or for himself, though she'd agreed to marry him.

'You're the healer, isn't it your requirement to be here?' he said.

'Yes.'

'Well, then tell me, healer, will he live?'

A soft noise, but he couldn't tell if it was in agreement or non-committal. In the end, all she said was, 'There are hundreds of different tinctures and concoctions that could have been used.'

Her voice was strong, but he heard the strain behind it. He didn't know this woman. Not at all, but he knew she had a spine and opinions. She'd been giving them since the moment they'd been introduced and now she didn't give him one at all. 'Tell me.'

'I'm trying. If it is poison—'

'It is,' he growled.

'It could have been his food.'

There it was. An opinion and wrong. 'It hit too fast, it hurt only him. That isn't food.'

Absolute silence behind him, but he didn't move, didn't take his eyes away from Paiden. When he woke, Rory wanted to be the first person his friend saw.

'It could have been in the wine,' she admitted. From her voice she was still in the corner. Sitting or standing, he didn't care. 'I don't know how much he drank, what the properties were or how long it was in his stomach.'

'We saw him drink,' Rory said. 'We saw him fall. And you know how long it was in his stomach because you were right there watching him die!'

A noise cut short. She wanted to say words and held herself back. Why now? 'Say it.'

'You want me to say it's your fault because you held a sword to my neck and didn't let me get to him quick enough?'

The truth burned him, but he wanted that. He could have been the one to kill his friend.

'It's not true,' she quickly said. 'I don't know for certain if those moments counted. We emptied his stomach until it ran clear. That is what counts.'

'Don't,' he spat out. 'You think to soften me to you? You think I'll forgive this. Ever?'

Did she think he'd forgive himself? What had this day brought him? He leaned his elbows against the bed and rubbed his face. Nothing. This day brought him nothing. No battle. No land. No wife. His friend at death's door. He came here to prove himself. To prove his worth to his father. He'd started to hope and now he had less than he came with.

'I don't ask for forgiveness,' she said. 'I've done nothing wrong.'

He remembered the moment she knocked the goblet out of his hand. She'd also worked tirelessly fingering and identifying his friend's vomit while Lochmores and McCrieffs yelled and pointed fingers. Still, she was not without blame. 'Your clan has done something wrong.'

She gasped. 'We don't know that.'

'You think Lochmores could have poisoned one of their own?' Rory looked over his shoulder. The woman was sitting cross-legged on the chair with a pillow in her lap.

Her hair had fallen loose when she tended Paiden in the hall, she'd discarded the cut gown when the woman, Hannah, brought in another. Though she had thrown the new gown over her head, she had never bound it and the brown fabric swirled around her.

With her red hair and her fine features she looked fey. As though a sprite had entered the room.

'Are you saying Lochmores never harm Lochmores?' She arched her brow. When he remained silent, she continued. 'That's what I thought. It's certainly feasible that a Lochmore would harm a Lochmore to start a war between us.'

'We are already enemies—throwing kindling on a roaring fire is futile.' He turned a bit more so he could see her fully. 'You can't possibly believe a Lochmore harmed one of his own?'

When her lips tightened and she remained silent, he repeated her words, 'That's what I thought.'

He turned around. Paiden was still as silent as a grave. He wanted to beg for him not to die like this. Not here on McCrieff ground without a sword in his hand. But there was a McCrieff at his back and he wouldn't give her the pleasure of seeing his grief or his anger.

He didn't trust her though he allowed her to tend Paiden and he'd locked them in the room together. A risky move if he wanted to annul their betrothal later. He'd seen the calculation and cunning in Frederick's eyes as he, too, recognised Rory's actions, but Rory hadn't cared at the time—his immediate concern was his friend.

He cared now as the hours went by and his friend didn't wake. More and more he didn't want to tie himself to this clan. To the falsity here. He had sensed a trap, he had sensed wrongness and still he'd agreed.

Now he was here. It was still day, but they had been alone for hours, the tension between them palpable. She'd warned him that there was nothing to do but wait, but he'd never had patience nor had he had to learn.

Ailsa, on the other hand, sat quietly in a chair. There were shadows under her eyes that weren't there before. Had Paiden's poisoning put those shadows there or did something else concern her and cause sleeplessness? He suspected both. There was...duplicity here.

After all, though she argued Lochmores could harm Lochmores, it was a feeble attempt. She, too, suspected McCrieffs would harm Lochmores despite inviting them to their table. More confusing yet, she seemed surprised by that.

Her father, too. Despite the betrayal in the Hall, her father still wanted them married. Right now, Rory wanted to bundle Paiden on a horse and get them out of here.

His only consolation was that he'd sent notice to his father of the illness and his agreement to marry. Maybe he would receive counsel back.

Because though he wanted to leave, he couldn't. Paiden was far too ill to move. Marry a McCrieff? As if he would. As if he could now. Except the longer Paiden stayed quiet the more aware he was of her. She wasn't resting now, her eyes no doubt on his turned back. Watching him breathe as he watched his friend breathe. He didn't need to be told, but Paiden wasn't waking soon. Rory could feel it. His friend was next to him, but he was somewhere far away. He wanted him back.

And though he didn't trust her, there was no one else to confer with. 'Who did this to him?' Rory said.

'I don't know.'

'It happened in your Hall, with your wine—don't tell me you don't know.'

'I don't—' She sighed. 'It doesn't matter what I say, you won't believe me anyway.'

Was that true? No. Because he had locked them in

the room together. He trusted her enough to care for his friend. Some small bit inside him trusted her. 'I do.'

'That doesn't make sense. There's no reason for you to.'

She questioned his sanity. He did to.

'You're direct, aren't you?' he said instead of answering her question. The truth was he didn't know the reasons. Not fully. He'd known this woman for mere hours, but he'd seen her in the shadows of the doorway, watched her pretend to descend the stairs for the first time to the hall. Since then they'd been in constant disagreement.

'Yes,' she replied.

He wanted to laugh—even that was blunt and to the point. 'Headstrong. Stubborn. Determined.' If they could talk about something, anything else, maybe he'd get through these first moments until Paiden woke. He needed his friend to wake.

'Why are you talking to me?' she asked. 'Why did you leave me in here and order everyone else out?'

Why did she stay? Why did she tend his friend if McCrieffs hated Lochmores? 'You're the healer.'

'Yes, but I'm a McCrieff. Why?'

Stubborn. He saw that when she fought her father on his proposal. Reasonable. He realised that when she made her argument on their marriage.

Could all of that been false? If so, he couldn't believe in anything. This woman was…honest, for a McCrieff. He'd do the same.

'You knocked the goblet out of my hand, out of your father's hands.'

A stunned moment. 'I didn't think you noticed.'

'Not then.' It was all he thought about now. That and how Frederick looked at the time. His eyes not on his daughter tending a dying man, but on the rest of the Hall as if it would mutiny. As if the battle that should have been in the field would erupt between dining tables instead.

'Why did you knock it out of your father's hands? If this is merely a McCrieff against a Lochmore, why did you suspect the wine to be poisoned for him?'

She was silent again and he imagined the tightening of her lips. No McCrieff would have allowed Lochmores on their land or to dine at their table. The poison was more in keeping with what had gone on in the generation before them. He'd been blinded by the marriage proposal, by the false hopes of his own future. And that was the bitterest truth of it all.

Nothing would take him by surprise any more. The first matter that needed to be understood was why, after generations of hate between the clans, did the poisoning surprise Fredrick and Ailsa?

'What is happening here, Ailsa?'

A pause. 'I don't know.'

Still mistrust. Still a McCrieff and his friend could be dying. Enough of this. Enough of indecision and nothing happening. Enough of not knowing what his past was. This day was to be his future. This morning he thought it would begin with bloodshed. In that room, he thought it would be done by marriage.

Bloodshed or marriage, he didn't care. He merely wanted it to begin. He stood and faced her. Her complexion was pale and she clenched the pillow in her lap.

He couldn't trust anyone. They couldn't trust him

either, but he was promised something this day and he
would take it.

'We'll marry. Tonight. I'll allow for you to arrange
what needs to be done, but it will happen.'

She threw the pillow on the floor and stood. 'I'm
not marrying you.'

'You will go back on your word?'

Ailsa yanked on her gown as it snagged on the chair.
In her worry for Paiden, she hadn't tied the laces and
now it hung indecently. 'Your friend—'

'Just because you marry me, does that mean you will
no longer be the healer?'

This man who stood before her wasn't sane. He
couldn't be. He'd come here to conquer the McCrieffs.
To wrest the land a king had given to his clan. Instead,
he'd been welcomed and fed and given fine ale.

He'd been given *her*. Another tug and her gown was
free, but she clenched it to her chest like some maiden
in a tower. What was happening here today? She had
no idea. Her father had sold her and, though he'd acted
with guilt, he'd meant every word. She refused to believe it was with ill intent, so there must be a reason
for the secrecy and betrayal. Never could she imagine
a marriage between the clans that would be sanctioned
by Hamish or the majority of elders.

This plan and decision came solely from her father,
who had protected her all her life. This decision could
not have been made lightly and came at a price to him.
Her father wouldn't sacrifice her for the clan. No, he
was Tanist, that was true, and a rightful heir to the clan.
He'd always been a good father and, after her mother's

death, he'd been devoted to his children. He wouldn't, couldn't simply sacrifice her. But he would protect her.

When she told Rory that she didn't know what was happening here, she meant it. 'You want to marry me when you must be worried I'll murder you in the marriage bed?'

'Worried isn't the word I'd use for how I feel right now.'

She couldn't tell how he felt right now. His words were clipped as if he said them through a clenched jaw, but his hands were unclenched, his body almost relaxed. His dishevelment, brown hair loose, clothes dusty from the ride, from the day. Stained from the armour that he had worn earlier and now was piled in the corner as if it wasn't valuable. He was half-careless, half-dogged. Who was this man and why had she readily agreed to marry him?

From his silence it was obvious he wouldn't share the truth of his feelings...if he had any. She should have fought more against the proposal. It wasn't only the leaders or the men who had gone mad, it was everyone. Hastily, she adjusted her gown, found the laces and clumsily tied them. She didn't care if they were crooked, she just couldn't storm out of here naked.

She felt exposed now though the fabric swamped her. He might not share his feelings, might be able to keep his expression neutral, but she couldn't. She wasn't trained in the art of lies and deceit. In truth, she encouraged open dialogue to better heal.

How could she ever know if Rory spoke the truth? One moment, he didn't want her, then when no facts were changed, he did. He hated her, but he also wanted to marry her.

And yet, a part of her still wanted what they had agreed to in that small room downstairs. Outwardly, she had agreed to the marriage to end the killing, to possibly stop future strife. Inwardly… She wanted to curse at the old healer Rhona for telling her stories and filling her head with possibilities that there wasn't only hate in the world between McCrieffs and Lochmores. That there could be something more. Daydreams from a child. Every one of them.

She wanted to curse herself for listening and begging to be told more. Because she couldn't get the idea out of her heart that a Lochmore and McCrieff marriage could be something good. But more than that… much more. There was something about Rory that intrigued and beguiled her. Something that had started in that courtyard…

She yanked harder on her laces, cursing herself for not having Hannah take care of these when she handed her the gown. But she'd been so aware of the intimacy of the room, of how close Rory was. His focus had been on his friend, but her focus had been on him. A man in the room and she only wore a thin chemise.

She'd been aware of him since the courtyard and even more so in the adjoining room. Once he agreed to marry her, she began to think of him as her husband… as someone to share a marriage bed.

It was more than how he looked, it was the way he moved. How he'd sat in the chair and stretched his legs. His easy gait, the drumming of the fingers on his left hand. When he'd leaned forward in his chair, for one wild moment she'd thought he would snatch her out of hers.

At her father's announcement to the Hall, Rory's bearing had been magnificent. He'd faced the crowd, his expression stunning her, and she couldn't—

'Do you need help with those?' he said.

Ready to give him a pithy retort, she raised her chin and lost whatever cutting words were waiting to be said.

This wasn't the man who had entered the courtyard or ate at the table or negotiated for marriage. This wasn't the man who had wielded his sword or shown such a moment of raw vulnerability when his friend fell it pierced her to think of it.

This was a man who was watching a lady dress herself. And everything in her knew it.

His eyes were on her sides where her fingers had gotten hopelessly tangled and trapped. His body was still held in that easy manner of his, but there was an alertness about him now. There was colour in his cheeks, and his brows were slanted down.

His lips were slightly parted to let in air and they looked slicked somehow as if he licked them before she had turned her head. Slick, soft, and for the first time in her life she wanted to kiss a man.

She braced herself when he took a step forward and another until his fingers were at her side, there with her own fingers that he slowly released from the laces.

Startled at the intimate touch, she wanted to step away, then realised she hadn't answered him if she wanted help. He'd taken her stunned amazement at wanting to kiss him as acquiescence for him to dress her.

Lowering her arms, she answered, 'Thank you.'

He yanked a bit, jarring her already unsteady stance against him.

'Sorry,' he whispered and helped her right herself. 'The strings are knotted. How did you get them like this?'

How did *they* get like this; from arguing of poisoning and intrigues to her wanting to touch his lips? To feeling for an instant her body curve to his before she found her balance again.

'I've never been good at them because I've never had patience for them. At least with these gowns it's expected to have another person dress you. If not for that, I'd feel a complete fool.'

'You haven't...ordered them to behave?'

She felt the curve to her lips. To laugh now? Impossible moment, impossible day. 'Countless times.'

He tied the lace and moved to her other side. 'There aren't any la—' She gasped when she felt the back of his fingers glide down her side. There were no laces, only the smooth seam of the gown. He'd caressed her for no purpose other than to touch her.

'Do you have an answer for me, Ailsa?'

Rory stood in front of her, asking her to marry him. Rory was here in her home, in this room. If Rhona were here now...

No matter what she felt like as he stood before her, there were more important matters than daydreams. And yet her logical response still held.

In the end, there was only one satisfactory answer. The one she had already given him. The reality was that if King Edward was willing to give away part of the land, there was no stopping him from giving it all away to the Lochmores. With her marriage, she could secure something for her clan. The land at least would be certain. Any peace between clans or a real marriage all but certainly doomed with the poisoning of Paiden.

Who could possibly have done it and why? Had it been planned before, or had it been an impetuous act when the announcement was made? And *what* was he poisoned with?

The world had gone mad; she needed to remember Rory was her clan's enemy and there was no trust between them. For his friend's sake, he might even hate her. Yet even so, she'd would make the sacrifice because her father had her loyalty, her clan had her loyalty. Despite what she wanted for herself, despite the dream of something greater, the logical choice still held.

'I'll marry you. Tonight. For the clans.'

Anger flashed in his eyes when he locked them with hers. 'For the clans then.'

Chapter Seven

'Take off your gown.'

His voice was no more than an order and with a tone she imagined he gave to his men when in training.

Ailsa had heard his voice in its many tones. The negotiator when he agreed to the land and to her. The wrathful warrior when he thought his friend was irreparably harmed. And when he said his vows, his voice resonated throughout the chapel. It had sounded as though he meant them.

Had that been less than an hour ago? Everything had happened so quickly. Her father and two Lochmores had been standing outside the door when they emerged from Paiden's room and announced that they would marry that very night.

Her father had looked relieved, the Lochmores surprised. She was properly dressed, but had been alone with him. If Rory hadn't announced it, her father would have forced the issue.

Oh, to be not at the whim of men and customs! But even men were at the whim of those higher than them.

Lochmores and McCrieffs were together because of a king's decree. But that did no good now.

Not for her, the wife of a Lochmore. *This* Lochmore who was full of concern and wrath because his friend was poisoned and would not wake. There was no trust between them. She knew it in every part of her being. A marriage for peace this was not. The most she could do now was to ensure her clan did not lose any more to King Edward.

Still, she did not bend to any man. 'And so I'm to simply take off my gown. No polite conversation, no offers of ale?'

A muscle clenched in his jaw. 'What more is there to say between you and me?'

'We could talk about tonight…exchange pleasantries.'

'You want to talk of the weather or perhaps leeks?'

Impossible night. She'd always done her duty to her father, to the clan. By marrying this man, she'd done it again. But maybe she should have stayed selfish. Maybe her first instinct to run out of the room was correct.

Her friend had died years before. Crushed under Lochmores' hooves. Just months ago, a skirmish occurred and two McCrieffs died. Now she had married one?

'Is it so wrong to ask you to be pleasant?' she said.

A rough exhalation. 'I did not thank you for requesting the return of our swords.'

He wasn't thanking her now.

Maybe this was how marriage nights went when a man from an enemy clan came to conquer land and married to gain more instead. Except, she'd seen a different side to this man. Was that man now gone because his friend might die? If so, for her it did not matter. She would not be treated so callously. He spoke to her as if she was a nuisance, a chore. She would not stand for it.

'If you are a reasonable man, you will understand I will not take off my gown. I will not be raped.'

They stood in her room that seemed so much smaller with his presence, though he wasn't looking at her, nor did he seem to be taking in the room that she once prided herself on. Instead, the moment the door closed and locked them he began pacing from one end to the other. His movements were of a caged animal as he demanded that she strip as though it was chore he needed hastily over with.

A part of her understood that caged feeling. For she herself was forced into this predicament. She was never asked to marry, there were no soft words of love between them. Her father had negotiated her as if she were of no more consequence than sheep. And, yes, her father did have control over her and, if she married, her husband as well. But she was more than property and whatever she wanted of her marriage would begin here.

'Do you think a gown would hinder a rape?' he said.

She did not know this man, but she recognised his anger. If he still suspected and hated her for his friend's health, why did he continue with this marriage? Ailsa could only come to one conclusion: this was, as she first said, a political alliance. She came with land and a title. His friend's life didn't alter that. He might resent that it was she who came with such a price, he might hate her if Paiden died, but he was a Lochmore, his father's son, and so he did his duty.

But she refused to be a duty and he needed to stop walking away and turning his back to her. 'A gown wouldn't stop a rape, but it's a far cry from a willing woman,' she said.

'Do you think of yourself as unwilling, Wife?'

There was no possibility to feel like a wife. He had arrived this very day and was still her enemy though her father forced her to see reason. Even with such a logical decision and agreement to save her clan, Ailsa could think of no diplomatic reply. As for unwilling or willing…

Rory must have seen her indecision for his upper lip curved sardonically. 'That's what I thought. We both know what must occur tonight. Take off your gown.'

She wouldn't. Not because she had some fanciful dreams of what her wedding night would be, but because she was worth more than this.

'You first,' she replied.

That stopped his frustrating pacing. 'What did you say?'

Wanting him to stop his pacing and look at her and him turning to her were two different things. Now she felt pinned by his gaze. No heat, no warmth. It wasn't restlessness that caused his curt words. He was angry. Still. Despite the fact she'd agreed to the marriage and saved his friend with a blade pricking her neck.

She could be angry, too. None of this was her fault. She'd explained that to him already. If this was how they married, with him blaming her for matters out of her control, it would stop right now or there would be no wedding night.

'I said you first to undress. Why should it be only

me? If any of this is to happen between us, it must come from both of us.'

His widening gaze swept over her and then again. Whatever he was looking for, he didn't find it because he still bore the stubborn perplexed look. 'You are direct for a virgin.'

She was told her speech bordered on insulting, but she had never been insulted in turn. They wouldn't dare. Everyone here knew her status and what her father would do. 'You think I talk like a common whore?'

He blinked. 'I meant no—'

'You did mean offence. I'm a healer; I've also been a midwife. Since I was young enough to carry rags and herbs, I've been at the beginning and the ending of lives. I've seen everything in between as well. I may not have engaged in the act, but I know what needs to occur.'

His brow furrowed, but he kept silent. If he wanted it all to be told to him, she would. 'So for us to lie together, *both* of us have to take our clothes off…at least to some extent. If you want me to take off my gown, then I require you to take off an article of clothing as well.'

'Women do not talk as you do.'

'These are words, are they not?'

'Not in any order I've heard before.'

Lochmore wasn't that far from McCrieff. She understood him perfectly, but perhaps he had been in other lands and wasn't used to native speech. Maybe she wasn't being reasonable and making assumptions. 'Have you travelled far?'

This time his mouth pursed. It didn't, however, soften his countenance at all. 'I've never left our land.'

Ah. This was an argument she'd heard since the moment she could speak in sentences. 'You think I talk too bluntly.'

'Decidedly.'

'For a woman or a man?' she asked.

'Is there a difference?'

That stopped her. She couldn't count how many conversations she had with villagers or those travelling through on how a woman should talk. Now he was suggesting there was no difference between a man or woman. Something in her eased at his words. If he was like her father when it came to her independence—

'You talk too bluntly for both sexes,' he continued.

Enough! He wasn't so different from other men. There was still time to show him another way of being with women, with his wife.

'You should get used to the way I talk.' She was a great warrior's daughter. First born and given freedom. She knew she would sacrifice a bit of that freedom by marrying another, she knew she lost some of it when her father became Tanist. But in this, in the private chambers of their bedroom, there would be no ordering or reining her in.

'I talked plainly instead of in riddles,' she continued. 'Wouldn't this make it easier between the two of us if we use plain speech?'

'I don't think anything between the two of us will be easier regardless of the way you talk.'

'How would you know?'

'You have yet to comply with my request.'

Now it was her time to be perplexed. All she had heard since the door closed was him ordering her about. 'Request?'

'It is our wedding night, yet you've not taken off your clothes.'

There was no air inside her lungs. She needed to talk to this man she didn't know and he ordered her to remove her clothing so he could continue with his duty. As if this meant nothing. Since his arrival there had been too much chaos on McCrieff soil, she would take back some control now. 'And you say I talk too bluntly.'

'I am a man and gave an order.'

'I don't listen to orders.'

'Nor to plain speech.'

Whatever political alliance her father needed, whatever she thought she knew of this man Rory, had to be wrong. There was no logic or reasonableness in him. She couldn't even hold a conversation with him. 'This won't work.'

'Our marriage? Too late for that.'

She stepped back as if he hit her. 'You think I deny this marriage? I gave vows before God and all my clan, including my father.'

His eyes narrowed. 'Including me.'

She opened her mouth to deny it simply out of spite; however, she might be blunt, but she was no liar. 'Including you,' she agreed.

He took a few steps away to face a wall before he braced his left hand against it. He stayed like that as she waited for him to continue. Another moment longer before he said anything at all. 'What won't work?'

She'd never seen a man with mannerisms such as his. He was large, formidable, and though it looked as if he pushed against the wall it felt as if in some way the wall gave him some support.

'What do you mean?' she asked though she wasn't truly paying attention. Rather, she avidly watched him drum his fingers against the plaster.

'You mentioned that this won't work,' he said.

Ah, yes. 'I meant our talking wasn't going to work.'

He turned his head to look at her and a lock of his brown hair fell across his forehead. 'I admit this conversation is confusing despite the number of words we're using, but it does appear we're conversing.'

'I meant the ones we will have in the future.' She wanted to put her hands on her hips. 'Do you intend to get used to my bluntness?'

More drumming of his fingers before he huffed out a breath that could have been a laugh or annoyance, she didn't know him well enough to know the difference.

With a shove against the wall, he stood. Then with his eyes on her, he seemed to come to a decision.

Something in her braced for it. Would he accept the way she talked, or had she married an intolerant man? Would there at least be some understanding between them even if trust was tenuous? Or would he—reach behind him and yank his tunic over his head.

Rory revelled in his wife's slight gasp. Her blunt words were none that he ever heard from a woman. As the Chief's son and heir, he was used to women catering to his words. If he did give them notice, they minced and blushed. Even his own mother was soft, gentle.

This woman, this wife of his, did nothing he'd ever encountered. She wanted to speak her mind, but it seemed her stunning eyes wanted to take their fill of him as well. And just as he heard every word she spoke regardless of whether he agreed with them, he felt every brush of her gaze against his bare skin.

He couldn't explain his rash action of taking off his tunic. He had entered this marriage knowing what was expected and needed of his role. He said his vows and closed the door to this bedroom understanding precisely what needed to be done tonight to honour his vows and protect his clansmen.

For though he'd bargained to marry her, he knew he could not, should not, consummate the marriage. How could he when a betrayer was in their midst? For Paiden's sake, for his own, he had to leave a way out. For though the McCrieffs dangled a bright future for him, they also took it away when Paiden collapsed to the floor.

More the fool he if he blithely denied that traitorous fact. But facts blurred when he was in the same room with Ailsa. He had not expected her and whatever it was between them. In the end, it seemed his reaction to this woman was also traitorous. Being in this room shook whatever convictions he'd intended.

Who was he fooling? Nothing had gone according to plan since he'd stepped across the stream bordering the lands. And all his intentions seemed foolish as he stood in this room and faced his wife.

He wanted, and though his friend could be dying in another room, he still wanted her.

The sounds of revelry were quieter now, the candle flames lower in their wax. The room's shadows thickened around them, cocooning them. He felt the quietness, felt the air in the room against his skin. It changed the longer they stood there staring at each other. Heavier, thicker, and harder to pull into his lungs.

He knew what this was becoming and what it shouldn't be. Where were her words now? 'You're quiet.'

She gave a wave in his general direction. 'I didn't expect—'

'A man?'

'That isn't what I meant. I mean…'

The longer she looked, the longer desire coiled around them. His own skin felt branded by her few words, by the gasp of breath she took.

This wouldn't do. He agreed to marry her, he didn't agree to trust her. It was a betrayal of his friend who still did not wake. Of his clan until he found the coward who poisoned him. And those were the truths she was aware of. There were more untruths he never intended to say because a wife should not have been his future.

Yet here she was and he didn't need to notice the flush along her cheekbones or the elegant way she turned her hands. 'Surely in all your help with life and death you've seen a man's bared back?'

Ailsa went quiet before her whisper. 'Not like this.'

'No, I imagine not like this.' She was his wife and he her husband. Politics. Paiden. He felt the pressure of both fade as Ailsa's eyes took in every contour. He might never have battled, but he trained for it, he'd been born for it. It was his right as a Highlander and ruler to brandish a sword, to take a life before it was taken from him. His body bore proof to his perseverance and training.

His body, however, wasn't thinking of battle or politics, it wanted something else entirely. And even that was mired with other layers that should be heeded, but were also ignored.

Despite her demand, despite her words, Rory knew Ailsa was inexperienced. A knowledgeable woman would never look at him the way Ailsa was, with a greedy innocence that caused his heart to thump in his chest and his blood to pool hot and fast in his groin.

Her eyes didn't stroke his chest in a blatant perusal, but flitted, darted, dashed from the curve of his shoulders to the tapering of his waist. Her eyes, her parted lips, were friction to the flames that made the heat between them erupt.

'Your clothes,' he ordered, his voice rough; his words cut short. He was amazed he could say that much.

'Are you saying it's my turn?' Ailsa replied, her tongue folding along the seam of her lips before pulling her full lower lip deeper in her mouth.

Tracking that move, he could not say a word, so gave a curt nod.

She walked slowly to the bed and sat, and his mind blanked. Her hair, her gown against the contrast of the bedding was mesmerising. He'd not intended to undress at all this evening. Resolved to make this marriage in name only until justice was met, he'd counted on her innocence to make that plan easy.

Instead, he found an experienced virgin. An innocent siren. How was he to give her pleasure only when she demanded his tunic so those eyes of hers could caress him?

Her beauty and grace affected him as no other woman. If they kept silent and he knew nothing else of her, perhaps with heroic effort, he could gaze and touch without losing himself.

But he knew her spirit. Her strength. He'd held a blade to her neck and she'd still ordered him about so she could tend Paiden. Now she sat on her bed covered in the softest of white and green linen to unlace her shoe.

Her movements were quick, efficient, and she looked every inch the Chief of her own clan or a goddess from tales past. He was a fool to think he could control this wedding night. He hadn't been able to control watching her in the courtyard or as they'd dined on supper.

And far worse than that, he hadn't been able to control how his hands had trembled just that bit, just enough, when he'd taken her hands in his and said his marriage vows.

Her flaming hair bound, her green eyes searing him as she'd whispered her vows in turn. He might not understand her, his mind fighting against hers at every turn, but his body…

His body resented that he stood still, that he didn't take the few steps towards her and press her back against the bed. It took every ounce of will to merely watch her toss her shoes in the corner and roll down her hose with fingers he wanted on his own skin.

When she stood, he swore he lost his breath as he waited for her to take off the rest. He'd never wanted this much, desired like this before. It was that lack of patience, that forced him to say the words. 'Your gown?'

She tilted her head. 'You want my gown off?'

'Is that not what I asked from the very beginning?'

'I asked something as well.'

Did she mean for him to accept her words? No man would accept such bluntness in a wife. He wasn't about to start. He'd been raised to believe that men were the providers, rulers, leaders, and women had different priorities. Of home and hearth. His mother was soft spoken, delicate, frail.

Ailsa, however, could be a warrior on the battlefield. She surprised him to the point he didn't know if he wanted to get his bearings or be left reeling. Agreeing with her demands for him to remove his clothing was mistake. He knew it, yet he leaned against the wall, shoved off his shoes and kicked them to same corner she did hers.

She glanced at his feet and looked back up. 'I've taken off more clothing than you.'

His skin was bare to her eyes and though her shoes and hose were more clothes than he'd shed, that cursed gown covered all of her. 'But not nearly enough.'

He took in the hem of her gown to the curve of her waist to the flush of her cheeks. Her eyes were equal parts ire and heat.

She knew what he wanted, but still defied him. She asked him for clothing as well, but didn't know what was at stake. Even if his doubts on his past were no more, there was Paiden. There was an enemy about and this alliance was for politics only. As such he needed to remain in control. Removing his breeches wouldn't happen. He'd stand here all night if need be.

'You want more,' she said as bluntly as ever. To him the words were a siren's call.

He closed his eyes on that. Always. He always wanted more and how was he to say he did and still deny himself? Apparently, he didn't need to, for he heard the tug of fabric and an impatient huff of breath.

Ailsa was struggling with her laces.

'I know I said I have troubles,' she said, 'but usually not this much.'

She looked so…frustrated that it eased something in him. Helping her was something he could do. Something simple. 'Let me.'

When he drew near so they almost touched, she turned her head. It made the closeness a bit easier. A bit, but not much. Like this he could see how many colours of red her hair contained, he could smell the lavender and evergreen that was brushed in her gown.

She exhaled. 'This is a very strange evening.'

The laces weren't so tangled and since they were made of silk, they unwound with a few simple tugs. 'Most husbands and wives undress in their chambers.'

'Most husbands and wives do not negotiate for each item of clothing. We didn't have this much negotiation when we agreed to marry.'

'True,' he answered because it was the truth and saying anything else would bring light to the lies he already had to protect.

Saying vows was no negotiation, but a swift sword of duty to the only son of a Highland chief. He had no power to avoid it. Everything else, however, he'd negotiate to ensure he kept the little power he had left. For no matter what, he would resolve the wrong that was done here and he wouldn't make any more mistakes.

To do that, he had to leave his breeches on, but with a few more tugs the ribbon pulled free and something within him did as well when Ailsa stepped away and flung the surcoat to the ground.

It was his control slipping as he realised he would touch, he would taste this woman with her green eyes and red hair that beckoned him. He'd feel what it was like to press against her, hold her and discover what it was about her that compelled him to her.

With a huff to her breath she straightened her shoulders which pressed her breasts against her chemise and he was glad for the ribbon still in his hand so he could hold on to something. He would find this *more* between them. The only question was whether he would also find his resolve.

Rory held so still, he could be carved marble. Ailsa didn't know why he'd grown quiet or didn't take off the rest of his clothing…or hers.

She didn't know much, but this couldn't be normal on their wedding night. If they were in love, kisses would be done and there would be passion. She had heard of both in abundance from scullery maids to cordwainer's mothers. She didn't expect that between Rory and her, yet even in an arranged marriage shouldn't there have been pleasantries? Some wooing?

The act of lovemaking was intimate and, though she had bared more before him than any man, he still felt like a stranger to her. Would they touch, would he take her maidenhead and she know no more of him than this?

She tilted her head to him and noticed the changes as they stared. No man had stood this close before so that she could see in minute detail the colouring of his skin in contrast to the dark discs of his nipples.

She felt the warmth of him as well and the slight rasp of his breath. This close she could also catch the hint of leather, of steel and something of the man. Something that reminded her of the cliffs heated by the sun.

She was reminded of those cliffs in his eyes as well. Dangerous with a forged strength to withstand the elements. That awareness pounded in her heart and rushed from her head to her toes and back again. Licking her lips at the dryness suddenly there, she asked, 'Aren't we to lie on the bed?'

He moved so slowly she could watch the ascent of his left hand, the one that held the ribbon, before he brushed his fingers against her jaw and just behind her ear. 'Perhaps I should kiss you first.'

A soft tilt of her chin raised her gaze. She kept her eyes open to see the descent of his head towards hers and saw the quirk to his brow as his eyes kept to hers.

'Are you watching us kiss?' he asked. 'You are bold, are you not?'

Boldness, no. Curious, yes. Unsteady, most definitely, and she placed her hand on his shoulder. His skin was warm, almost hot beneath her. It surprised her, but not as much as him if the widening of his eyes was any indication.

'Very bold,' he murmured against her lips. Now he would kiss her as expected and the strangeness of this day would be like it should.

Instead, he tilted his head and kissed just to the side of her lips. Then up along her jaw with a delicate, deliberate precision she was helpless not to be affected by.

To give him access, she arched her neck, placing her hand on his other shoulder.

A growl of approval as Rory shifted closer to her, his right hand supporting her lower back, shifting her weight to support her against him. As he kissed along her neck, his left hand caressed and she felt the ribbon he held brush against her shoulders before he pulled back.

A soft chuckle. 'Still watching?'

She couldn't seem not to. This man, this stranger who was touching her as no other had before, as she experienced shivers and heat along her skin as she never had before.

'See this, then.' Stepping back, he gathered her chemise and tore it up and off her body.

'Ailsa,' he said as he tossed the garment even as he kept the ribbon. She stood naked and vulnerable. Feeling the air and this man before her, she was aware of the prickling of her skin and the tightening of her nipples.

His eyes darkened to impossible depths as did the flush along his chest and cheeks. Then he closed his eyes and eased his breath through parted lips.

Was this how it was? How could she know this was how it should be between a man or a woman? As a healer, she seen many women naked and tended to some males as well. There'd always been chaperons and the older healer usually tended the males until her death. However, in a marriage situation, she didn't know what she was to do.

Should she have taken off his clothes and closed her eyes as well? 'What is it?' she whispered.

He opened heavy-lidded and unfocused eyes.

'I don't know...' she started to say. 'Is there anything...?'

His eyes cleared and he gave a rueful shake to his head. 'You're untouched, Ailsa. Am I frightening you?'

'A bit.'

He clenched the ribbon. 'Sorry, lass, do not worry. You're beautiful.'

'You've told me before.'

'I did?'

'When we stood before the priest.'

He frowned. Did he not want to say such sentiments to her? Maybe not and for some reason that hurt. She'd liked that he said such a compliment in front of their clans. But he didn't. Suddenly she wished she denied him taking her chemise off.

A rough exhalation and he cupped her jaw. 'You are more than beautiful, Ailsa,' he said. 'So beautiful I could barely keep my eyes from you when I entered that courtyard though your father faced me and arrows were pointed at my back.'

'You saw me, then?'

He caught a tendril of hair and let it flow through his hand. 'This hair.'

'Everyone sees my hair.'

'I shouldn't have been noticing you at all when faced with enemies. Yet I can't help noticing you like this, the bounty of those breasts, the flare of your hips...'

His words weren't praise, but the tone of his voice made her flush as if she was truly beautiful. 'I don't understand. Haven't you seen a woman's form before?'

'Are you asking if I've had lovers?' At her quick nod, he continued, 'Yes, but I can't remember any of them.'

'We all have breasts and hips.'

He leaned forward and for some reason she stepped back, then again each time he moved forward until her legs were pressed to the bed. When she didn't move, he gathered her in his arms to lay her down. She moved over to give him room, but he didn't take it. Instead, he stood over her with that same heat intensifying between them as she admired his wide shoulders, the ripples of his stomach muscles, the dark trail of hair that arrowed into his breeches.

'You're beautiful,' he repeated. 'Stunning. And I wasn't expecting this much…' He looked away, his left hand caressing the ribbon still in his hand. 'I guess it's safe to say that everything about this is unexpected.'

She felt her own lips curve. 'True.' But she welcomed it. This wasn't the man who told her to strip when they entered the room. This was Rory, whom she had glimpses of. Like now. Talking to her, easing her concerns.

Turning them into something more. This evening seemed full of surprises, from the emotions of her wedding vows, to the heated exchange to just…this heat between them.

She'd seen men's bodies before as she tended wounds and illnesses, but this was different. This was her husband and she wanted him undressed to fully see him, to touch him not as a healer, but as a woman. 'You're still clothed.'

He frowned, swallowed. A flicker of something went through his eyes that sent a fissure of warning through her overly warm thoughts, but it was gone before she could grasp what it was.

'Yes, I am,' he said, placing one knee on the bed. 'And you still are talking.'

'Bluntly?' she gasped, as he lowered his head and hovered his lips along her collarbone.

'Talking at all,' he whispered against her skin.

She expected him to kiss her. To make the contact he seemed at first to want when he leaned over her. Instead, he pulled away and carefully knelt between her legs. He didn't even ask for her to spread her legs for him. She simply did, as if she knew what this part of a marriage bed was about.

And she thought she did, but she didn't understand at all when the cool slide of the silk ribbon fluttered along her collarbone sending warm chills to every bit of her.

'What are you doing?'

A curve to his lips. 'I'm touching you, Ailsa.'

'No, you're not.'

'You don't feel it? I thought you'd like the feel of the ribbon along your shoulders.'

He dangled the ribbon down one arm and up and down the other. Every time it reached her hand, she felt like curling her fingers around it to see if it truly felt as warm and soft as it did when he wielded it.

It was maddening, especially when he dragged the ribbon down between the valley of her breasts to pool around her navel and then back up again. It affected her.

It seemed to be affecting him, too, if the darkening of his eyes and the flushing along his cheeks was any indication. His lips had parted again and they looked wet and slick. Tempting.

Was this what he'd thought of when he tied her gown earlier? To touch her like this? To see her like this? She felt the same. It made her feel as though she wanted to touch his lips again, to feel some of that soft slickness he had yet to give her.

'Kiss me,' she said.

His eyes flashed to hers, stayed there as he un-wounded the pooled fabric and wrapped it along one breast and then the other.

'Still talking,' he said, but she saw his gaze dip from her eyes to her lips and back again. Felt the brief stut-tering drag of the ribbon along her skin as if he couldn't quite keep control because of her request before he found it again.

Around and around, in some pattern only he could see. She didn't want to watch what the ribbon was doing to her body, she wanted to watch him.

She could, however, feel the effects of that ribbon. The goosepimples ever increasing, the tightening of her breasts as if she had laces binding her entire torso and then binding her again. Her nipples taut to a near unbearable level. The chill of the room almost accost-ing in comparison to the ribbon that was warmed her, but not in all the places she ached for it to.

He seemed to want it to touch her elsewhere as well for he wound most of the length around his left fist, giving himself more leverage to wield the soft fabric. Then he touched the tip of the dangling fabric against one nipple before he unwound the fabric to let it drip and slide along her breast.

Then he gathered it again to repeat it on the left breast. Then again…and again until the soft silk tip became almost sharp against her sensitive nipple, the warm glide almost soothing as it slid along the sides of her breasts.

Though she wanted to close her eyes at the sensation, she watched him. His gaze was narrowed and riveted to what he was doing. His lips had parted that much more and she gasped when she saw that hint of his tongue touching his lips.

Brown eyes returned to hers. Not so brown now, darker, so dark and within those depths, something was going on that she suspected was happening with her as well.

She didn't need to see her body to know her skin flushed like his, her eyes had darkened, her lips had parted to take in needed air. She felt it.

The only difference between them was that he remained nearly immobile and she couldn't remain still at all. The next touch to her breast and her back arched into it. Another glide of the thin silken strip and her hips rose as well.

He detected the changes in her body, her restlessness, her eagerness for another caress, and yet he didn't lower his eyes from hers. 'Is this better, Ailsa?' he whispered, his voice raspy. 'Is the lace better free like this? Loose from your gown?'

A flip to the ribbon and he dragged the band along her sides and up again. Down to where her hips undulated and then further along her outer thigh. Up again to encircle her other hip then along her inner thigh.

Closer to where he knelt so the ribbon now touched him, too. His breaths quickened, increasing the golden expanse of his chest. His skin gleamed and an almost unholy light entered his eyes.

'Turn over,' he demanded.

She was a midwife, a healer, she knew about the human form, but she knew nothing of this. Of how her own body simply did as he asked before she could think why or how she could do it with him between her legs.

She was clumsy with it. There was no way to manoeuvre otherwise than to draw her legs in and turn before lying flat once more.

The sound he made didn't make her movements seem clumsy or too hurried. A rough groan choked off, a harsh swallowing. She knew then, that he'd seen everything. The cradle of her hips as they tilted towards him, the curve of her behind. How wet she was.

She lay there and waited for the ribbon, knew it was coming, but he held it aloft too long. He was doing something else now. He was gazing at her. Why she felt more vulnerable than when she had first stood naked before him, she didn't know. Maybe because she couldn't see him or know why her back would be so interesting.

'Women have backs, too,' she said, trying to recall their earlier conversation.

'Not like this,' he said.

His words heated her more and she lost more control of her thoughts, more control of what was happening between them. 'You remember the others, then.'

'There was never one like you. There couldn't be.'

When he lowered the ribbon to her skin, it was different this time. Different because that slight stuttering he made with the silk before was now almost constant. He, too, was losing control as he brushed the ribbon along the back of her arms, between her shoulder blades and along her spine. Brushed it along her until he pooled the ribbon in the small of her back, then wound it around and around until she felt as if he wound the silk between her legs, low down, and much, much deeper.

'Lift your hips,' he said.

He'd claimed that she spoke bluntly, but he bludgeoned her with his rough rasped words. Her body instantly responded, knees drawing in, elbows pressing into the mattress more, giving her leverage enough to tilt her hips up and back.

Into the calloused grasp of his hand against her right hip. The shock of the sudden contact making her gasp. Pant. The ribbon was warm, but his hand was hot, searing her.

Another clenched sound from him. From her. And then... And then a brushing of something just at her centre. Too firm to be the silk. Too slender to be his thigh. She guessed that he had somehow released his breeches and he was there, there to finally press forward into the ache that her body had become.

She arched her hips to give him more access and felt the scrape of his breeches against her inner thigh. He was still clothed. Once she registered how he touched her with one lone calloused finger, she understood the intimacy of his touch. Sliding around her outer lips and circling in. Sliding around and circling in. Like the pooling of the ribbon.

It was too much. 'Rory.'

He hummed a reply that wasn't a reply. This wasn't how it was done with her body tightening to some unimaginable degree. With her knees almost digging into the mattress and her hands gripping the quilt. He needed to be undressed, she needed to face him. They were meant to join their bodies and bind their marriage.

But his finger that had drummed along the surface of her skin now curved along her wetness, winding her body like the silk of a ribbon. Coiling everything inside her tighter and tighter.

'We have to stop now. Please.'

'Ailsa, let it go. You must let go before I… I'm here. This…*this* is what was meant to be.'

'Rory—'

His hand gripped more firmly against her hip, grounding her. Centring her. Another finger added and he pressed more firmly.

She couldn't catch her breath. Her hips wouldn't stop their own movement that mimicked his fingers. But her hips weren't as gliding and insistent, they trembled and juddered until she felt something else.

The ribbon. He'd wound the ribbon around his hand. It was there, too at her centre. Just as insistent and de-manding. Soft. Silk surrounding the bluntness of his hand that pressed and rubbed against her until it was all too much.

'Rory!'

Chapter Eight

'I hope you don't intend to use that ribbon to secure my gown when we leave this room,' Ailsa said.

Raw with denied need, Rory felt like chuckling despite the fact his wife had somehow shifted their positions and turned partly on her side to make that comment.

She was still underneath him, but her legs were stretched so he straddled her long limbs. The move had bared her shoulders and breasts to him, showed the soft curve of her belly and hips and gave a hint of what was between her legs.

He felt the wet hint still on his fingers though he'd practically flung the ribbon away once her pleasure was done. It didn't help his need to free himself of that ribbon. It only made him aware of how his fingers were now unbound so he could touch and reach every bit of her. His wife, this night, wasn't supposed to be like this at all.

They had started as enemies. They still were. Paiden was proof that this marriage wasn't to be trusted.

He couldn't even take comfort that he had somehow

remained in control, that he remained clothed because that made this point in time all the worst. Damn politics and clans. To see her like this, how she responded, to know what they could be together...

Shoving away his need, forcing away the want for more, Rory knew he must extricate himself from this bed, from this room. He must pry himself from the woman. His loyalties couldn't be divided, not when his friend's life was at stake.

'I've no intention at all.' He hoped they found the ribbon and burned it before he forgot all his loyalties. 'Does that please you?'

'Please me?'

'Because you don't like laces.'

She smiled and it punched him in the gut. Her green eyes almost slumberous with the desire that wasn't quite sated. He knew it wasn't because they'd begun that flitting thing again, making him aware how bare he was to her still and how undone he must seem.

He was so undone.

'I might have changed my mind,' she said. 'I might add more laces to my gowns now.'

He probably would be overcome with lust every time he saw one binding her body. The thought of her like that shuddered through him and his knees gave. Which was a mistake because it brushed that part of him that needed her against her stretched legs and her eyes widened and locked on him.

Ailsa thought she knew what happened in the marriage bed, but Rory had showed her otherwise. She thought there could be no more pleasure, but the burning heat of him against her leg proved that idea false as well.

'I didn't know it could be like this,' she said.

He tensed and his gaze, which was now pointedly over her shoulder, glanced to her again and then slid away. 'I'm glad I had the experience to bring you such pleasure.'

A sharp stab that she didn't want to identify pierced her. Ailsa didn't want to think of him with other women though it was foolish of her to think he hadn't been. Even if he wanted to stay away from women, his status and looks would have women coming to him.

He adjusted his legs to sit beside her and she immediately missed the heat and feel of him there.

'Why did you ask if I'd had another lover?' he asked.

Did he hear that she didn't want to think of his lovers? His tousled hair fell heavily along his jaw and shoulders, his eyes held just a hint of the heat they had before, but more of a puzzlement she couldn't understand until she remembered his question.

'I didn't ask if you had another lover,' she said. 'I asked if you had seen the female form because I had seen the male as well.'

'What do you mean, you've seen the male form? Do you mean naked?'

She shrugged. 'Of course. I'm a healer. I've seen lots of bodies and their parts over the years.'

He raked his hand through his hair, controlling the wild locks she'd been admiring. 'I don't like it.'

She couldn't have heard right. 'The fact I'm a healer?'

'The fact you've seen other males.'

Was he jealous as well? Could he be feeling the same as she did? If so, she'd ease his concerns. 'I've seen females, too. I've tended children…animals. Any living creature injured.'

'Your father, your clan, allowed this?'

Allowed. That wasn't a word she appreciated. 'Of course. It was either that or, when the old healer died, which she did, there would be no one to tend injuries. Would that be preferable?'

A rough exhalation and Rory turned away, so his back was to her and his legs were over the bed.

That was an answer as good as any. He obviously didn't want to argue. That was fine with her. There would be all the time in the world to discuss what she was capable of as a healer and a woman. He seemed intelligent and, after her discussion regarding the benefits of her marriage, amenable to listening to her, but maybe now wasn't the time.

Maybe their time now was for something else. She was struck by the definition of his back, the tapering of his waist, the fact that seeing him like this made her want him more. Ailsa propped herself up to touch his arm.

He flinched, but held still, and she took advantage of it to caress his skin as he had hers. To watch him turn his head to gaze at her hand as she stroked his shoulder and traced her fingers down his spine. He fascinated her. All of this fascinated her not as a healer, but as a woman discovering the different textures of a male's skin and the fact his body didn't give at all underneath her touch.

So wonderfully different than hers and the more she touched, the more different he became. No longer pulling away, but almost leaning into her touch as if he welcomed it.

She welcomed it though she'd found her pleasure. Simply curving her palm along the blades in his back had her needing more. Didn't he need more?

'Rory,' she said. Was her voice threaded with desire?

Must be since his riveted gaze locked with hers. 'Ailsa.'

'Yes?'

'You keep...' He gave a hard swallow. 'You keep saying my name.'

'I thought you wanted me to say your name.'

Brows drawn in. 'The way you—' He shook his head.

Oh, she wanted him to finish that thought. When he didn't, she spread her fingers to reach more of his back, his skin, to feel the way his ribs curved around his side.

The way he imperceptibly shivered when she did so. Did he feel the desire like her? He must. They were strangers and newly married, yet here they could talk, they could know each other...discover each other.

She wanted that. Very much. So why did he turn away?

'Why are you not touching me?' She sat and released the quilt so she could feel the ridges of his abdomen, the narrow trail of dark hair. The way his—

He grabbed her wrist, which pleased her. He tried to stop her, but she'd felt his response to her touch and knew he was as affected as she. Now they could join and bind their marriage to make their vows to each other and their clans complete.

She lay down again and stretched her limbs. Since Rory kept hold of her wrist, he had no choice but to turn just that bit to see how she lay before him. To see how much she wanted him.

Like this she felt vulnerable and powerful as his deep brown eyes caressed her legs, her hips and breasts and down again. Slowly, she took his hand and laid it on her stomach and felt the warmth, the heat seep down deep into her. 'Come lie with me now. I want you to.'

'Ailsa, you don't know what your words do... I can't...' A hiss and his fingers curled. It sent shivers through her and she wanted him more. 'You keep... surprising me,' he said, sounding puzzled. She wanted to ease his concerns.

'You keep doing that to me as well.' Something in her bubbled to the surface. They were strangers, but there was some connection between them. All would be well. 'Come lie with me. Let's complete our marriage vows. After all, it's not every day I get married to the man who vowed to kill me.'

It was a mistake. Any confusion or heat in Rory's eyes disappeared. Almost flinging her wrist, he launched himself off the bed. Chilled, she yanked the quilt around her.

'Rory?'

'Don't,' he bit out. 'I need to see Paiden.'

If he checked on Paiden, she would remain a virgin. He couldn't want that. Surely, after all she felt? All that he felt, too.

'Don't you want to...?' She gestured around the bed and patted the space beside her.

Grabbing his tunic, he shoved it over his head.

He wasn't understanding. Taking a breath, she continued, 'I may be an innocent, but I know we aren't finished.' She paused. 'I know you're not finished.'

Carrying his boots, he sat in a chair. 'You found pleasure.'

'Except you—'

He looked up at her at that and something naked and raw surfaced before he shut it down. 'It was pleasurable for me as well.'

'You're leaving the room'

He shoved his boots on. 'Yes.'

'Do you not intend to honour this marriage? Tonight they'll expect...' She clutched the bedsheets closer to her. 'There's no seed or blood.'

'I vow I've never heard a woman talk as you.'

Ailsa bit back her retort. Arguing the benefits of an intelligent and verbal wife wasn't the issue. The fact that if he walked out of this room without taking her maidenhead was.

'You married me so that no blood would be spilled. I'm holding you to that.' His eyes were almost murderous.

And she felt it, felt as if she'd been murdered, but she wouldn't stand for it. 'What of your political alliance?'

'Maybe I would care for my alliance if my friend wasn't poisoned mere moments after the announcement of our marriage.'

'You insisted that we marry. Why are you doing this?' And then she knew. 'You agreed to marry me knowing this would be our wedding night. You never intended to make this a marriage in truth.'

'Not right now,' he said.

'Maybe not ever?' she said.

At his silence, Ailsa wanted to gut him with a thousand shears. His friend was poisoned and could be dying, and there was still a part of her warning her to give him leniency. But she had lost Magnus and still married the enemy of her clan, expecting to make a true marriage. She was willing to make a true sacrifice for her clan, when he hadn't intended to at all.

Because now she realised everything depended on who had poisoned his friend and whether he lived or died. Her friend had been trampled. Many other Mc-Crieffs had died since then. If they didn't make this a true marriage, then her vows to Rory, and her lying in his bed tainted all the loss and pain in her past. She wouldn't allow him to do this to her.

'Your friend sleeps,' she said, lacing her tone with as much accusation as she could. 'He's not dead.'

The string of curses was more a growl than words, but she understood them all the same as he turned back to her again. Every bit of him was as menacing as when he had entered the courtyard that very morning. 'Yes, Paiden does sleep, McCrieff. But will he wake or sleep for ever?'

She had no answer to that. None at all.

'I thought so,' he said, closing the door behind him.

Chapter Nine

Hours later, Rory left the quiet of Paiden's room. Too quiet. Too still. Barely his friend at all despite the jolt of joy and relief when he first entered the room to see Paiden sleeping in a different position.

All hope dashed when Hannah, the servant tending him, recited the litany of tasks she done since the wedding. One of which was to move Paiden's prone body so he did not get sore.

His vibrant friend adjusted by a woman. When he woke, he'd give his friend hell for missing the opportunity. Hannah, with her ample curves, was a woman Paiden would try to woo.

Why hadn't he fought Paiden harder to stay behind? They'd all known it was a trap when the field had been empty of McCrieffs. Because of that they'd all stayed on their guard, even during the feast, his men had carefully watched the food, the McCrieffs, the doorways.

It wasn't until he'd announced his wedding that they forgot themselves. Forgot that they were on enemy land. It wasn't until he had lowered his guard, had gazed like a lust-filled fool at Ailsa that his friend was poisoned.

All his fault.

Out of all the Lochmores, Paiden was the only one who accepted him, who made him feel as if he belonged. He should have ordered his friend to stay behind, but he'd been weak. If Paiden died, Rory wouldn't want to return to castle Lochmore because he wouldn't have a home.

Forcing his thoughts away, he turned in the hallway, intending to go outside, when Duff came around the opposite corner.

'You've returned,' he said. When he announced they would continue with the marriage, Rory had directed Duff to return to Lochmore land and sent a message to his parents.

'It was quick, they were already mounted on the other side of the stream. There wasn't a battle, and they'd heard nothing.'

So they'd intended to storm McCrieff land to rescue them which would have nullified all their careful planning to keep to a negotiation first.

Duff gave a quick grin. 'It's not as if they'd risk your precious neck.'

As an only heir. Of course because he was an heir and now they were here. It was early morning. They must have packed and travelled by night. He thought he'd completed everything quickly enough that his father wouldn't interfere. He was satisfied that he had at least managed to wed the McCrieff woman before he was stopped or his father demanded more terms.

He'd done the best he could under the circumstances.

Except Paiden's health was in the balance and that would take some explanation. The missive he'd sent explained most of his reasoning, but not all. He wished for more sleep, not for endless discussions and strategies.

'Tell my father—'

'Your father's not here.' Duff gave a slight shrug. 'Neither is your mother, but that was to be expected.'

Rory was tired, exhausted. He ached… He woke yesterday morn with thoughts of battle. To lose friends and comrades. To gain some bit of McCrieff land. And instead he'd gained a wife. So of course, he didn't understand Duff when he'd said his father hadn't come.

'You carried my missive to my father.'

'Aye, and I stood before him as he read every word.'

If only he could have been there to see the expression on his father's face. 'And?'

'He rolled it up and handed it to your mother, who opened it twice as slowly and read it twice as long as that.'

This was why he gave the missive to Duff, not because he thought he could fight off whoever stopped him along the way from McCrieff lands to there. It was because Duff had the observation of a hawk and the tongue of an ale-doused whore. Nothing would get past him and he'd freely give Rory the details he craved without losing his pride in the asking.

Still, he felt like asking, his exhaustion making him impatient, not the need to know his parents' reactions to what he'd done. 'Then what?'

'Your mother placed her hand on your father's arm and acted faint. Your father leaned over her and with some words to his man—'

'Harold.' His father's man-at-arms and advisor. The man Rory talked to more often than his own father.

'Yes, him. He bid me good eve, told me to rest and thanked me.'

Rory couldn't come up with further words, but something on his face must have given his shock away because Duff continued.

Shrugging, his friend said, 'Then he…gave me a nice coin and left. I didn't sleep, but got straight to work with what Harold wanted me to do.'

'And that was?' Rory said through the closing in his throat.

'To bring more men and a trunk. It seemed your mother wanted to give the bride a token of appreciation. I didn't know where to put it, so it's with the men now in their quarters.'

'That…is welcome.' Rory said as evenly as possible. 'You rode hard, Duff, I'll see that you get another coin. After fast, bring the trunk to my chambers and leave it there. After that, get some rest and I won't be bothering you for three days.'

'Three?'

'I saw that black-haired lass giving a pout when I sent you out the door and, if I'm not mistaken, you noticed her as well.'

'Black hair, you say? I think I was looking at the way her—'

Rory held up his palm. 'Spend your time well. You can regale me with the details later.'

Duff turned abruptly, if unsteadily, and was gone in an instant. Duff was built like an oak tree. If he was that off balance, he'd ridden hard and fast.

This part of the hallway was empty, with only faint distant sounds coming through. It appeared most of the keep was still asleep. And so, for the first time since he'd begun the long journey yesterday, he was alone. The halls were narrow and dark, which Rory hoped hid some of his reaction to the news he received as he slapped his hand against the stone wall to support himself.

He was exhausted. Drained. His father gave no congratulations or asked questions on how he accomplished a feat no other Lochmore had achieved in all the years before or after the Great Feud.

Centuries of living next to the clan and nothing of this had ever been thought of or attempted. Except that one time, the one time which started this endless warring.

The story was that around seventy years before, a Lochmore lass was betrothed to the McCrieff Chief. How they met no one knew, but just before the wedding, the lass returned to Lochmore where the Chief took her in. There were plenty of rumours of mistreatment and abuse leading to her escape and subsequent return, but she and the Chief fell in love and married soon after. All seemed well until she grew fat with a baby and died in childbirth, the baby as well.

When the McCrieff Chief heard of the news he rode up with a few of his men. Drink was involved. Pride was as well. Now there were witnesses aplenty and the story didn't waver or fail from fact or fiction. It was told the McCrieff accused Lochmore of stealing the woman he loved and wished to marry.

Lochmore would hear none of it and roared that he

wanted McCrieff off his land to mourn his wife and child. McCrieff refused and Lochmore drew his sword first. In the melee, Lochmore's nephew Rory, for whom he was named, tried to stop the two drunk men and McCrieff's sword sliced clean through the young man's stomach. It ended in more tears than it started with, McCrieff's men tearing him away and Lochmore broken in grief.

And for seventy years only more falsities and slights had been done by McCrieffs to Lochmores until his father had sided with Edward and was granted some of McCrieff land.

It was a decided victory and one that the Lochmores never thought to ever achieve over the cruel McCrieffs who caused a grieving man to break after killing a young man who simply wanted to stop two drunken men from killing each other.

Now Rory meant to bring peace to their clans. To marry a McCrieff and end the feud. More than that. An easier relationship with the Tanist would help prosperity and gain wealth no other Lochmore had before.

To bring pride to his clan and to prove to his father he could rule it one day. Except...he hadn't achieved any of it. It appeared his mother sent kind words, no doubt more polite than actual happiness for her son, and his father sent nothing.

Worse still, he had a wife whom he couldn't trust, but who he wanted more than anything. After Ailsa found her pleasure, he'd nigh on almost lost his mind with the want and need firing through him. She was well tousled, a flush to her cheeks and her lips swollen from kisses. She was so lovely his heart ached.

Until she reminded him that Paiden lay at death's door. She could not have said words more chilling to his ardour and adding more to his confusion than those. She was a McCrieff. She was the enemy and, to prove it, Paiden was in another room, possibly dying while he trailed his fingers along soft skin and longing to kiss parted lips.

He didn't want this. He didn't need this. The land, the power, yes. The confusion, never. A McCrieff, his wife, and one who might have poisoned his friend. Except the wariness, fear and confusion in those bright green eyes of hers told something else. So, too, her knocking the goblet aside. She had not been the poisoner and possibly had worries over who was.

She seemed unsettled by it as well. A different reaction than the outrage and surprise she'd given her father when he suggested they marry. By no means could Ailsa be part of a conspiracy.

Yet years of mistrust did not go away simply because he felt something for her, because he hoped she was honest. So he'd held back last night, but they'd argued all the same.

He shoved himself off the wall and brushed his hands against his breeches. No matter what he did between his family and his wife, there would always be failure. However, he wouldn't fail his friend and he would find the culprit who poisoned him.

That meant talking with a few important people. Hamish McCrieff for one. Last night before their vows, he and Ailsa had been escorted to his room, only to see that he was asleep.

Frail, grey and waxen with a weak rattle to his breath.

Here was another fact that proved true. Hamish, Chief of Clan McCrieff, was truly ill. Which meant Frederick, as Tanist, was in control.

If so, why invite him, offer his daughter and then try to kill a Lochmore? Perhaps even kill him. He did not know what was in the goblet that Ailsa had shoved away.

That, out of all of this, was the most perplexing. So why was he visiting Paiden this morning, why wasn't he confronting Frederick, why even now did his feet take him to Hamish's room first?

He feared that it was because of Ailsa. Because without thinking this through, he had married her. Without thinking, not even once, if he proved the poisoner was Frederick, how could he face his wife?

Not his wife.

A thought that didn't sit well with him. Rory raked his fingers through his hair. However, it was possible by not consummating the marriage, he'd done something right by her clan. He'd only thought of Paiden and Clan Lochmore, but he realised now Ailsa had a chance out of the marriage as well.

A deed done for the rightness of Clan Lochmore, for Clan McCrieff. To have a chance to right wrongs to their clans.

He wondered, however, if by denying them both last night, what wrong he'd done by them?

Chapter Ten

'I don't know why he is like this today.' Ailsa snapped the linen off Hamish's bed.

This was a task she would have delegated to others, but Hamish wouldn't have it and so, along with his waste bucket, she often replaced his ruined clothing and sweat-laden sheets. She didn't do it because he was the Chief, she did it because it was her duty to God and to her craft. Hamish ordered her to do it because she was the Tanist's daughter.

'Last night, I couldn't rouse him for the pain tincture,' Hannah said, grabbing the other side of the fabric.

That was unusual. As was him still sleeping on the mattress that was laid on the floor as they replaced his bed with the new mattress. To keep his sores at a minimum, they did this often, and he just as often complained. Now they exchanged mattresses and he didn't once wake.

For him to remain sleeping this long was concerning. He also hadn't been awake last night when they went to talk to him before the marriage.

'I thought you were seeing to Paiden?' Ailsa said.

'I was, but he was sleeping so I checked on Mary... just in case. She, I and Kit also helped get Hamish to the floor this morning before Kit left and Mary went to care for Paiden.'

It would have been helpful to have had Kit, the falconer's son, stay to also get Hamish back on the new bed. 'Did Hamish wake at all?'

'Mary said that last night he woke to relieve himself and take some broth, but that was all,' Hannah replied.

'Anything else?'

Hannah scrunched her lips. 'His breathing has changed since yesterday.'

Hamish was sick with an illness that was deadly and painful, but familiar. His uneven breath and deep slumber wasn't usual. Something was wrong. 'You should leave now, you've been up far too late and have done too much going from room to room.'

'If I leave, who will help you with the mattress and Hamish?'

'It's not as if you can help lift him, either, and you need your sleep.'

'I have slept some,' Hannah said quietly.

'You did?' Ailsa said. 'You never sleep. What brought that on?'

A pale blush went to Hannah's cheeks.

'Is there something you aren't telling me?' Ailsa said, dripping much humour into the words. Hannah with her generous curves loved to flirt and was pursued by many a male. If Ailsa didn't find her at her duties, it was because some interest pulled her away. Maybe the blush was why Kit didn't stay...

'It wasn't—' Hannah flapped her hands in front of

her. 'I slept some because I didn't know how long you'd be gone. I thought I'd help Mary with the linens this morning. It was your marriage night. I didn't expect to see Rory enter Paiden's room or for you to help with Hamish so soon.'

At the reminder of her marriage night, it was Ailsa's turn to blush. As for the rest, she knew that Rory would go to Paiden first. He said he would and nothing in his countenance made her believe he lied. In fact, he forsook the marriage night altogether to see to his friend.

Her emotions were as tangled as her laces. Her reason warred with her heart. She'd exposed all of her body and part of herself to him, and she felt— No. She didn't want to think about last night.

She'd think about here, now, and that Rory should be with his friend, but not Mary. 'If Mary's there and you're here, we don't have enough help for the daytime.' Old Rhona would have planned their care better. But Rhona didn't have to marry without a moment's notice.

With Hamish on the floor and needing care, she couldn't keep an eye on Paiden as well. There was no possibility Hamish would allow the Lochmore to share his chamber so that she could care for them both. 'We'll have to sort our shifts. Is it possible you could sleep—?'

The door to the annexed room burst open. A few heavy footfalls and Rory strode into the bedroom. Ailsa didn't know why she should be surprised—after all, she was here when she had promised she'd care for Paiden.

'I'll be done here soon enough,' she informed him.

He peered at Hamish on the floor. 'What is he doing there?'

'We're changing his mattress. Sometimes it gets wet despite our efforts and it isn't good for his skin.'

Rory glanced from her to Hannah and returned to Hamish.

'He still sleeps,' he said.

'When I'm done, I'll help with Paiden.'

'I'm not here for you.'

He was here for Hamish. Why? She could read nothing from his manners now. Fully clothed, his expression impenetrable, even his hair which curled was held back. Controlled. This wasn't the man who had been in her bed. This was a man who grieved. She shouldn't have avoided seeing Paiden just to avoid seeing Rory.

'Is Paiden worse?' she asked.

'The same.' He pointed to Hamish. 'Can you wake him?'

'No,' she replied and that was troubling. Hamish's breath was uneven, but he wasn't restless or curled in pain. In truth, there wasn't much she could do other than to observe him. 'It's better for him to sleep. Shouldn't you be talking with my father?'

He frowned. 'It's early yet and I didn't know whether he was about.'

'He always wakes early to break his fast, you can find him in the hall.'

'I didn't see him there.'

It was her turn to frown. Her father was old and set in his ways. At this time of day he was always in the hall. Something…perhaps everything, wasn't as it should be.

Turning to Hannah, she said, 'Who else could we call upon to help with Paiden right now?'

'Beth, perhaps,' Hannah replied. 'She won't know all

what we do, but she's dependable and can fetch water and food if necessary.'

'Go find her and get her to Paiden's room.' She turned to Rory. 'Help me get him on the fresh mattress.'

'Won't that wake him?'

'He didn't wake when they moved him to the floor and hasn't stirred since. I doubt we could wake him now.'

Rory looked to Hannah, who scrambled around the bed to the door. 'I'll find Beth.' When the door closed behind her, he said. 'What is wrong with him?'

'It's a sickness I've seen once before. There's no remedy for it.'

'Is the sleeping common?'

'It's not uncommon.'

She lied. Rory knew it. 'I'll help you with him.'

'He's tall.'

'But half my weight. I can move him.'

'If you wish,' Ailsa said without looking at him.

Rory bent and laid Hamish on the newly made bed. Carefully he arranged him, all the while the Chief of the McCrieffs remaining silent.

Pulling the covers over Hamish, Ailsa gestured to Rory to follow her into the adjoining room. He did, watching as she partially closed the bedroom door. It was enough to give them privacy, but also enough to hear if Hamish woke. Feeling restless, Rory didn't sit when she indicated for him to join her on one of the two chairs.

'Why are you here, Lochmore?' she said.

'Rory,' he said automatically. This room was too small to pace—with the barest stretch of his arm, he'd touch the ceilings and all the walls just by standing in the centre. 'I need to talk to Hamish. We both do.'

'You want to talk of who poisoned your friend.'

'Talk is too light a word for what I want to do for my friend,' he said. 'Whoever did this needs to be found. Since we are married, it does no good if there is someone undermining it. This is a matter for McCrieff's Chief.'

'We're not ma—'

Rory held up his hand and, after a stunned moment, Ailsa's hand went to her belt. No doubt her shears were there. 'You think to harm me?'

'I should after last night. Do you think to shame me further by coming here today?'

'Shame? I protected your reputation and have said nothing. Your honour is still intact.' Unlike his own which felt frayed.

'You'll never claim me. And you're a fool thinking I care for my reputation. I told you I've been around males. I'm a healer and have more freedom than many women in this clan.'

'Then what is this about?'

'So you ask questions of me. Do you know what marrying you cost me?'

'It cost nothing. McCrieffs gained everything with our marriage.'

She pulled her shears and pointed them. 'We. Are. Not. Married.'

Not married. It was the truth, but he wouldn't say it out loud and it was best she didn't either. Especially here. Hamish might appear to be asleep, and they kept their voices low, but who could truly tell?

'Quiet, or you'll sacrifice everything.'

'Don't talk of sacrifices, Lochmore. You aren't the only one with conflicts or burdens.'

In the meantime, it was essential that everyone believed they were married, at least until the one who had poisoned Paiden was found. Until then, he had to remember they weren't. If in the end it was her father who'd harmed Paiden, well… He'd address that if that time came.

For now, he knew Paiden was still alive and it appeared that Hamish was as well. He should leave to find Frederick, except Ailsa was here, and he found himself reluctant to leave her just yet. It didn't sit well how he'd left her last night.

'I should tell you my family received my message regarding our marriage,' he said. 'My mother sent her congratulations along with a trunk and I had it moved to our room. We could go open it if you wish. There would be gifts in there for you. I suspect something of great value, too.'

'Gifts? Do you think me that simple?'

Simple, never, but what was between them warred with what must be. Conflicts. Betrayal. Treachery. He'd married her to gain control over his future, over his life—instead, he was even more powerless than before. He wouldn't apologise for what he'd done because he'd done it out of loyalty and honour to his family and clan. However, this woman was his wife in name at least, she'd been working since his arrival and he knew she'd gotten little sleep.

'Do you need food?'

'I need to stay here.'

'Won't a servant return?' When Ailsa shook her head, he asked, 'What of your sisters? Do they not help?'

'They're young. Twins.'

'I don't remember seeing them at evening meal.'

'They weren't there,' she said.

'Because Lochmores were dining?'

'What do you think?'

They could argue over many things, but protecting children when swords were drawn wouldn't be one of them.

'I'd do the same,' he said. 'If I were a father, I, too, would keep the young protected.' Then he remembered the other red hair that had caught his eye. 'But they were there at the wedding.'

The tension in her eased a bit. It wasn't forgiveness, but it was something. 'They were in the crowds.'

So they could see their sister being married, but also kept at a distance to be swept away if tempers flared. Trust. Mistrust. If the Lochmores felt uneasy, so must the McCrieffs. The question was, how much did his wife trust him?

He looked to the open door to Hamish's room and then to the closed door behind him. He didn't need to be here now. He needed to be planning for every scenario with his men. At the very least, he needed to be at Paiden's side, just as he knew that Paiden would have been there for him.

Instead, he was in the bedchambers of a dying man whom he had never met, but whom his father hated.

'You don't need to stay here with me,' Ailsa said.

He whipped his head around. 'We are married. Where else would I be?'

'I can tell you wish to be elsewhere. You're drumming with your fingers against your leg and staring at the doors.'

He stilled his left hand. 'Is this what you do? Stay in this man's room?'

'I'm a healer and he is ill.'

'We, too, have a healer,' he said. 'But she's there for everyone, not cloistered away for one man.'

'I was requested to be by Hamish's side as much as possible.'

Except this was excessive. No healer would stay all day like this. It would be a waste of resources and certainly, in a clan this size, the healer would be needed elsewhere.

Hamish was the Chief, but her father ruled and it didn't seem as if there were numerous visitors or clansmen worried about this dying man. In fact, the hallway was bare. Hamish was hated by Lochmores and it didn't appear he was much loved by McCrieffs either. Yet she stayed by his side.

'Who requested it.'

She jolted. 'What does it matter? Our Chief is sick and needs someone.'

Trust. Mistrust, but he wanted an answer and wouldn't let this go. 'The Chief would be sick even if you tell me.'

'Hamish,' she said tersely. 'He requested it of my father and so my father granted it.'

Requested, or ordered. It was Hamish's right to make orders. A chief was Chief until he died. A Tanist was only heir apparent. But Hamish was dying and, from the time he'd been here, Hamish was bedridden, and Frederick had been making decisions. How much control did the Chief have?

'Who is in charge of this clan?' he said.

'Hamish,' she said too quickly.

'Ailsa,' he prodded.

'Don't think to reprimand or demand answers from me.' She glanced at Hamish's door. 'My father is a great warrior and well respected. Hamish is our Chief. There is nothing else.'

A change of power wasn't 'nothing else'. He'd seen enough last night to know that Frederick had power here. Many McCrieffs raised their goblets at his announcement and there were no open denials or interruptions when he'd given his speech. If there was disagreement, Rory hadn't noticed it.

It appeared the Chief did not have control. If Frederick and Hamish agreed on matters, the transfer of power would be unproblematic. If they held differing opinions, however... No, the results would be too disastrous to even think about, let alone be true.

'You have a person who tried to murder a Lochmore,' he said.

'I know,' she said more quietly than him.

Her honesty jarred him. Just a few hours before she'd prevaricated about Paiden's poisoning. Had she thought about it some more or did she know something more?

He hid secrets, but there were some here as well. 'Ailsa, your father invited me here. If he poisoned—'

'He didn't!'

When he raised his brow, she huffed. Her vehement response was an answer. So there were other factions here. Some who upheld the old story, who wanted to keep the hatred. Was it Hamish? He seemed too diminished to make such demands.

'They could poison you, too,' he said. 'Because

you're married to me, a Lochmore, they could come after you. Did you think of that? Did you think I would tolerate it?'

She kept her quiet. He let her; it was a lot for him to think about, too.

'Come. If Hamish sleeps, we will talk to your father.'

'I *can't* leave the room,' she said.

Her father was Tanist, but Hamish was Chief. Where did that leave his wife? For as much as she was direct and seemed to have independence, it appeared she was kept as a prisoner.

'Is it like this every day?' he asked. 'Are you here every day.'

She looked at the window. 'Yes.'

'Then we'll wait until someone brings you food and make them tend Hamish while we talk to your father.'

'My father brings me food.'

Frederick wasn't in the hall, and might have missed the morning repast which meant Ailsa would as well. Where was he and why would a warrior cater to his daughter?

Rory stood. 'I will bring you food.'

Ailsa released her shuddering breath the moment Rory strode out the door. He seemed angry that her father brought food.

Was it wrong for family to wait on each other? They'd all grown very close since her mother died. At first, she'd been surprised when her father brought her food, but after a while, she'd looked forward to it. It was a time when they could talk. Now, however, because Rory asked her about it, she questioned it as well.

Because ultimately, her father wouldn't be waiting on her if Hamish didn't demand her time. Just how much power did Hamish wield? Something was amiss. Other Chiefs had gotten ill, other Tanists gained the control of clans, her own observations could be skewed.

But she knew, absolutely knew, Hamish was undermining her father's rule. She knew that Paiden's poisoning wasn't an accident. That it had been done just at that moment to ensure he died so there would be a battle, that there would be no peace.

Her father often whispered that he wanted her to have a future he and his father never had. Hamish had no issue and cared not for the future of the clan. He had blind pride and revered the past when McCrieffs were strong, wealthy, honourable. It was…possible for Hamish to have ordered Lochmore's demise.

Except for her interference, Paiden would be dead. She wished she knew what ailed him, but his stomach contents had been too jumbled for her to guess correctly. Whatever the poison was, it was well hidden and, until she knew what, she feared any antidote.

In the meantime Paiden slept on, but for how much longer? Someone didn't want her—a McCrieff, the Tanist's daughter—marrying a Lochmore Chief's son. They wanted war.

From Rory's storm-ridden countenance, she feared he'd guessed that truth. Arrows pointed at him, he'd entered the McCrieff courtyard anyway. Paiden close to death, he'd married her anyway. He and his men had been threatened the moment they rode on McCrieff land. Yet, he was angry now.

Her heart wondered if his anger was from the fact

that she now was threatened. He said he wouldn't tolerate it. However, the way he said it… As if he wanted to say something stronger, more dangerous, and just held himself back.

Could Rory have feelings for her? Too soon. Not possible. Not given the history between McCrieffs and Lochmores. He'd said he'd married her for power.

Except they weren't married and he seemed to think he was the only one to make sacrifices. She knew his, he didn't know hers. Nor had he asked. And in truth, she wouldn't even tell him of Magnus now. He didn't deserve to know after what he'd done on their wedding night.

But now he meant to break her fast and last night he had preserved her honour.

Married or not, the real question was, in the light of day and knowing what happened afterwards, would she still have done it? She still believed some alliance with Lochmores would stop future battles. Lives would still be saved, maybe there was a chance at lasting peace.

Or maybe it was true, what Rory had said, and their marriage would expose how deep the hatred was between the clans. Paiden's poisoning certainly revealed animosity; maybe someone would try to kill her for marrying Rory.

Marrying Rory. She wasn't married. She hated that he held that control over her. More fool her if it did come to light. Despite her father's leniency when it came to her being a healer, he would not forgive if his only child's marriage was false.

Everything about this circumstance was false. They were simply strangers. Except…was that true?

Neither had been held to sword point. Her father had alluded to Rory suffering consequences, but she knew her father would never harm anyone invited to dine. Her father was a great warrior who had survived many battles. Other men had looked up to him long before he became Tanist. He'd earned that respect because of his reasoning as well as his sword.

In the end, it was she who agreed to the marriage. And yet, why? She couldn't lie to herself. She hadn't married him solely because it would bring the clans closer to peace, or that it would make the King's decree an easier transition for her clan. If Rory had been proved cruel, or showed no reason, she would have begged her father for alternatives. She would have denied it outright and not heeded his words to think.

No, she hadn't married him simply for the clan's sake. She'd married him because he…affected her. The moment he'd entered the courtyard alone and yet undeterred, the instant his eyes had caught hers and the distance between them hadn't mattered, something of him had pierced her.

Oh, she'd been infuriated by his comment on the leeks and him being a Lochmore from the clan she'd hated all her life, she'd would have gladly shown him out the gates. But she could not avoid her curiosity, her fascination with him in the small room.

She couldn't avoid her attraction to him in her bedroom.

Except now after a night spent together, she had to question what part of her decision was based on her meeting Rory, or on a secret told to her by Rhona the former healer.

On her deathbed, Rhona had been ill, half-coherent, but enough of her words Ailsa understood. Rhona had confessed a secret that affected the Great Feud between the clans about a baby, named Rory, given away in the dead of night.

That name. Rory. Could that baby be her husband?

His name was too significant. Too much of a coincidence and he lived near McCrieff land. Then there was also the fact he drummed with his left hand. That he arranged his food, touched her intimately with his left hand.

Could he be left-handed? It was rare, so rare. She couldn't be certain. For it appeared he used his sword with his right, his dining knife with his right, yet she was an observer. He wasn't as fluid with his right hand as he was with his left. As if he forced himself to use that hand instead of his dominant hand. Why did he do it?

It was almost as if he was trying to prove himself. He had nothing to prove. All she knew with certainty was that his name was Rory and he was left-handed. If what she was just beginning to guess was true, however, his very existence changed everything.

When the Great Feud began seventy years ago, the story as she'd been told was that a Lochmore woman fell in love with the McCrieff Chief and grew ripe with his child. For unknown reasons, she married Lochmore's Chief instead. When the McCrieff child and woman died, it broke the McCrieff Chief's heart. She'd found the story sadly tragic as a child, but it was the baby's death she mourned the most. That baby was also named Rory. What if he had lived? As a child herself, it had

made her think about life and death and she'd often
asked Rhona questions.

However, when Magnus was killed, she knew without a doubt she wanted to be a healer.

So she'd followed Rhona, the clan healer, who
couldn't at the time have been that old and was dis-
gruntled that a pesky child hounded her. They soon
became very close. Years later, she was able to care for
Rhona when she was dying.

Ailsa took great pains to care for her alone, for
Rhona, as a healer, knew many clan secrets and at the
end of her life she mumbled when she hurt, when she
slept. And Ailsa heard many secrets, especially one that
would change the course of their clans for ever.

Ailsa couldn't get it out of her thoughts now. That
Hamish had raped a woman named Marion from the
Clan McNeill, that the babe born of that rape was given
to another family and one outside the clan. Never liking
Hamish, Ailsa had been fiercely glad that child escaped.

Yet, could that babe born of hate have been given
to Lochmore's Chief and passed as his own? Could
Rory be Hamish's son? For Rory was large and left-
handed like Hamish. To have one or the other traits
was unique—to carry both was rare. Rory would be
fully a McCrieff then. There would be no need for a
feud or poison or finding a killer. He wouldn't have to
prove himself.

She was tired, worried. Perhaps even grasping at any
ideas to make her marriage to Rory work. There was
danger here and she was married to a stranger who was
kind one moment and cutting the next.

Though she felt something for Rory, she didn't know

him. At first, she thought there could be peace, but not as long as Paiden lay ill and possibly dying. She felt so helpless with his care, hopeless she couldn't have just married a man she fell in love with.

And she couldn't call him by his name. That was telling how deep her conflict went. She knew, he, too was conflicted. They'd said their vows, but he hadn't taken her maidenhead.

She knew her secrets, what were his? It was too much to think about. Too many uncertainties. Maybe her mind was playing tricks on her.

Under no circumstances could Rory be Hamish's son and a McCrieff. Under no circumstances could he be named after the McCrieff babe who died in the Great Feud. It was too fantastical to be true.

Chapter Eleven

'Where are you going?'

A child's voice chimed behind Rory as he stormed out of the almost-empty castle. A few of his men had been at the end of the hallway. Enough to give privacy and security. With so much unsettled, he ordered them to stay.

'You're him, are you not? You're the one everyone's talking about.' Another voice. Just as young, just as avoidable.

'Of course it's him. We've seen everyone else.' Two childish voices, girls, moving in close behind him. Their words beginning to register, though he continued to ignore them. Where was Ailsa's father? The keep was small, the rooms mostly empty except for those cleaning from the night before.

Paiden and Hamish were both sleeping beyond that of normal rest. Was it a coincidence? Ailsa didn't seem surprised that Hamish was sleeping, but she did seem concerned. Hamish could merely be suffering from his illness...or he could be suffering from the same poison as Paiden.

'We haven't been allowed to see everyone. He could be anyone.'

'You know that's him. We saw him yesterday with Ailsa.'

'From a *distance*.'

Louder, a hint of that tone and pitch only children arguing could hit. He'd walked away from the keep, around a corner, and they were still there. He wouldn't find Frederick at this rate. Stopping abruptly, he turned.

Only to be almost ploughed into by two girls with longer limbs than bodies.

The one on his right immediately straightened and brushed her skirts, the other pointed her finger at him and announced, 'You're him!'

Eyes with more brown than green. Hair with more orange than darkening sunsets. But there was no mistaking them for anyone other than Ailsa's identical sisters.

'I'm him.'

The one who pointed hit her sister in the chest.

The one who straightened her gown merely jutted her chin and raised her brow. 'Ailsa's not out here.'

Rory blinked. These girls were mirrors of each other and they equally shared their older sister's blunt speech, but their mannerisms were very different.

He'd been trained as a warrior, a man to follow his father into battle, a man to lead. His first reaction to such directness was to immediately answer. A habit he would break. He was married to a McCrieff and McCrieffs didn't seem to obey the same niceties.

'And you are?' he enquired instead.

The stiff-backed one sighed as if put out, the one

who pointed her finger sniggered. 'It won't matter because you won't know.'

'So you are impolite?' he said.

One blushed, the other did not. 'It's not as if you told us who you are.'

'True, but being clever you already guessed. So my guess is that you are my wife's sisters who were ordered to stay away from me.'

Now both blushed.

At least when it came to these McCrieffs he could retain some control. 'So, if you want to keep in my good graces, or if you wish me to keep secrets, the least I can acquire are names.'

Silence from them both. If they stood out here much longer, they'd be discovered and any secrets they wanted to hide would be lost. Of course, maybe they wanted to be discovered in his presence. Though he didn't know why their identity was being kept from him. Was it simply him being a Lochmore or something else?

A slight shuffling of feet, an elbow in the ribs, and the fussy one sighed. 'We're Gormlaith and Grizel.'

Ah, so that's how it was to be played. With a nod towards the more violent one, he said, 'Well, good hunting day to you, Grizel.' When she gasped, Rory nodded his head to her sister, who straightened her spine. 'And a pleasant day for you, Gormlaith.'

'Who told you?' Grizel said in equal parts awe and cross.

Rory shrugged. 'Just as you've been kept away from me, I've been kept away from you.'

'Then you guessed?' Gormlaith said with an imperial brow raised.

'That's for you to find out, isn't it?' he said, turning away. He was intrigued by the two sisters. Very much so, and in the brief time since he met them, he envied their sibling rivalry. He'd found that kind of comraderie with Paiden, which was why he wasn't about to lose him.

'What if it isn't for us to find out?'

Rory turned back to face the two girls who hadn't moved. How old could they be? They were so much younger than their sister and it begged questions. He had so many already.

'You were meant to stay away from me—what will happen if we're caught?'

Grizel gave a grin. 'Nothing. Father told us to.'

Gormlaith scoffed. 'Grizel! He shouldn't know!'

Yet he did know. Ailsa almost confirmed it.

'Why not?' Grizel said. 'It's not as if it hasn't been amusing.'

'Amusing,' Rory repeated. 'Since you both stayed away so well, I thought it was Hamish who ordered it.'

Both girls paled. Grizel managed to shake her head, but Gormlaith looked ready to faint.

The girls' response only confirmed what he needed to do. 'Amusing or not, I'll make my way so we don't get caught…' He gave the girls a wink before he turned to leave, but the uneasiness prevailed.

There was much wrong in Clan McCrieff and Hamish, though bedridden, was still ruling or at least people were obeying because they feared him. It wasn't unusual for chiefs to rule when sick, but Hamish was truly ill if not dying while Frederick commanded the clan and sat at the high table.

But that simply revealed the difficulty he found himself in. Was he to believe Hamish, who couldn't wake, or Frederick, whom he couldn't find, when it came to King Edward's decree being honoured? If Hamish still ruled, then why did he feel that Frederick wasn't ruling according to the Chief's wishes? There was much to support this. The girls' paling, Frederick's proposal and then his guarding the door of the small room.

Too many questions and too much at stake, and he'd married into this. Whatever this was. It could be a folly or he could bring great fortune to Lochmores.

To Lochmores. Could he say that any more? He'd married a McCrieff. The Tanist's daughter. He shared a night in her bed. Folly or not. Marriage consummated or not. The curiosity and intrigue he felt with Ailsa only increased with desire and need. Something he either needed to end now or be completed. But first, he would talk to her father.

In the end, it wasn't Rory who found Frederick, but rather the old warrior who found him. Hours had passed, Rory was hungry, worried for Paiden and restless with an understanding that he been too long without Ailsa. At first, he'd wandered, believing he'd find Frederick naturally, but as the sun continued to rise, he asked his whereabouts. From some, he was given different directions from others, a narrowed gaze or a tightened jaw. He suspected this, too, had something to do with the clan differences, but what he didn't know.

More seething frustration until he turned another corner. 'Ah, there you are!' Boomed Frederick as he emerged from a nondescript hut. It was neither in ill repair nor in a fine state. It also did not look like a home or a building to hold wares.

It was, however, the perfect location if a Tanist needed privacy from a dying chief, or from a new son-in-law who was from an enemy clan.

Rory waited for Frederick to walk closer. 'Yes, here I am,' he said, as if Frederick was truly looking for him. A lie and they both knew it. He continued the ruse for other ears by saying, 'I apologise for not being where we agreed. I don't know my way around yet.'

Frederick's brow rose, a tiny gleam of relief and wariness in his eyes as he nodded. 'The mews are not as large, I'm sure, as Lochmore's, but they are very fine indeed. I'll show you the way and next time, you'll not be so lost.'

The mews. He didn't care for birds. They were useful for small game, but too unpredictable for him to find any fascination with. He lived with enough uncertainty in his life, he didn't need to add any more to it. Birds frustrated him, as did Frederick's discussion of them. Rory wanted to confront the spies that kept their eyes and ears on them, not talk of birds.

He was at a disadvantage with too many unpredictable perils surrounding him. Too many dangers and Paiden had been the one to pay. Even now his friend could be drawing his last breath and he was out here being followed by two children and a man who had answers, but didn't share them.

'We need to talk,' he said.

'Your man still lives?'

Rory nodded. 'Or we wouldn't be talking.'

Frederick's lips thinned, but he gave a curt nod. 'How fares my daughter?'

'Why do you ask me of her?'

Frederick's gaze pierced his. 'It was her marriage night.'

Ah. Tanist. Father. 'You have many roles here.'

'Not as many as some.'

Rory suspected he had more. 'You should ask her how it went if you truly want to know.'

A flush upon his wrinkled cheeks. 'Probably not.'

They kept their pace slow, steady, allowing many to see them. Villagers, some he recognised from earlier, greeted them. Most went about their day, but many stopped and simply watched. Rory resented their gawking, but not as much as he resented being manipulated.

He might not have had a sword to the back of his neck since he arrived, but he felt it all the same. Still, it had been his decision to marry Ailsa. There was much to gain here, but only if he did it on his terms, not the McCrieffs' and certainly not Frederick's.

'Is there a reason you avoid your daughter this morning?'

A frown. 'I did not avoid her.'

'Then it is I whom you didn't want to see.'

An abrupt stop as Frederick pointed. 'Here we are.'

Rory gazed at the simple, tall building that he'd walked past many times today.

'You don't want to go in,' Frederick said.

Mews smelled, feathers flew and, if the birds inside were loose, he'd have waste splattered on him. 'It would be my pleasure.'

Smiling, he pushed the door and walked in and Frederick quickly closed it after them.

The building was large, the bird collection...not so much. Three hunting birds at most. Not enough to foul the air or his clothing.

'So this is where we talk?'

'This is where it is private with also a plausible reason to be here.'

They were followed through the village. 'We won't have privacy for long.'

'No.'

So what to talk about? Why Frederick had avoided him this morning, or about his youngest daughters or should he talk about Paiden and the possible killer? There had been no outbreaks today between the Mc-Crieffs and the Lochmores, but he'd talked to his men, they were taking turns at watch. Thus far there was a temporary truce, but they could not keep that schedule and remain safe. Eventually, someone's guard or temper would slip and either a sword or poison would fell another Lochmore.

Paiden. Everything in him roared to help his friend. Instead he asked, 'What was the meeting about?'

Frederick folded his arms. 'I'm Tanist. It is common for council to be conducted.'

It wasn't a usual council and they knew it. 'I married your daughter; we've gone beyond those border conflicts, haven't we?'

'You're not a McCrieff. The border still exists. As I said, I'll remain Tanist and I'll keep the control of this clan.'

Rory stepped back in agitation. The birds skittered on their perches. 'And the King's decree?'

'It will stand with no dispute. This I promise you. Can you promise not to claim more?'

Rory should have expected this, but hadn't. He'd kept his eyes so focused on the future for his own issue, he wasn't thinking about now. Striding to the opposite wall, he leaned against it, settling in as the birds settled. 'My father is Chief and he will decide on Lochmore's clan. But I offer you congratulations that you married me to a McCrieff, thinking he'd be loath to fight against my chosen family.'

Frederick gave an audible sigh and released his arms. Rory wouldn't give him the benefit of relief.

'But know this, if Lochmore's interests are compromised, it won't matter whether I married your daughter or not. If you keep your power, I, too, will keep mine.'

'What are you, then?' Frederick said. 'Lochmore or McCrieff?'

'Shouldn't you have figured that out before you offered her? You may hope for a peace in the future, but we're both involved in the present. Right now, I have the right to know what the secret meetings are about.'

'Secret?'

Rory made a pointed glance to the door. 'We have little time, remember?'

With a glance at the airways above their head, Frederick moved to the wall Rory leant against.

Rory kept his posture casual as Frederick approached. Even so, he could see that he was a large man who had maintained his training. Which begged the question, how much control and power did Frederick wield? 'Are there stronger warriors than you here?'

'Hamish. In his prime, he was as large as a mountain and no one would argue with him.'

'But he's not in his prime, is he?'

'He's been ill for many seasons now...'

'In body or mind?'

Frederick huffed. 'Wise, aren't you?'

'You wouldn't want your daughter to be married to a simpleton.'

'It would be simpler.'

'Because you need deception.'

Frederick raised his finger to his lips. 'I have followed my Chief all my life. I am Tanist, true, but Hamish still rules.'

'But he doesn't know of my marriage to your daughter.'

'She is my daughter. Whom she marries is of no concern of his.'

Ah. 'Except when he poisons my friend or will you suggest your own people did that?'

Frederick rubbed his hands over his face. The years were showing on him, but it was the toil of the situation that weighed more heavily. Rory felt the weight on his own shoulders, but he'd have no mercy.

'Hamish will not survive the year,' Frederick said. 'Edward made his decree and there was no time to waste; otherwise, everything would have stayed as it had been. I would not have willingly gone against the wishes of my Chief.'

'There would have been a battle for the land,' Rory said, no question in his voice. No question in his gut as well. It had been easy to traverse McCrieff land because it should not have happened.

'There are men who follow me here, Lochmore,' Frederick said. 'Strong, good men and their families. Many of them—enough I hope, to support my decisions.'

'You hope.' Rory dug his shoulders into the wall behind him, felt and welcomed the bite of rough timber. It was enough to keep his temper. 'Yet you took the risk of inviting me here and offering marriage, knowing those who follow Hamish would not accept it.'

At Frederick's brief nod, Rory shoved away from the wall. 'You fool, you've divided loyalties and then brought in an enemy clan. You expect me to repair this?'

'By marrying my daughter, you already have. Maybe not in my lifetime, but I hope in hers. I would do anything for her. There are possibilities for you as well.'

Ludicrous. Fanciful dreams. 'The possibilities are there only if we live through this. And know this, if my friend dies, your possibilities are meaningless. I am Lochmore's son.'

Frederick shook his head once, twice, as if answering his inner questions, but confusion laced his expression. 'You married her.'

Rory was tired of being held at the whims of others, of trying to get approval. He might not have control of his past, but he would take control of his future.

'I said my vows, but that is all that occurred last night,' Rory said, his stare unbending until Frederick's eyes widened in recognition. Until the father knew the marriage was unconsummated and could be annulled.

'Know this as well, Tanist.' Rory stepped to the door,

his hand on the latch. 'I will never meet privately with you in the mews again. When we meet, it will be in front of all so that every McCrieff will know our collaboration. As for you, there will be no more secret meetings, no behind-my-back negotiations. You invited and proposed a Lochmore to marry your daughter. We're family now.'

Chapter Twelve

She shouldn't be here, not at this time of day. Now was the time she should have stayed by Hamish's side, but Hamish slept as if dead. When she checked on Paiden, saw that he remained the same and that Beth was taking care of him, Ailsa knew she couldn't just hide inside the room. Something had to be done.

That something led her to these rooms down below the keep. Mostly they were open spaces: coffers made empty by Hamish's poor choices, a few stocked with wine for celebrations only and then this room…the one worth any value at all. Shelves upon shelves of scrolls and journals. Costly items and for years it had been suggested they be moved to the chapel. Hamish, greedy man that he was, insisted they be kept under his domain. They were worthless in trade, but a source of vain pride.

For her, they were priceless. In here were kept all the healers' journals; Rhona's was the thickest and most worn. The journal should be in her rooms, but even knowing it could mean life or death if a cure was not found quick enough, Hamish had declined her possession.

He'd announced it was done to protect the knowledge, but she knew he did it to retain power over her as he did to everyone, but for her, she believed it was personal.

Hamish had never married, never conceived or at least none outside of Rhona's story. Because of that and her father's ancestry, it had been expected for her father to become Tanist, even as it was expected that his issue would rule. Though she was a woman, she was the healer and had retained her own influence with the clan. Though her purpose was pure, Hamish never saw good in anything or anyone.

Therefore, to show she was lesser than him, he had decreed that she request his permission to enter this room. Permission that couldn't be granted now. So she had taken his keys and left him in the care of another.

She had the Chief's keys. Just that alone could earn her punishment. That she left him not in her care as he ordered could earn her death.

But she'd had to come here; there were too many truths needing discovery. She needed to investigate Hamish's and Paiden's symptoms, find what could have caused their illness. If it was poison, they should both have died or recovered by now.

Nothing she knew of caused this constant continual sleep. Nothing she knew of caused any sleep like this unless it was taken in massive doses. If that occurred, Paiden or Hamish would have noticed the taste.

Unless…unless they continued to ingest the poison, but how? And if that was the case, wouldn't she have noticed it by now? So either the means of poison was just under her nose and she'd forgotten or it was something she'd never come across before. Whatever the poisoner gave, if there was a cure to be found, it would be here.

Which led to the next troubling thought. Who would attempt to murder her husband's friend and the Chief? There was no connection between a Lochmore and a McCrieff who did not know each other.

Having nodded to the guards in the courtyard, Ailsa quietly closed the door. The first obstacle had been met because they assumed she had the right to be here. The second obstacle for today was privacy. An open door would make the room more comfortable with light and fresh warm air, but she couldn't risk it.

She needed to be left alone for there was more than herbal remedies and tinctures in this room. Here was the reason the chapel wanted possession of the documents: here were official clan announcements, including important births.

She shouldn't look, didn't have the right. If what she guessed was correct, what would it prove?

If such a thing had occurred, she couldn't imagine it being written down. Though if Hamish had had a child, it would be claimed because Hamish never wanted her father to rule. If the child was born secretly, then the mother hadn't claimed Hamish as the father. Thus, again, there would be no point in writing the birthing down, let alone that the child was given away.

Still, she needed to see. Too much depended upon Rory's lineage not to.

Ailsa reached for the first flat satchel containing various parchments and unwound the package. Inside was a bound cartulary regarding the building and upkeep of McCrieff Castle. She carefully placed it back on the shelf.

She grabbed the one next to it—this book was on the parish. That, too, she returned. Her eyes roved the shelves. There were other satchels, some bulky, most likely containing scrolls versus books.

None of it was in order. Church lists, with flecks of brittle parchment in pieces too small to read. Still precious enough that she didn't dare just toss it to the side. She could ask for help. There were others here who knew the documents, could probably guess by sight which she needed, but she felt this was something she needed to do herself.

Hours later and Ailsa stretched her arms and back. She'd stopped long ago placing the cartularies back on the shelves. At one point, she thought she'd organise it. Now the room was untidy. Some books hadn't made it back to the satchels, nor some scrolls, and she stood back and surveyed the room. As the time crept on, she'd become impatient. To think to organise it was madness. For now she was tired and carnage laid at her feet.

She was also no closer to the truth. She'd hoped that she could discover something of import on her own. There was a part of her that purposefully felt she'd been kept in the dark. Her father overly protective, Hamish controlling, Rhona reluctantly sharing her remedies and hiding secrets until her deathbed.

The records of her birth she found, as for—

'I thought you'd be in Hamish's room,' Rory said.

Ailsa started at the sound of his voice and the closing of the door. She turned to face him. 'I left.'

Gazing roughly around the room, Rory stepped forward.

She raised her hand. 'Wait. The documents are scattered.'

'I can see that. Why?'

'I was…organising records.'

He'd changed since she saw him last. His clothes different, his hair a bit damp, but it wasn't simply his physical appearance.

He'd strode from their bedroom full of outrage. She'd expected Rory to return within moments with something from the kitchens and news of a confrontation with her father. Instead, hours later there was a predatory stillness about him.

Shadows played havoc here and she shouldn't be able to see everything about him so clearly, yet she did. His dark brown hair was loose and framed his unshaven jaw. The bristles there darkening and casting him further in shadows. His eyes just a shade lighter held some burning emotion that shifted too quickly for her to discern. She wanted to say frustration, but it was held back, simmering too hotly for that emotion.

Nothing of this moment could she fully understand. All she knew with certainty was that he sought her out and found her here…alone.

'Did you find my father?' she asked.

'I didn't get you food.'

'I didn't expect you to.' She swallowed. 'Did he have much to say?'

'What makes you believe I found him.'

That stopped her. 'You said you'd find him. There's been some time since then, so I thought perhaps you had.'

'And you believe I'd do as I'd say?'

What was going on here? So much more under the surface with this man, but what, she didn't know. She'd wed him though they approached their marriage differently. She, trying to protect her people; he, trying to secure the lands owed to his clan. Then she'd laid with him, bared her body and he had rejected her.

They were strangers with mistrust between them, but still she'd undressed before him, still allowed him in her bed. Accepted his kisses, his touch…and the *way* he touched. Yet now, she couldn't understand what he meant then by 'This is what was meant to be'?

She had never felt such pleasure before, had never allowed herself such vulnerability and exposed her very soul to him. When he had said those words, had he meant that what she felt, what she perceived they both felt, *that* was how it was truly meant to be between husband and wife? Or had he known in that moment he would deny their marriage?

'Do I believe you'd do as you'd say?' she said. 'Within reason.'

His brows drew in. 'I always do as I say.'

'You brought me no food and, though vows were exchanged, we aren't married,' she said and quickly wished she hadn't. They weren't here for that. They weren't here for anything. Except they said words before her clan and he had never meant them.

'I met your sisters.' Rory took another step. This room was meant for papers and perhaps a few people inside, but Rory was so large just that slight step further into the room made it seem so much smaller.

'How are they?' she asked.

He reached down and picked up a single parchment, laid it back. Picked up another, then let it fall to the ground. 'They're alive and well, if that is what you ask. I think you and your father do not credit them enough with intelligence. I found them rather interesting.'

Suddenly needing more room, Ailsa stepped back. Rory noted her movement and raised a brow. What had happened between this morning and now? Exhaustion had blurred her earlier indignation and anger, but she was still shamed and he was still in the wrong. Now she felt as if he set a trap and she merely needed to set foot in it. If he had originally approached her like this, she would never have agreed to marrying him.

'They are interesting and quite opinionated.'

'Where is your mother?'

She thought he'd know some of the clan's interests, but then, when had there been time? 'Dead. She died giving birth to them.'

'I'm sorry.'

She almost felt that he meant it, but he was a good liar. 'She was a gentle soul. I think if she had lived, we would have given her a very difficult time. My sisters especially. They are a bit more…free.'

'Than you?' He took a journal off the shelf and flipped through it. She'd held that journal just moments before. It looked diminished in his large hands. From here she could see the scars along his knuckles and in the tender crook of his thumb, and knew he'd earned them. He was a warrior now, but at one time he'd had to train, at one time he'd made mistakes.

'I'm free.'

'Apparently, because here you are instead of in Hamish's rooms.'

Here was one of her mistakes. Forgetting the passing of time in this room, allowing Rory to find her. She was married and it was conceivable he would search for her. The other mistake was walking further in the room and allowing Rory access to the information.

'I told you why I was here.'

'You're not organising. You're searching for a cure.'

She wouldn't lie to him, but that didn't mean she would tell him the truth. Last night proved that he didn't trust her. She'd never been more vulnerable in her life. She said she'd help him, gave a vow before God, and he'd...hurt her. 'I said I would help your friend.'

'But you didn't come here when he was struck down, only when you thought McCrieff's Chief needed help.'

She would grant some allowances for their differences, the fact they were strangers, but never this. 'Don't you dare accuse me of such a thing. It was you who demanded we wed immediately. You who barred me from reaching your friend. Since that time, I've done everything I can for him. This clan has continued to stay by your friend's side to care for him as well. I'm here to find a cure for them both.'

'Both?' he said, a note to his voice. 'So you, too, believe Hamish suffers from what Paiden does.'

She was unused to politics, to subterfuge. Everything she said felt as though it was cloaked in lies. On the surface, her husband should know everything, but he'd shown he did not trust.

Could she blame him? His friend could be dying. Still, with last night unresolved between them, she would not expose herself or her clan again. 'Hamish has been ill for many seasons.'

'But it has worsened overnight?'

'What are you accusing me of, Lochmore? Shouldn't all of this have been discussed before we said our vows?'

'We're not married,' he said.

She couldn't hide the flinch as his cutting words struck right where she had stewed all day, but she did turn her back so she didn't have to see the simmering rage in his eyes boring into her. She'd placed some trust when she married Rory, even more trust when she'd lain beneath him. Now this? 'If you've said your piece; you should go. I have work to do here.'

Silence, but she refused to turn again to see if he left or stayed. She did have work to do; kneeling again on the cold floor, she attacked another stack of papers.

Rory bit back a curse. He'd been manipulated since he was a baby. As the son of Lochmore's Chief, he'd been shuffled and positioned to take over the Clan's interests. Over the years, he'd suspected he wasn't even his father's son, which meant he was more manipulated and controlled than anyone knew.

With no way to earn his right on Lochmore's lands and under Lochmore's rule, he'd come here to secure his future, to gain some respect from his Chief and clan. If he wasn't a chief's son, then he could earn the right to rule. A gamble to be sure, but there was enough incentive here to make it worthwhile. Except he was being directed and controlled again. What made it worse was he hadn't known how far or gravely until his conversation with Frederick.

If McCrieffs themselves were divided, there was no solution to the problem between McCrieffs and Lochmores. He'd married believing there could be a chance for some future, but there wasn't.

Lies everywhere. Even his wife lied to him. She told him she couldn't leave Hamish's room. Yet here she was, telling him she did it to organise mouldy parchments. That was another lie.

Some of the records she'd disturbed were certainly on gardening, and herbal combinations, but some were documents that usually were in churches. Lineage on families, births, deaths, acquisitions.

Her purpose in this room wasn't for organising, but to find information and not only on herbs. Controlled again. Would nothing be his own? Yet he didn't feel the same wrenching frustration towards her as he did towards her father, or his own father for that matter.

It was because of that moment in the courtyard. It had skewed everything he'd done since then. Her beauty, her intelligence more tempting than the control of McCrieff land. Then he'd touched her, kissed her, held her to him while his body burned. To accomplish what he needed to, to unveil truths, to help his friend, he had refused to take her in their marriage bed.

But he wanted to. No, more than that, it was something beyond need…a longing. Here, with her vibrant hair half-bound, half not, her cream gown covered in dust and wrinkled beyond repair, she was as much a siren to him now as she had been in the courtyard.

More so because her pride would not tolerate his behaviour. And rightly so. He'd been heartless last night, cruel today.

How was she to be understanding, if they had no understanding between them? Yet how could he risk his friend's life, even if they could resolve what was between them? Someone had intentionally harmed his friend and it appeared also the McCrieffs' Chief.

His eyes scanned the room for answers, found nothing but dust motes floating in the dim light provided by the three lit torches. The room was filled with precious scattered paper and damp air, as if this room refused to let go of winter though spring showed its abundance everywhere else.

Ailsa was like spring to him. Danger surrounding him in that courtyard and he'd not been able take his eyes off her fiery locks. Dining at his enemy's table and he'd kept trying to catch her green gaze like some lovesick fool.

Last night, he'd demanded she take off her gown, to gain some control, but he wasn't in control, hadn't been since he undid her laces. Rory shut down those thoughts as he had all day. His body was still drawn tight with need and desire. Touching her only made him want more of his wife.

She was his wife. His future uncertain, but this…?

Since he arrived the division between clans made a division within himself. From one moment to the next his thoughts and actions changed, but since the courtyard Ailsa had been a constant.

Impossible possibilities here, but she, somehow, was a certainty within him.

Something righted itself inside him as the full resolution of his wants became clear. He wanted *this* wife. With a marriage not forced on him and one not full of secrets and accusations. But he'd hurt her—maybe now he needed to make some amends. Not everything, but a compromise so that there could be some peace between them.

'I could help you,' he offered.

Ailsa tied a scroll and picked up another one. 'You'd get in the way.'

True. He didn't like it though. 'I could organise—'

'Haven't you done enough, Lochmore? You need to leave.'

Rory stepped over the paper and watched Ailsa tense. He hated his large and clumsy body in places like these. When he reached the other side, he leaned against the wall. She kept her head down, her shoulders hunched. Did she think he'd harm her?

'I did meet with your father.'

Ailsa hesitated, before she shuffled more papers.

'I know of the divide now.'

Ailsa's head snapped up. 'Divide?'

She had to know. 'Between Hamish and your father.'

She opened her mouth, closed it. Opened again. 'You guessed.'

'He told me...but it wouldn't be hard to guess. My family has had dealings with Hamish. He's never been the type to allow Lochmores free rein on his land and invite them to dine.'

'Or offer the Tanist's daughter for marriage?'

He looked at her pointedly. 'Oh, he would, if it meant getting the Tanist's only issue out of the way. How long have you known?'

'Their differences? All my life. As to the marriage, you were there when I first knew of that.'

'You're a terrible liar.'

She jerked. 'Me a liar? You're the one who gave his vows before God and then didn't keep them.'

A stillness overcame him. An understanding. 'You're afraid. Why?'

Startled green eyes met his before she looked away again. 'What would I have to be afraid of?'

'You're not merely here for the cure, you're here to discover the poisoner. The documents aren't only on healing tinctures.'

Her eyes swept the room and the sudden tension left her body. It immediately alerted him. She *was* a terrible liar, but now he wondered if he had truly discovered the lie. It was his turn to search the room, but he could think of no other reason for her presence here. Why she looked at lineage documents as well as healers' recipes.

'You understand the difficulty of it,' he said. 'Who would want to murder a Lochmore and a McCrieff?'

'I'm here for exactly what I said I was…to find the cure and I'm also organising the room. And if you are thinking of blaming my father, you met with him today. You know what kind of man he is.'

'I know what kind of man he is and I can't rule him out. He has reason to kill Hamish.'

'My father is loyal and wouldn't harm his Chief!'

'Despite their differences?' he asked.

'They've always differed in opinions.'

'And always differed in power. But your father has some now.'

'Killing Hamish wouldn't serve the clan, nor would harming the Lochmores.'

'Harming the Lochmores would always serve the McCrieffs.'

'Not with our marriage, which was suggested by a McCrieff. My father will not harm you or yours.'

His wife was as direct as always. The room was cold, the wall damp and the stone he stood on was unforgiving. She'd been toiling here for hours. For him, for them or for her own interests? A wife he wanted, but could he chance his clan, his future with her?

'I won't harm you either, Ailsa.'

'Why are you talking of this with me?' she asked.

He sank a bit further on the wall, crossed his arms. 'You don't need to be afraid of me.'

She dropped the parchment in her hand and rested her hands on her bent knees. Like this she was so much smaller than he and almost fragile looking. But her gaze held his and he knew the falsity of that impression. His wife held unimaginable strength. After all, she had brandished shears at him.

'I think your family have underestimated you as well,' he said. 'I think your father has also tried to protect you.'

'Shouldn't all fathers protect their daughters?' She stopped, hesitated. Looked away as she said, 'For that matter shouldn't fathers protect their sons?'

His father. His lie.

His wife. Too far away, was his only thought as he sank to his knees next to her. He relished that she didn't move away. 'Ailsa.'

'What are you doing?' she whispered.

Taking a chance. 'I'm helping you. These documents are everywhere.'

She shook her head once, twice. 'Last night…'

He needed to apologise, but how to say it? Her hands fluttered in her lap and he took them. Her hands were cold and he rubbed them. Her lips parted as she watched his clumsy attempts. He was acutely aware of his callouses, how his hands engulfed hers, of the hitch in her breath.

How it matched his own. He didn't know this woman existed until yesterday. Couldn't imagine the way she felt, or the way her mind worked. All he knew was he wanted more.

A tug on her hands woke Ailsa from her reverie. Wrenching her hands free, she skittered back, not caring about the papers she bent. 'You must think me a fool, Lochmore.'

She had lost her friend years ago. Months ago, she tried to save two McCrieffs. Last night she lost a bit of her pride to this man. This was no time to be weak.

'You are anything and everything but a fool, Ailsa. As many differences as there are between us, that is truth.'

'Can you not just leave?'

'We're married.'

She pointed at him. 'And there you go, changing the story again. Are we or are we not married? Because I can't keep up with your moods even in such little time that I've known you. You may think me blunt, but you are everything but. Deceit is everywhere around me.'

'You are surrounded by your clan, your father and your Chief. Why would you think there is deceit?'

'Did you not think that I felt deception when my father held back clan information, when he handed me off to you? When you agreed to marry me, then didn't consummate the marriage?' She pulled a pile of documents on her lap. 'Leave Lochmore. Leave me to this. I'll heal your friend; I'll find the remedy in this mess I made. Then you can take Paiden and go. We'll pretend it never happened. Maybe our arranged marriage in name only will be enough deterrent for war between our clans over the land.'

He was silent so long, she thought he'd finally listen to her and leave. Instead, though he stayed very still, she felt as if he moved closer. She knew it was the size of the room compared to the size of the man, but this close, her awareness of him was something more than that. She was aware of him by the subtle heat coming from his tall frame, and the way the air seemed to move differently around him. And though she couldn't possibly see his steady brown eyes, she felt his measuring gaze on her.

And he kept looking at her despite her not looking back.

'For a moment, forget the clans. How did you think it would be between us?' Rory asked quietly.

'There is no us.' She kept staring at the papers in her lap. 'I only hoped our union would be enough to stem the differences between our clans.'

'And the differences within yours?'

Her gaze finally snapped to his. 'There are differences in every clan.'

'Not many clans have two rulers.'

'Hamish is ill.'

'But he was well enough at one point to order someone to poison my friend. If I'm to believe your father innocent, then the order must have come from Hamish. Maybe that poison was meant for me.'

Her thoughts muddled, her tears threatening. She didn't want poison or swords or talk of death any more. She'd had enough of it. Shuffling on her knees, she turned her back to him. 'Can you not leave?'

'You know of the secret meetings your father has been holding. Did you see Hamish have some as well?'

'Hamish is the Chief, he has no meetings that are secret.'

'But they are private.'

'I'm a healer; not part of the council.' A useless healer, for the documents in her lap she'd seen before. They were as worthless to her as this conversation. They didn't provide the answers regarding the poison used, or who administered it. They didn't even hint at what to do with this husband of hers, who sat with her on the floor.

'You're a healer, but you're also part of this divided clan,' Rory said. 'One that most likely will be even more divided upon Hamish's death. It is of little wonder why your father wanted to keep ruling, but what then with our marriage?'

'We're not married,' she said stubbornly.

He exhaled roughly. A few papers ruffled next to them. 'I felt married.'

She couldn't breathe at all.

'I felt married when I gave my vows, when we shared that bed,' he said, his voice low almost reverent. 'When I held you.'

She didn't want to hear this. There was no purpose for this. Not for her and definitely not for him. He had no need for the deceit here. And, if she was right, and he was Hamish's son… Hamish, who poisoned his friend, but might have wanted to poison his own child.

Was it possible that Hamish knew Rory was his son? If so, he needed to get as far away from her as possible.

'Save your seducing words, Lochmore. They are unnecessary. Leave now and there is nothing permanent between us. All can return to as it was.' She turned her head to catch his eyes which had impossibly darkened and held emotions that weren't there before. She wasn't prepared for them. A banked heat, a longing, a thwarted rage.

'How was it?'

Caught in the turbulence of his eyes, she answered, 'Last night?'

A soft huff of breath from him. 'Your past. You want to return to it as it was…but I know nothing of it. How can I know it was better?'

'It's not for you to know.'

'Then tell me.'

She didn't need time to think about the answer, but she tried. Yet nothing in this room or from the muffled sounds above would change the truth. 'It wasn't better.'

'You know of my hell. Paiden is my very dearest friend. He is a brother to me and I am terrified to lose him. I know you know this because you've seen it from the very first. You tried to shield me from your clan in the Hall that morning when he collapsed.'

'And you held a sword to my neck.' When he had been filled with so much powerful anger and anguish she'd felt it, she'd instinctually protected him. The end result of that was pain and uncertainty now. 'It doesn't matter how I felt then. You made it clear last night what your feelings between us are. Didn't you say, this is how it should be? So let it be, Lochmore, and leave me alone.'

His left hand clenched in a fist. 'You know my burdens, I don't know yours. Perhaps if you shared yours... Why won't you share them?'

She turned her head, her back remained to him. She didn't have to answer any of his questions. 'What will it prove?'

'Nothing, except... Nothing.'

It was Rory's hesitancy, his revealing of vulnerability that pricked something within her though her defences were up. What was it? Perhaps it was Rhona's story. Or perhaps it was the time they'd spent together or that moment where he'd seen her hiding when he arrived in the courtyard? Whatever it was, it compelled her. This man compelled her. She fought his demands, requests and stubbornness. But in the end, there was a part of her that wanted him to know. That part she had no defence against and so she told him.

'I had a friend once who was like a brother, though why we were close I don't remember,' she said. 'He was the least sensible friend I could have picked.'

She kept her head down, but could no longer touch the papers that were blurring around her. Lost in the past, defenceless against unhappy memories, she didn't want to remember Magnus, that day or what she lost. Because as much as she loved and was loved by her clan, other than her father, she never dared get that close to someone again.

'What happened?'

Rory's deep voice jarred her from thoughts. Exhaling, she said, 'You already can guess.'

'I want you to share this burden with me.'

His voice was closer, she felt his breath. For a flicker

of a moment, she thought to argue with him, to tell him to move away, but Magnus deserved to be known... even if it was by this man. 'Lochmores reeved. Magnus charged out to stop them and was trampled by horses. I was there with him when he let go of my hand. I saw and heard everything. His sharp cry, the crunch of his bones. He didn't...he didn't die immediately.'

Rory cursed, but she didn't care for his emotions. Only for hers and she felt too much. 'I've hated the Lochmores since that day. I hated you for coming on to the land and dining at our table.'

'But you married me.'

She pushed the papers off her lap, grabbed another scroll. 'We're not—

'We said our vows. You said them and meant them.'

She ripped the ribbon around the parchment. 'We were before Clan and God.'

But Rory knew the truth, she did it to save lives because she cared. This woman hadn't lied to him; she was incapable of it and he had treated her wrongly.

'Are we done now?' she asked. 'I have more to read and you are in the way.'

He watched Ailsa open the scroll and read the contents. She did her best to ignore him, but he was incapable of ignoring her. He wanted her, this woman, this wife, but again he asked himself, could he chance it?

If he confessed the facts to Paiden, what would he say? That he was a fool...no, Paiden would use a more colourful insult while also challenging him. Paiden most likely would want Ailsa to himself. Any man would. But after he treated her the way he did, did he deserve her? 'I don't want to leave.'

Ailsa lowered the scroll and finally, finally, looked over her shoulder and up at him.

'You're still kneeling next to me.' Her brow furrowed. 'And you're closer.'

All true. 'You told me of Magnus. I couldn't stay away.'

Great green eyes held him. How long had he known this woman? Mere hours, moments. Carefully, holding her gaze, he leaned forward until his body almost touched her curved back. Her eyes widened and then darted to his arms, as he cradled her and clasped her hands beneath his. Then one by one he lifted her fingers until the scroll fell into her lap and he brushed it aside. With so much revealed between them, he wanted nothing in their way.

She smelled of lavender and old parchment, she smelled of her, and he wanted a taste.

'I told you of Magnus, so you'd leave,' she said, her voice a shiver.

He relished that telling response. 'Are you certain?'

The heat of Rory's body sank through her skin, thawed her cold limbs. Ailsa felt the slight dig of his knees in the small of her back before he eased them open, edged forward and pressed against her hips, her thighs.

The rasp of their clothing was barely heard above the pounding of her heart, the choppy exhalation of his breath.

Then she heard nothing but the wet slickness of his tongue, felt nothing but the tiny flick against the back of her ear. Her body flooded with awareness, her skin prickled with need.

Another warm exhalation from him and the soft

press of his lips to the back of her ear, down her neck and to the edge of her gown. Another flick of his tongue before his lips followed the path upwards.

'Rory.'

With his lips against her throat, he growled, 'The way you say my name.'

Possessive. Territorial. Ailsa swore she could feel that very male sound to the marrow of her bones as it swept need, lust, desire through her.

Too much heat, too fast as he lifted his head, and she turned hers to see his eyes rake from hers to her lips, down the curve of her neck and along her spine, then back up again.

Despite knowing better, she asked, 'How do I say it?'

'As if you always wanted to.'

Every defence Ailsa held crumbled. Why bother when he saw her so clearly? 'What do you think you are doing?'

'What does it appear I am doing?' Rory asked, his gaze locked on to her lips.

'I think…do you want to kiss me?'

His eyes to hers again. Dark, so dark there was hardly any colour to them at all. 'Soon, but first I want more of this.'

More of this was more of those soft, heated kisses along the fragile cords of her neck until he was lifting her hair and kissing underneath. The warmth of his breath contrasted with the whispering chill of the room. Then he clenched her hair in one fist and the imprisoned tendrils swept against her overly sensitive skin until her body shivered. He groaned and continued his path on the other side, up to her other ear.

She couldn't touch, couldn't kiss him. She could do

nothing but bow her head to give him more access, of which he took advantage.

One of his hands contained her hair, the other now pulled on her gown, trying to expose more of her to his touch, to his kisses. The fabric cut into her neck and she flinched. He stopped immediately. 'Sorry.'

A heartbeat. Two. There was no one here but them, daylight still and she heard no one above. The door was secure; they were alone. 'Don't stop.'

'I don't want to hurt you.'

'I know.'

Another heartbeat. 'I meant what I said; I don't want to leave…ever.' His voice low, rough. A man trying to be gentle.

She turned her head. His cheekbones were mottled, his lips soft, his eyes, however, were hardened with a hunger she hadn't seen before, but that she wanted. Desperately. She'd lied when she'd said that she'd told him about Magnus to push him away. She'd told him to bring him closer.

'I said my vows,' she said. 'I meant them as well.'

He released her hair, his hands going to her laces. Fumbling. 'Did you tie these?'

'Yes.' He let out a frustrated breath and she laughed. Another tug and she felt the laces give way to his intentions. To hers.

He'd have access to her now if they weren't kneeling on the cold floor, if they weren't faced the wrong way. She shifted so she could turn and strong hands came to her hips. 'Stay.'

'But—'

He squeezed her hips, adjusted himself closer until

all of him was pressed against her back. 'Stay,' he rasped.

His hands pulled and tugged at the fabric of her gown, loosening and widening it. She felt the gaps along her torso and collarbone. Felt his expansive chest against her delicate spine, felt his need pressed hot and hard against her lower back.

Then his warrior's hands, calloused, lethal, greedy, pulling her up and back against him by her hips to clench and shove himself forward.

He shuddered. She gasped with pleasure. Her back to his front, it shouldn't feel like this, and yet she was sensitive, aware, needy. Reverently, he caressed along her waist, stroking upwards to gently cup her breasts. His fingers swiping across her nipples, his head bowing until it was side by side with hers.

Like this, she knew Rory could watch his hands rolling the sensitive flesh of her breasts which became full and heavy. Could observe her response as he flicked and swiped her nipples until they were taut and achy. Like this, she could see his hands rake down in the valley between her breasts, down further until his urgent fingers slowly dragged the bottom of her gown up and over her knees. She could watch as his hand crept under the cream linen of her gown and touched the bared flesh of her legs. As he splayed his fingers against her inner thighs to give him purchase to roll his hips again, then again.

Heat flared and again. She wanted so much, she cried out.

'I'm sorry.'

His stillness rather than his words, registered with her. 'Why are you…?'

Another flexing of his fingers against her delicate aching skin, his hips shifting as if wanting to move more, fast, hard. The tension in her mounted. His forehead skimming her shoulder, his kisses and hot fast breath striking the side of her neck. 'Ailsa, I'm sorry. I'm sorry. I can't seem to help rutting against you like some great beast.'

She wanted him like this. So different than he was their first time together. There he'd brought her pleasure and forsaken his own. There he'd remained in control and denied them both.

Never again. 'Rory, I want this.'

A rough exhalation, a stroke of his fingers, a brush against the juncture just where her thigh curved. Her bowed head, her eyes half-open to watch, to see him touch her. But the generous swathes of linen from her gown hid everything. Frustrated, she clutched the folds and swept them back. Revealing everything.

He shook, he spoke her name on a ragged whisper. So much desire. She shifted, tried to turn. He splayed his hands wide, held her still. Why? 'Let me turn. Let me…'

'I need to touch, to ready you. Holding you like this, I can control what is between us.'

'No more. I want this.'

A guttural growl, his body tense, a burst of his breath against the side of her ear, her cheek. She turned her head, beckoning for his kisses. He gave them.

One, then another, a litany of the same words in between. 'I know, I know.' An answer to her needs, his, *theirs*.

Where he could touch and kiss and watch, she could only clutch his forearms, her fingernails dragging down and gripping back up. She wouldn't soften her touch, couldn't when she wanted so much more.

As if hearing her need, he gave more caresses, rapid feather-light strokes through her growing slickness. His breath hot against her collarbone, his lips continuing their trail of kisses behind her ear. 'To feel you like this.' He delved his fingers deeper and she couldn't breathe at all. She was about to break apart, without him.

She clutched his wrist, hard, sharp, and he stopped. She knew nothing of a marriage bed. Nothing of how to bring as much pleasure to Rory as he brought to her. But everything in her knew he felt as equal a desire as she and she wouldn't let this moment pass like she had last night. 'No more.'

He eased his fingers from her core. They glistened with her need, the sight a jolt to her senses. Then he brought those fingers to his mouth. She slammed her eyes closed against the knowledge, against what flared inside her, against everything knowing he touched her, tasted her. Knowing that finally, finally there would be more. He had stopped and now there would be more.

Because she could move, *would* move, but he stood first and took her hand to pull her up.

Her gown fell to her feet, her chemise held to her shoulders, but she felt the looseness of it and the chill in the room. Without Rory's great body surrounding her, she became aware of her surroundings. That it was the middle of the day, that there was no lock on the door. That this wasn't a bedroom, but a storage room and the floor was covered in parchments.

'We can't… I don't want to leave.'

A small smile. 'We're not.'

He spared the room a glance, strode to a wall nearest a torch and sat down with his back to the wall.

'Come sit right here,' he said, indicating his lap.

She hesitated.

'Ailsa, the room is cold, the floor damp, hard, uncomfortable. There is no bed here for us. If we aren't to leave, this is what we'll have to do. All I can offer is my body to protect you from the ground, and the torch overhead which is giving off heat.'

'You want me to sit, to straddle you?'

His eyes grew heavy lidded. 'Your tongue. Your words, they'll undo me, but, yes, straddle me.'

'How are we to be together? You're fully clothed.'

'I'll release when I can. I need a few moments.'

She didn't want a few moments.

'I am…' he swallowed '…feral with need. I'll be no more than that rutting beast if I let myself out of my braies now. You're not quite ready, not yet, not how you need to be for this first time. I should be gentle. Maybe if I didn't want you so much, I could hold you up against the wall to take you. Maybe I could protect you from this damn ground, but I fear my legs would give.'

'Your legs are like tree trunks, Rory.'

'They are as weak as a foals—' another curve to his lips '—but there are other parts of me that are far too strong.'

Avoiding the parchment, she came to him on shaky legs. One foot on each side of his thighs, she pulled her chemise up and sat down. His need just there where she could touch him. So she did, watching his reaction, feeling hers in response.

'Can I touch you?' she asked.

'I think you already are.' It was all here, them, together, right here. She undid his belt and he whipped it away. Free, she ran her hands under his tunic to feel the corded muscles in his stomach, the strong curves of his chest. She leaned up to gain access to his shoulders, revelling in her breasts brushing against his skin. Further up until the tunic wouldn't give any more.

'The wall's rough,' he said.

She released her arms from their trap and gripped his thighs that flexed, so she rubbed harder. 'I want to see.'

He trailed his fingers along her thighs. Up and down again, then he went to his waist and undid his breeches and braies.

She stared. 'How can you…fit?'

'I thought you'd seen the male form before.'

'Never like this.'

He smiled. 'I suppose not. We'll fit. Like this, I won't be able to move as much. It'll be you who brings us there.'

She wanted it. Taking him in hand, she raised her legs. He cursed, his hands on her hips stopping her.

Frustrated with need, she growled, 'I'm ready.'

'What is done, cannot be undone,' he said.

Fascinated, she didn't take her eyes off him, of his response to the brush of her fingers, releasing a droplet that she eagerly spread. 'We're married,' she said.

'Look at me.'

She did. His breath was deep, his dark eyes filled with warmth, heat and something more than desire. He wanted her.

'Why are you stopping me?'

'This doesn't have to be here, now. We can wait.'

'No.' Her limbs trembled, her body shook. She could see what his stopping cost him as well. But more than that, she wanted him. 'I don't want to wait. I want this. I want…you.'

He shuddered beneath her. 'Then take me.'

She did. Her hand on him, his hand now coming to cover hers to hold himself steady. Slowly, she eased down. Rory ripped his hand away and held as still as his harsh breaths allowed. It didn't hurt like she'd been told. Instead, the pressure, the fullness was only pleasure.

'How?' She shifted, adjusting to him bit by bit.

His lips parted, his eyes raking from hers to where they were joined. 'Because you do this. Because your body knows what it needs.'

She knew so little. 'But…isn't…? This isn't usual.'

A slight curve to mouth, a slight exhalation. 'Some day I'll ask about what you know. But know that if we had a bed I'd want you underneath me. I'd want to—'

A pained look crossed his features at the same time as he flexed within her. She gasped at the quick movement.

With iron control, his eyes held hers. 'Last time, I had you on the bed. I…had control of the laces, of your pleasure. If we do this, if this marriage is true, I want you to have power and control. You have it. You take it.'

This man, who talked of power and planned with determination, relinquished what he most held dear. To her.

She rolled her hips and felt her body give way to him. 'But how—?'

'Like this.' He grabbed the back of her neck, pulled

her close and kissed her. Their lips joining, fusing as their bodies did the same. A gentle rocking of his hips until hers did the same, until she needed more and she raised on her knees to take more of him. To take more for her. A clash of breaths, a want, a need. She wrapped herself around him, just as he flattened his feet on the ground, bent his knees, and surrounded her.

She broke away.

'Rory.'

'Please,' he rasped. He shoved deep and her body tremored, tightened. One more roll of his hips and she'd be undone.

She pushed up from his shoulders; Rory braced against the wall.

'Let go,' he said. 'I'm right there, Ailsa, I'm there.'

She dropped, just as he gave another roll of his hips. Until the pleasure broke for them both and they were there.

'That was…pleasant.' Ailsa rested her head on his shoulder.

He hummed. 'It almost didn't happen at all. When you pulled your gown up so I could see my hands between…' He exhaled roughly as if the memory of it was too much. 'You undo me, Wife. I have no control when it comes to you.'

He clasped her hand so that his fingers played along hers, drumming down her palm and around her wrist, then back up again.

She liked that and he must have realised as he gave a low chuckle and splayed his fingers wide so he could play more.

'Our marriage is in truth now,' he said.

She could argue that their marriage had been in truth when they said their vows or earlier yet when they'd made their bargain. But the truth was, their marriage wasn't genuine until she'd told him of Magnus, of her loss and why she hated Lochmores.

Another play of her fingers against his until she must have hit a sensitive spot, for his hand jerked away and he wiggled it a bit before placing his hand in hers again. His left hand.

'Why do you insist on using your right hand?' she asked.

He made a disappointed sound.

'I told you of Magnus. Telling me that you use your right instead of your left shouldn't be that significant.'

'I am truly sorry for Magnus, Ailsa.'

Aware that he avoided her question, but also aware it was important to talk of their past, she said, 'Have you ever lost someone like that to the McCrieffs?'

'Paiden is as close as I've ever come to that loss and you know how well I'm faring.'

'You miss him.'

'Very much. I think he would have had some things in common with your childhood friend. Paiden isn't very practical either.'

She liked the idea of Paiden and Magnus being similar in character. It eased something more between her and Rory. 'Will you tell me now about your hand?'

'Would you let me keep my silence on it?'

'Never.'

That's what he thought. His hand was hyperaware from her touch, from her observations. Rory held it still and thought hard about how to answer her because why he used his left hand instead of his right was significant. The physical tests and challenges he'd overcome to force himself to use one hand over the other had been an ordeal and often excruciating. Even so, the why he did it…he didn't know if he was prepared to say. 'How did you know?'

'I'm a healer. I observe. You drum with your left hand, arrange items with your left…you touch me with your left. It comes more natural to you, doesn't it?'

She'd told him of Magnus; she deserved to be told of his family. 'My father, who trained me, insisted I use my right.'

'I can't imagine you bowing to any man.'

'You haven't met my father.'

'Your mother never stood up for you?'

'My mother is…' No, he wasn't prepared at all. 'I think we can do something more than talk of my hands.'

Cradling her closer, he revelled that she came willingly. So little time between them, so much more to tell. But this, her tugging her fingers through his hair, her eyes darting from one of his features to the other, as if trying to see his very soul, *this* was true.

Ailsa let Rory distract her with touches, with kisses. He'd told her very little, but it was enough. He must have changed his dominant hand when he was very young or else his body would have rejected such training. And he must have done it very diligently for he was almost as good with his right as with his left.

But it wasn't only that. Her heart ached for the little boy who must have questioned if he was lacking somehow that his father wanted him to be so different. His father, who obviously was not as generous of spirit as she. What kind of man was he to force a child against his very nature? To make him feel unworthy even for a moment?

She'd show Rory how worthy she found him. 'I think,' she said, giving him a shove on his shoulder so he'd stay still, 'that it's…'

Something in the corner of her eye caught her attention.

Rory let out an amused breath. 'Delaying can sweeten our time, lass, but the floor's damn cold and—'

'Wait!' she cried, pressing her hand against his chest to stop his reaching for her.

'Ailsa, I meant—'

'Not that.' Clumsily, she tried to extricate herself from him. She knew he was too large, too determined to move unless he wanted to. But he let her. Another revelation on the worthiness of this man. Scrambling over him, she swiped a crumbled parchment.

It was here. Right here and she had the answer.

She felt Rory's eyes on her, but she ignored him for now she was pondering the implications.

'What is it?' he asked.

'If it's made into an oil,' she said out loud. 'It's so common the amount could be…then if it's concentrated enough…'

'Ailsa!'

She locked gazes with her husband. 'I know what has harmed Paiden.'

Chapter Thirteen

'I can't believe you almost left like that.' Rory raced with Ailsa to the kitchens.

'I hate tying my gowns.'

'In the future you must learn to like it, unless you wish to display what only a husband should see.'

Around the bend in the road, avoiding the animals and people. Rory wanted to pick her up and run even faster. A cure. A cure. Was it possible?

'My clothing is what you want to talk about?'

He wanted to discuss everything. He wanted to stop time and hold his wife longer. His legs were unsteady, the fullness in his chest at his good fortune, making it hard to breathe. The moment she'd swiped that parchment, the look of unfettered joy and fear in her eyes…

'Ailsa, tell me.'

'In a moment, I can't…' She ran out of breath.

He shoved open the door to the kitchens. While she frantically grabbed mint, cloves, she ordered a servant to find Hannah and procure hot water and salt.

She hurried back to the keep, her arms full of herbs,

and he followed her. Running up the stairs, she barged into Paiden's room. Mary was there, a tincture in her hand, a spoon lifted to his lips.

'Stop!'

Mary jerked, the wooden spoon flew and thumped against the wall.

'How much did you give him?' Ailsa demanded.

Stumbling in her haste to stand, Mary blurted, 'Nothing yet.'

'Yet?' Ailsa felt her legs give under her and Rory was suddenly by her side. His arms steadying her though he couldn't know what was to come.

Mary's brows rose. 'Yet. I just lost the spoon.'

Ailsa pushed away from Rory and grabbed the spoon. It smelled of water, but the handle…

'It was you.'

She couldn't believe it. She trusted Hannah and Mary. They'd held conversations on scheduling Hamish's care, ensuring that they were all well rested. It was rare that Ailsa actually saw Mary. Their schedules didn't usually meet, except it happened recently when Rory arrived.

'I thought you wanted me to give constant doses of water to keep him hydrated.' Mary glanced to Rory, then back, her face calm, but something flickered in her eyes.

Fear? Most likely.

'Water, yes. Rosemary, no.' Ailsa brandished the crumpled parchment, handing it to the servant, who blanched, but quickly handed it back.

'It's only rosemary,' Mary said. 'Do you want me to administer—?'

'Stop. Did you give him rosemary today? I need to know.'

'You want to talk about herbs?' Mary clenched and twisted her fingers.

'Rosemary wouldn't harm anyone,' Rory said.

'High doses of it will,' Ailsa answered. 'Concentrated and continuous and a person might not wake up.'

She charged around to Paiden's bed. Smelled his breath, his hand, his clothes, the bed linen. 'It's all over him.'

The door slammed open. Frederick stormed in with Hannah carrying a steaming bucket which she placed on the floor.

'Rory, you've got to change his clothing and the linens. I won't be able to move him. Hannah, can you gather fresh ones, but smell them first. There can be no rosemary, do you understand?'

Hannah's wide eyes glanced to Paiden, then Mary. 'I'll go now.'

Ailsa pointed. 'Father, bolt the door and stand by it.'

Mary's eyes darted towards the exit, but her father didn't question her request. Once Hannah left, they were all locked in a room that suddenly was as silent as a tomb and just as ominous.

'What is the concern, Ailsa?' her father asked. 'Hannah found me; brought me here.'

'I need you,' Ailsa said. 'As Tanist you need to listen to this, doesn't he, Mary?'

The servant's eyes were suddenly frantic. 'I didn't. I am—'

'You made an undiluted oil from rosemary,' Ailsa interrupted. Right now they had relative privacy. The parties that must hear the confession were here, but whatever information was coming needed to be divulged quickly. Other clansmen would have been alerted with Hannah running around the grounds and her father's charging up here.

'Did you give any to Paiden today?' she said.

Rory swept the linens off Paiden and placed them both on the floor. His attention seemed to be on his friend, but Ailsa knew he was aware of every nuance given by Mary and her father.

He was aware of everything. The moment she exchanged words with Mary, she felt the tension in him. Her warrior was bracing for a battle, but this wasn't something that could be solved with a sword, or with swift retribution. His priority was his friend and so she made Paiden's hers as well.

'Mary, he can't die.' Ailsa stepped closer to her. 'Right now he lives, but I need to know, so I know how to proceed.'

A gasping choked sound. 'N-no.'

'What is going on here?' Frederick demanded. 'What has Mary to do with this Lochmore?'

Ailsa glanced to her father, picked up the bucket, smelled the contents, and the metal spoon. 'We won't use the salt then.'

Rory knelt and lifted his friend. 'You trust her.'

'I believe she is speaking the truth.' Ailsa administered the tiny drops of fresh water to Paiden's lips.

Mary's choked sounds turned to sobs.

'Why not give him the salt as you did before?' Rory said.

'There are other complications that could occur

from forced sickness. He is weak. For now, we clean his clothes, linen and anything he comes in contact with. We clean him and then we give him fresh water and food to digest.

'Was any other herb used?' Ailsa raised her voice, but kept her eyes on Paiden. Right now she needed to coax as much information as she could from the frightened girl.

'Clove,' Mary whispered after a heartbeat.

'You talk of herbs, of oils. Am I understanding this?' Frederick said, his voice booming against the stones of the room. 'Mary, you've given this man poison?'

Paiden groaned.

'There you are.' Ailsa handed the spoon to Rory.

Rory jostled him closer. 'Friend!'

'You meant to kill a guest of Clan McCrieff!' Frederick roared.

Stumbling, crashing, Mary fled to the corner of the room.

'Tanist!' Rory said. 'You make it no better.'

Ailsa met her father's eyes, put a finger to her lips to beseech him to remain quiet while she crouched near Mary.

Sentences and punishment, if need be, could be announced in front of the clan. But if what she suspected was true, then the information might need to stay locked in the room with them.

'You made the quantities of rosemary potent enough to poison to cause sleep. You had access to the kitchens that day, knew what was to be served for the meal. There was rosemary lacing many of the dishes. So all you needed to add was the oil to one particular goblet.

The chances of it being enough to cause distress heightened by what was already served.'

Mary's eyes were downcast, her arms wrapped around her knees. She was at least five years younger, but she looked as fragile as a child when she nodded.

Aware of Rory's and her father's eyes on her, Ailsa knew that no matter how innocent Mary looked she wasn't. But to find the truth, she needed to force it from girl, who would have run away if she could. Now was the time for confrontation.

Sinking in as much venom as she could, she asked. 'How easy was it to rub that oil around the goblet, Mary? Did it take so little of you to commit murder?'

Mary's head snapped back, her eyes wide with fear and agony. 'No, never that. Never!'

That's what she thought. Mary's family was deeply loyal to Hamish. Ailsa knew this. Her age and her loyalty made her a good caretaker for the Chief. But it didn't bode well for any Lochmores.

Still, she couldn't understand why Mary had committed such an act. Even with loyalty or her family's dogmatic urgings, she was a gentle soul.

Keeping her voice accusing, she continued, 'Why would you want to murder a Lochmore clansman?'

'It wasn't meant—' Mary blurted, her eyes darting from one person to another.

'You wanted to murder me,' Rory said.

Pressing her lips together, Mary slammed her head on her clenched knees.

Ailsa felt as though she was missing an important fact. Mary had access to the rosemary. Ailsa, herself, taught her much of healing, but Mary was too young and hadn't the inclination that Rhona had required of a healer. So she hadn't taught her of the more complicated tinctures or any of the poisons. Ailsa had always thought to teach Hannah and so she had gone into—

A gentle knock on the door. Frederick slowly opened it, allowing Hannah, with her arms full, to emerge into the room.

'Did you and Mary talk of remedies?' Ailsa said.

'Did she do it?' Hannah said, clutching the linens to her.

'Did you?' Ailsa demanded.

'I said nothing!' Hannah cried out. 'All these years, you taught me, told me... I said *nothing* to her.'

Frederick gently pried the linens and clothes from Hannah and carried them to Rory.

Three men, one about to be naked, and three women in this room. It was large, but not that large. There was no privacy for Paiden who hadn't made a sound or movement since that one exhausted groan, but there was no time to waste.

'He'll need to be cleaned, Rory. Rub the salt on his skin until it shines red, then rinse.' Ailsa said. 'Use the water in the bucket.'

Hannah glanced that way, then returned her gaze to Ailsa and Mary. Mary's eyes were clenched tight. Ailsa shifted so her back was to the men. It would have to do.

How had Mary known how to make the undiluted rosemary in the correct concentration? The answer was obvious.

'You had access to the journals,' Ailsa said to Mary's bowed head, but her feet went up on their toes and her heels slammed once.

She'd take that as a confirmation. 'You were in that room the day the Lochmores came. You talked to Hamish and he gave you his keys.'

'Hamish!' Rory growled. 'He's bedridden, ill, barely alive.'

Ailsa shook her head. 'He was ill, but aware until the day you arrived. He—'

'So Hamish caused this,' Rory interrupted. 'He harms Lochmores, he poisoned Paiden. My father was right not to trust McCrieffs.'

'Careful, Lochmore's son,' Frederick said. 'You are married to my daughter.'

'All the worse,' Rory said. 'You'll allow this, Tanist? You, who invited us to dine at McCrieff's table. I married your daughter and therefore all treachery is forgiven?'

'Never, but… Ailsa, how long does it take to make the oil?' Frederick said.

'Hours,' Ailsa said. 'Days if done right, which means she had it ready when they arrived.'

'Hamish knew of the King's demand. He may have known that Lochmores arrived on McCrieff land that day, but as for the rest…' Frederick stood, his feet heavy against the wood floor, his body towering over her, over Mary.

'It was meant for me,' Frederick concluded.

Mary howled.

As the cold truth of it swept over her, Ailsa lost the ability to kneel and sat heavily on the ground.

'Ailsa?' Rory asked, concern sweeping away all anger from his voice.

'I'll be well,' Ailsa said, still averting her eyes from

Rory and his friend, who would appreciate knowing he had some privacy when he woke. 'Care for Paiden.'

'The bastard's heavy. He'll hear of this later.'

Ailsa welcomed the relief in Rory's voice. Despite what occurred in the room, if all went well, Rory would have Paiden well again.

Still… 'My father. You meant injury to my father?'

'Hamish meant ill to your father,' Frederick corrected. He placed a hand on Mary's shoulder. She startled.

'Talk to me,' he demanded. 'As Ailsa's father, tell me what happened.'

Mary raised her head. 'Hamish. He ordered me to.'

'How much did he tell you?'

'He knows what you wanted from Lochmores.' She gulped, rubbed her nose on her sleeve. 'He knew that when they came, you would not oust them from Mc-Crieff land. That you…intended to grant them the land.'

'Were you angry about my decision?'

'My father wouldn't like it.'

'Did your father know?'

'Hamish told me to be quiet.' She wiped her face, glanced at Ailsa and then back to Frederick. 'He didn't mention the marriage.'

'How did the goblet get to Paiden instead of Frederick?' Rory asked.

Mary shook her head. 'I don't know. I was so specific. I couldn't be there because I was supposed to be caring for Hamish as Ailsa told me to.'

'You couldn't be there because you didn't want to watch my father collapse to the ground!' Ailsa said, the venom in her voice not feigned this time.

Mary met her eyes. Agony. Regret. 'Yes.'

'What happened since then?' Frederick said.

'I thought Paiden would wake,' Mary said. 'I haven't been giving him any more, honest. Just that once and by accident.'

'Why isn't he waking?' Rory said, a grunt to his voice, a thump of a leg or arm flopping to the floor.

'Because—' Ailsa started, the truth of it all sinking in. 'Because he's been getting it from other sources. The clothes, the wash water to take care of sores. We've been using cloves as well to help with stomach ailments. Our curing has been harming him.'

'And Hamish?' Frederick stated. 'He's not waking either, is he? Did you give him the same oil?'

Mary raised her chin. 'I couldn't… I wouldn't allow him to make any more orders.'

'Ah…' Frederick pinched the bridge of his nose. 'You were ordered to harm me by Hamish and you did it because of your own family, because you are loyal to the Chief.'

At Mary's quick nod, her father continued, 'You should be loyal to the Chief, child.'

It was true. If the Chief gave an order, it was punishable if it wasn't followed. Ailsa felt all the hatred drain instantly. Her father didn't seem surprised or angry that Mary had done what she had. Her father acted as if he'd expected it. From the 'others' he'd mentioned, perhaps?

Frederick cleared his throat. 'But the poison accidentally went to the Lochmores and Rory married Ailsa. You care for her, don't you?'

Mary nodded, tears pouring from her eyes. 'I wasn't go-going to murder Hamish, just keep him sleeping until the marriage was done, until matters were…settled. I don't know why he isn't waking.'

'It's because you haven't been trained, Mary,' Hannah said. 'It's because he is already sick!'

'I'm sorry!' Mary burst into tears, her face in her hands, her shoulders shaking. She curled up even tighter in the corner.

Rory scrubbed Paiden from the top of his head to the soles of his feet, between his toes and fingers. He poured the water over him, grateful there were other buckets here for other uses. They didn't smell of rosemary or clove, but the water was ice cold. He knew it because he'd poured almost half of it on himself.

Paiden didn't wake through it all which Rory was grateful for. He wanted only one of them to remember this and even then he hoped enough ale and time would allow him to blur the details. He wasn't trained to put braies on another man and Paiden would have new bruises. But the deed was done; his friend was out of harm's way.

As for Hamish, as far as Rory was concerned, he would never be out of harm's way. To lose Paiden would have been to lose family. Paiden…

At Mary's apology, he tore his attention from Paiden to his wife and watched Ailsa stumble over to the sobbing woman to clasp her close.

Anger mottled her cheeks, but his wife, the healer, gave comfort where it was needed because she cared. When Mary cried harder, Hannah flew to her side. Ailsa murmured words he couldn't hear, but Frederick's oath was firm and resolute. 'How far my clan has fallen. My God, I will repair this.'

Rory knew, absolutely knew they wouldn't ferret out all the deception. Even here, Mary confessed to her intention to poison the McCrieff's Tanist because of her father's loyalties. Even Mary, not quite a woman full grown, was divided. The entire clan of McCrieffs was divided. With his marriage to Ailsa, he had tied his own clan to lies and deceit, murderers and traitors. He was helpless to fix any of it, to slash his sword and order executions because there were innocents here as well. Mary was both loyal and a traitor. Their future was dark.

Then Ailsa turned her head to look his way. Her eyes were green like spring grass, new and full of promise, and Rory knew, no matter the future, he'd marry her again if he could.

Chapter Fourteen

Ailsa was beyond exhausted, but so were Hannah and Mary. A fortnight had gone by since she'd made her discovery and all of them had been working, ensuring that every bit of food, clothing and linen was free of rosemary.

It had been found in everything. It was in the trunks containing folded linens. Laundry, put out to dry, had been draped over the sturdy rounded shrubberies. According to Rory, Paiden often brushed his teeth with the fragrant herb. If that were true, it wouldn't have taken much more to push him over the edge.

Frederick ordered everyone to keep quiet. Not much could be kept hidden, but Frederick waited because he wanted to confront his Chief first. However, though everything they'd done for Paiden had been done for Hamish as well, the Chief never woke. He still slept, his breathing laboured, his cheekbones sunken. Bone broth was given to him in tiny droplets, but most now just dribbled down his chin.

Paiden, however, had woken within hours of Mary's

confession. It had been a happy moment for all, but joyous for Rory. Once she ensured Paiden's breathing, eyesight and memory were restored, she left them alone in the room. Right before she closed the door, Rory caught her eye and the look he gave her was full of warmth, gratefulness, and something more...something she dared not think of now.

For though Paiden was mending, Hamish still slept and looked ready for the tomb. Her work was not over with.

In the meantime, Rory and Frederick were seen together. There were no more secret meetings, only open council sessions which they both attended. Such open co-operation also brought open disgruntlement and scathing remarks. Ailsa feared there would be no resolution between the clans and no peace within the McCrieffs.

Yet in the evening, when the doors were closed, she and Rory discovered their own peace. Fragile. New, but there was now some understanding between them.

The only fissure of worry was the matter of Rory's parentage. In the midst of it all, Ailsa could not forget. Maybe it was because, with Hamish's illness, it brought back memories of Rhona's dying words. Maybe...she more than cared for Rory now and wished for him to know the truth even if he didn't know his life was false.

Was there a right answer here? With Hamish looking as though he'd never wake, maybe the answer would never come. Thus far, she'd found no records on McCrieff land that Hamish had fathered a son or that a boy had been given away. Maybe Rhona's murmurings were just that. Dreams and imagination cloaked within her illness. Maybe it was all made up. And yet, Rory's—

'You've retired early.'

Ailsa spun around. Rory closed the door behind him. His clothes were dusty which could only mean that he'd helped with the fields or with training. 'It appears so did you.'

'Your father had nothing else on his agenda, I thought I'd take advantage of it. Why are you here?'

'Mary and Hannah are looking after our patients.'

'Is Hannah with Paiden? If so, I should warn her that he can be quite charming when he wants to be.'

She had no doubt. That man was all too free with his smiles. 'Hannah can take care of herself. Moreover, Mary still wants to tend Hamish, though I don't fully understand why, after what he ordered her to do.'

'In my years, I have seen great men do terrible things and terrible men rise to occasions,' Rory said surrounding her in his arms. 'People are surprising with their actions.'

'You surprised me,' Ailsa said. 'When Mary said it was Hamish who ordered the poisoning, you didn't demand retribution.'

'Because quickly after, Mary confessed Hamish targeted your father. It wasn't about me or Paiden then.'

It was about her. Generations of strife and hatred worked to keep them separated, yet she and Rory... She didn't dare believe there could be more, but when he said things like this, she couldn't help but hope.

Which made it all the worse when she remembered Rhona's story and the fact she kept secrets from him.

'How is he faring?'

Rory chuckled. 'He asked about the bruises. I told him I didn't know where they came from.'

'He believed you?'

'No, we've known each other too long, but I won't be telling that story until we are well drunk and years have gone by.'

None in the room told of what Mary had confessed to. That Hamish had given the order. What it would have taken for Mary to lace the goblet knowing the harm she could do... Ailsa couldn't comprehend it. As for then turning the poison on to Hamish, Frederick couldn't fault her. It aided his proposal of marriage between the clans. Further, it protected his daughter and her new husband.

Knowing that it was her father Mary had intended to harm, Ailsa tried to find some vengeful emotion within her. Her father was very dear to her, but Mary was broken, and her remorse so great, that even if Ailsa rained down all the wrath she had on Mary, she could do no worse than what Mary was putting herself through.

As for her father, he'd had a discussion in private with the servant. What was said, Ailsa didn't know, but some understanding was between them now and she left it alone.

'Here we are with the whole evening ahead of us,' she said, enjoying the dusty scent of him. Knowing that soon he'd wash the day away, and then it would be just them. 'Because I told my father he needed his rest.'

Rory gave her a wolfish smile. 'Truly?'

She nodded. 'He looks tired, but I didn't know if he'd do it.'

'Well, he decided to so...' Rory stroked down her

arms and back up again '…we can work on giving him grandchildren sooner rather than later.'

Ailsa felt her skin flush. Even after all the nights they spent together, each of them with very little sleep, she couldn't believe her good fortune that this man was her husband.

And yet… 'With Paiden mending, you'll be able to return home soon.'

Rory's arms dropped. 'Home?'

And here was the other matter. So much shared between them, but not Rory's past or his future. He was the acknowledged son of Lochmore's Chief and that was something they could not avoid much longer.

As much as she wanted to stay in his arms, to while away the night as they had been doing, there were some matters that needed to be discussed. Ailsa strode to the bed and sat down.

'We're married,' she said.

Rory moved to a chair to unlace his shoes. 'For some days now.'

One lace, then the other as she gathered her courage for what she needed to say. 'I know of the letters to your family. I know you wrote them…but they weren't returned.'

Rory threw his shoes in a corner, the heavy clunk sounded with finality. 'My family is complicated, Ailsa.'

'Any more than mine?'

He stood to unhook his belt, to remove his trousers. She waited patiently, knowing when he finished this task, he'd go to the water basin warmed by the fire and clean the dust away as he had done every night.

She waited, knowing these tasks were necessary for

Rory as he thought about her question. After all, he obviously never intended to talk to her about his family.

But then he ripped his tunic up and over his head and her thoughts turned from Rory and his past to just… him. The sunlight was dimming and the firelight was taking over their room. His body carried many scars and many more bruises, recent ones from training his men, yet she'd never known anything more magnificent. Except maybe the way he made her feel when he… 'Are you trying to tempt me?'

'Perhaps.'

She wouldn't answer him. She couldn't as she watched the way he strode to the basin.

'You're being quiet for you,' he said.

'Just being patient. I'm on the bed and you like your sleep. You can't avoid me or my questions for ever.'

A rough exhalation. 'I don't want to.'

It was a start. Maybe this something new she felt, he did, too. 'Your family didn't come to the wedding, Rory. They didn't come knowing Paiden was on his deathbed. Do they hate you?'

'Thus enters my blunt-tongued wife.'

'I thought you liked my tongue.'

It almost looked as if Rory flushed. 'I'm baring myself to you and washing the dirt of the day away, Ailsa. Don't put images in my head unless you're prepared for the consequences.'

'I like…consequences, just not now,' she said.

He tossed the linen aside. 'This is important to you? We have enough with your family. Your sisters are rather devious and your father works harder than twenty men.'

'Hamish will die soon from illness or from poison and my clan is severely divided,' she said. 'But I still want to know about you.'

He glanced to his clean clothing, and then strode to the bed. She shifted so he could come between her legs. The dark of his eyes darkened further and she knew it matched her own. 'Ailsa,' he growled leaning forward. 'You can't look at me the way you do and think I won't respond.' He was going to kiss her and she wanted him to. But just before their lips touched, he suddenly pulled away.

'There's something I need to show you,' he said, opening the trunk at the base of the bed and pulling out a rectangular flat box. Eyeing it, and her, he held it aloft.

'You want to show me that now?' she asked, knowing she sounded disappointed.

Rory's lips curved. 'My family sent it when we married, but with everything happening, I forgot.'

'I gather it's important?'

'It could be.' Rory eyed the box which had been in the large trunk that Duff had brought over from Lochmore land. It was different than he remembered it, but it had been years since he saw it last. If his father honoured his marriage, the box would contain Lochmore brooches. One for each of them indicating their position in the clan, and the unity with each other. With an almost giddy eagerness, he couldn't wait to pin the brooch to her gown.

'I'm happy then.'

She meant it. All this time, he'd raged against his life. He came to McCrieff land wanting to secure his own future, only to realise with the McCrieff clan's division that future was wrenched away from him. Positioned by Lochmores, manipulated by McCrieffs.

But this woman, what had she done? Only offered to save her clan, Paiden's life…his own. By marrying Ailsa, he had gained something important for his future, a family he had always wanted.

His own family hadn't come to his wedding, but she offered him the possibilities of a future where he could be happy, have children. Where the strife around them would be something they would face together. And at night, they could privately find peace. With the contents of this box, however, the Lochmore familial brooches, no one would question what she meant to him, what they meant to each other.

With a snap, he opened the lid, only to see…

'What is it?' Ailsa asked.

A white roaring filled Rory's head and his vision narrowed as he focused on the contents. The box…the box wasn't the one that he remembered.

Ailsa huffed as if greatly wounded. It wasn't a sound she ever made so he glanced to her. A teasing light was in her eye. He couldn't reciprocate it. Shock, anger and now this gut-wrenching emptiness wrested away his hope. If someone had taken a sword to his gut, he'd feel no different.

'If you think I'm disappointed with that necklace and ring you're mistaken,' Ailsa said, peering into the box, her tone as light as her eyes, 'I would have preferred something more practical. Still, I could make do if—'

Rory slammed the lid and tossed the box on to the trunk. Division here, division in his family. And one he obviously created by marrying a McCrieff. There were no brooches in the box. It was clear his family did not recognise their marriage. He'd done everything he could to please his father. Even marrying this woman, in part, had been done for the clan. Why did he even try?

A gentle tug on his bare arm and he fell into green eyes and a gentle expression.

'Where did you go?' she asked.

If he explained, he'd sound like a bitter mad man. He'd worked tirelessly with the intrigue here, he'd braced himself for poison to hit him, or a sword to come slashing down in the middle of the night. He was on McCrieff land and he had expected betrayal here.

Never, not once, from his own family. Yet that is what they had done. They hadn't come to his wedding and they didn't offer the brooches that would acknowledge his marriage. Maybe his suspicions were true. Maybe he wasn't his father's son, and this, now, was how they told him.

Another tug, this time behind his neck as Ailsa pulled him closer. 'Rory, you're mostly naked.'

Her hand was warm, her words finally registering. His *wife*. Deceit from the McCrieffs. Betrayal from Lochmores. Caring…a chance at love, with Ailsa.

That thought, that certain bone-deep knowledge pulled the sword in his gut free and he felt a sudden dizzying freedom. This blunt-tongued woman whom he wanted more than anything or anyone just told him she wanted him. He'd take her.

'You, however, are clothed,' he said.

'Of course I am, this gown has laces,' she said, pressing light kisses along his jaw and down his neck.

'Not for much longer.'

Chapter Fifteen

With Ailsa curled up next to him, Rory could want for nothing more. Everything about this moment, about this woman, was right. As for the rest, his family be damned—by her side was where he needed to be.

'Are your feet cold?' he asked, aware that she kept sliding one foot down his leg and then back up again. Every time, the movement slightly dislodged her from his hold so he curled her tighter into him.

A muted laugh. 'I was wondering if our feet could touch like this. You've a considerable size to you if you hadn't noticed.'

He'd wondered when his size would bother her. It hadn't taken long. Shifting, he tried to give her room so she could extricate herself. In response, Ailsa dug her nails into his arm and curled closer.

'You don't like it that you're taller than most?' she asked.

He couldn't get much past his observational wife. 'It is something I have been both pleased and ungrateful for my entire life.'

'Like the colour of my hair.'

He twirled a lock between his fingers. 'Never disparage your hair.'

'So stop leaning against walls to make yourself look smaller.'

It was his turn to laugh. 'That's not why I do that.'

'Then why?'

'It's because none of the furniture at home fitted me.'

She gave a slight hum before answering. 'Hamish's furniture fits you.'

'Hamish's furniture? Maybe I should have measurements done for Lochmore's castle.'

'I never thought of that,' she said. 'Where we would live.'

Rory loosened his hold enough to look at her. 'After everything, did you think we would live here?'

'I suppose with Hamish here, you wouldn't want to stay.'

'It's not Hamish. Your Chief will soon die, but your father is well and has many years left. It is right that he rules and takes proper control of his clan.'

'With fewer Lochmores to poison,' she said. 'I don't know if Hannah knows enough.'

Her clan would be without a healer. That was something he had not thought of, but it was the right decision to return to Lochmore land. 'You can travel back and forth, it is not very far. Your family is here and they will want to see you.'

Ailsa pressed her palms to his chest to look down at him. What she could see of him in the darkness, he didn't know. Yet she looked at him for so long, he al-

most wanted to joke like Paiden, but her expression
was serious.

'While you remain on Lochmore land?' she finally
said.

There was no satisfactory answer to that. It would
cause more problems for her clan if he remained on
McCrieff land. His own personal reasons why he didn't
want to return to Lochmore were inconsequential.

At his silence, Ailsa laid down again. 'You seem…
reluctant to return home. What was it about the box,
Rory?'

Blunt tongue and too observant despite the darkness.
'We can think more on where we live. And do not worry
about the box, the contents are yours.'

'That is for the better, I already have plans to carve
out the stones and melt the silver so that I could share
it with my sisters.' She patted him. 'Your mother won't
care, would she? Maybe we should go to Lochmore
Castle to ask her.'

'Ailsa,' he growled.

There was frustration, teasing and a warning in that
sound that he could not suppress. He could tell, immediately, Ailsa took all those emotions as truth. 'Am I
the reason you do not want to return home?'

He didn't want to return to Lochmore Castle because
he didn't believe *he* belonged there, not her. Never her,
yet his family had not given him the brooches. They did
not acknowledge his marriage. They did not acknowledge her. 'Lochmore clan will adore you despite your
past as a McCrieff.'

'My past,' she scoffed.

So much separated their families. So much might

separate their future. It was a great weight that had been placed on *their* shoulders. 'Will the past…will a story always separate our clans despite what we do?'

She sighed and he felt her warm breath against his chest. 'Despite how many babies we have, it seems one McCrieff babe may always haunt our lands.'

'McCrieff babe?'

'The baby from the Great Feud.'

Surely she couldn't believe the baby born seventy years ago was a McCrieff. Rory shifted to get a better view of her, but Ailsa held firm to him and all he could see in the dark were the tendrils of her hair against his chest and her hand, gently roughened from years of tending gardens, laid flat against his stomach. Though he dearly wanted to see her expression, he didn't dare dislodge himself from her hold.

'We *are* talking of the Great Feud?' He kept his voice light.

'Unless you know another one?'

This couldn't be. Ailsa was so straightforward. Direct. She didn't lie ever and she didn't tolerate any falsehoods either. So for her to believe the baby to be a McCrieff and not a Lochmore was something she thought was the truth.

'You believe the baby to be McCrieff's versus Lochmore's? Tell me.'

She glanced up at him, her eyes reflecting amusement and confusion. 'That's how the story was told to me. I believe it to be true.'

It never dawned on him that the story could be different. But why? It was naïve to think otherwise. 'I want to hear it as you were told.'

'You don't sound as if you do.'

'You've surprised me is all. Again.'

She patted his chest and settled her head down. 'Well, then. The McCrieff Chief loved her. Wanted to marry her. I think she was scared and went back to her clan and married Lochmore's Chief.'

Rory placed his hand on hers. 'So the baby—?'

'Was certainly McCrieff's. Why else would he have flown to Lochmore land and challenged him when they both died?'

'McCrieff challenged Lochmore because he was spurned. Because of his pride. Because the woman he cast aside found happiness and he couldn't tolerate it.'

Ailsa propped herself up to look at him. 'That woman broke his heart. He let her go because he loved her, but that babe was his. He knew it as sure as anything.'

'Never.'

'Thus, the McCrieff–Lochmore Great Feud contin-ues between us. Except...' Ailsa started. 'We could end it. Between us.'

Rory couldn't see how it was possible. 'Once Hamish dies, Frederick will rule.'

'Yes, but as much as I don't want to talk of it, once his rule is done, Frederick will have free rein. I think he was waiting for you. I think that's why he invited you here.'

'He invited me?' Rory asked. 'He almost started a war by ignoring a king's decree and a chief's missive.'

'Possibly,' she said. 'But you have to admit, it was rather clever.'

'Your father certainly saved face by marrying you to me to justify the giving of such precious lands,' Rory said.

'Do you mean that?'

Old beliefs didn't just disappear. Especially not when motivations such as greed, power, control were at stake. 'It all comes back to the land that the King granted to Lochmores.'

'Do you want war?'

'Never, but we can't stop bloodshed even with Lochmores controlling the land. Why is the land important for you?'

'Watercress. Mint. Thyme. The water's important. McCrieff healers have been planting there for centuries.'

'So not land, but herbs for healing. That's not an argument I'm going to make before the Lochmore council or my father.'

'Why not?'

'Because I'll be labelled a fool.'

She raised her hand as if to slap him and he grabbed it. 'Won't do much damage without your shears.'

'It'll still sting.'

Chuckling, he studied their hands. Like this, their differences were acute, but still she curled her hand until it held his. He welcomed that warmth, but not for the first time Ailsa's brow was furrowed, her thoughts elsewhere. 'What is it?'

'Will we still be able to use the land?' she asked.

'There is no denying the King's decree. Ultimately, my father is Chief. He will listen to opinions, but in the end he will decide. I'm married to you, however, and, despite rumour, he is a fair man. But I don't have a say in the matter for your water basil, dear wife. Despite our marriage, we are still Lochmores and McCrieffs.'

'Hmmm,' Ailsa said.

Rory waited for her to continue. He knew her well enough to know she had more on her mind. He didn't have long to wait.

'Rory, do you ever…do you ever wonder if you were named because of the Great Feud?'

Strange conversation. 'I know I was… You looked shocked.'

'I am. I didn't think the Lochmores would ever use that name. Why would you be named after McCrieff's baby who died?'

If she said she could heal the dead, he could not be more shocked. Keeping their hands linked, he sat in the bed, leaning against the back frame. 'It's McCrieffs who believe the baby was a McCrieff's. For Lochmores, that baby had no name. It died along with its mother. Thereby, I was named after the nephew who attempted to stop the fighting.'

Ailsa adjusted herself around him, but she, too, kept their hands linked. 'More differences. Tell me the story as you know it.'

'It's a tragedy, Ailsa. I'd rather not talk of tragedies right now.'

'A tragedy?'

'The Lochmore lass rejected the McCrieff Chief, and married Lochmore's. In childbirth, she and the Lochmore baby died. When the McCrieff heard of her death, he stormed our castle. He did it out of pride for being spurned. At sword point he threatened our Chief. Thinking he could protect him, Lochmore's nephew, Rory, interceded and died by the McCrieff's hand. Mc-Crieffs yanked their Chief away. As for my clan, the

Lochmores were already mourning and now there was another death.'

'The story from our side was the mother was pregnant with McCrieffs' babe and died in childbirth, but not before she named her son Rory.'

'More differences between Lochmores and McCrieffs,' he said.

'It appears so.'

Ailsa gripped his hand. 'It is tragic the nephew's death escalated the strained relations even though McCrieff killing him was an accident.'

'Not if you look at the fact McCrieffs' Chief shouldn't have been there at all. If he hadn't been there, he wouldn't have killed the Lochmore nephew named Rory.'

Ailsa wasn't silent at his words, instead she did that low humming sound she made when she was deep in thought.

He gave that to her. There was much to think about. From Paiden's recovery and Hamish not waking. His family's brooches, his obvious disappointment, her comforting him after everything. Him unable to express what she was beginning to mean to him.

To this… More revelations.

'Rory, do Lochmores have written records?' she asked.

It had never occurred to him to search records before because the Great Feud was so well known. 'We have them, but… Was that what you were doing in that room, searching records about the feud?'

A hesitation before she answered. 'Mostly I was there to search for remedies.'

She was a good wife and far more intelligent than him. Brave, too. To set herself in amid all the conflict to try to heal the present and the past.

His family might not acknowledge his marriage or his wife, but he refused to let this continue. She was a healer. If she could be so brave, so could he. 'Ailsa, I want you to meet my family.'

Chapter Sixteen

Ailsa had never spent much time on the border between Lochmore and McCrieffs. As a child, her father
warned her of the dangers. As she grew older, she and
Rhona planted and picked water herbs and quickly left.
Often, she wondered if Lochmore's children were also
warned not to approach the stream, for she never saw
another soul on the other side.

Now she would cross this border which was rather
unremarkable for such a contested piece of land. No
brambles or briars. Certainly, no arrows shot or battle
cries. It was merely Rory and herself, a few McCrieffs
and Lochmores leisurely riding towards the stream.

All very uneventful. Perhaps it had to do with the
King's decree. Perhaps it had to do with her father taking care of the Clan, or the missive Rory had sent ahead
to his family.

Whatever the reason, they were here now. As for
the land, she intended to talk to Lochmore's Chief on
whether McCrieffs could use it. It had taken years to
cultivate some of the plantings and she'd be grateful to
not have to start again.

They weren't half across the water when Lochmores emerged from the trees. One man was in the centre of it all.

'My father,' Rory said low for her ears. 'Lochmore's Chief.'

The man held authority tightly to him and his clothes were as fine as she'd ever been witness to. Yet there was no resemblance to her husband, not in stature or in colour. Whatever misgivings Ailsa had to Rory's parentage were rapidly becoming truth. With the surety of each steady beat of the horses' hooves, she felt the need and the burden of telling him. But after all the betrayal he'd experienced since arriving on McCrieffs' land, what would he think of her withholding the information.

Would Rory be angry or shocked? They had discussed the origins of his name. He hadn't appeared angry, but he didn't know they talked of him.

Were Rhona's words pain-filled ramblings or truth? She wasn't certain they were true. They'd see the records first and then, no matter what they found or what she said, Rory would want to talk to his mother. The burgeoning trust they shared because of the marriage and the efforts to end Hamish's ill deeds was too fragile. The little time they'd shared in this marriage meant that she couldn't, shouldn't, bluntly step forward and tell him what her thoughts were. For once, she wouldn't be direct or straightforward. For once she'd be patient and wait. For if she was wrong? She could hurt the man she was beginning to—

Love. Did she love him in so short a time? She feared it was true. They approached matters differently, but they also shared much. And if what she did feel was love, her withholding Rhona's last words might harm any chance of a true marriage.

Her horse's steps along the stream bed were uneven and slippery and Ailsa concentrated on that rather than the approaching confrontations. She was on Lochmore land now. As far as everyone was concerned, she was married to Lochmore's son.

All her life she'd thought only as a healer, a McCrieff healer. Now her path was different, being here was different. Except being here didn't *feel* different. Though everything in her knew it should be, the land on this side of the stream felt the same as on McCrieff land. The Lochmore men rode their horses the same as the McCrieffs. The wariness, the locked gazes. All similar.

But Rory stopping his horse in front of Lochmore's Chief wasn't the same at all.

She and her father had never been separated before, but often their days would be filled with tasks and they wouldn't see each other until evening meal. Even with so short an absence, there would be warm greetings between them. There would be banter about their day and she was always pleased to see her father.

Rory and Finley sat proud upon their steeds, facing each other. Neither spoke nor smiled. Instead, Rory merely nodded his head in acknowledgment to his father. If she hadn't been watching so closely, even that would have been missed.

The years hadn't been kind to Lochmore's Chief. Time and weather grooved his face and the extra weight softened what once had been a warrior's form. Still, she saw a proud man who ruled his clan, but who also looked and felt the years he lived and the few seasons he had left.

Her father, though aged, had kept his vitality. Lochmore's Chief was indeed older. But it wasn't only his health, she noticed. She also saw a father surreptitiously observe his son who rode beside him.

Just a slight tilting of his head, not enough to be obvious to Rory, who didn't look pleased to be returning home. If anything, her husband's bearing was even more rigid, his expression impenetrable.

Adjusting the reins in her hands for the umpteenth time, she loosened her grip once more. It wasn't her lack of riding experience that caused her unease with the horse. It was that she shouldn't be witness to anything this private. Except there was nowhere else she could ride without causing more scrutiny. Enough wondering eyes were on her as it was. Even Rory spared her a glance.

Did he gauge to see about her welfare or if she turned to retreat? They'd shared intimacies and some of their past; they were married, but she still didn't fully understand her husband though she wanted to. He was a man who was loyal to his friend, to his clan. And there were moments it seemed he was loyal to her. Allowing her to use the information and heal Paiden. To confront Mary, to accept her judgement.

Last night he'd held her. The drumming of his fingers along her shoulder blades after they'd made love told her that he'd found some contentedness in what they were creating.

Now there was no hint of the Rory she was beginning to know. Fearsome. Daunting. He hadn't even been this formidable or cold when he'd first entered the McCrieff courtyard. Except for that one moment in their bedroom when he'd opened the box, he'd given no indication that this was the man he was at his home.

He said his family was complicated; this was more than complications. Her heart ached to see Rory like this. Among his family once again, he looked alone. She received no answers as to why from their surroundings either.

Lochmores and McCrieffs together. Though there was still a firm divide, a few attempted conversing. Tentative. Wariness. But this was so much more than what was possible a mere fortnight ago.

Such a turn of events. She hadn't believed, after what Hamish had attempted, that the McCrieffs and the Lochmores would ever ally with each other. Some of the animosity had also been eased by Paiden's recovery and easy manner.

So true as well, Hamish's lack of recovery took the sting out of revenge. The Chief was ravaged with the illness now. There was nothing left to take of him. As for Mary, she had been manipulated in Hamish's games and was forgiven, but even so...

Even with Ailsa's marriage and Rory and her father holding council together, there was an underlying animosity that lingered. Old bitter memories and Hamish's plots had made true cuts in her clan.

It hurt her in a way she didn't think possible. Her clan...wasn't her clan. If they didn't accept Rory as her husband as she was beginning to accept him, then what would be their future or their children's?

Because as much opposition as Rory incurred on

McCrieff land, it didn't appear as if Rory was accepted by his family on Lochmore land either. She didn't dare guess what his life had been like before now. Rory and his father barely spoke. And for her?

Chief Lochmore hadn't acknowledged her until Rory almost demanded him to. Not overtly, and the words exchanged were outwardly polite, but there was a rigidity between the father and son she didn't understand. It was as if Rory expected Finley to criticise or disparage her. He hadn't. Rory's father only nodded his head, as she had seen Rory do to him, then ignored her.

As a child, she'd been told of the Great Feud. She mourned, as a child would mourn, for the baby who died. If that child had lived, he might have changed the fate of the clans. Changed the fate of her and Rory. Now they were married, but in a clan that might be divided for ever.

And yet if they hadn't taken the step to marry, there'd be no chance at all for the clans to make amends, to stop the skirmishes and reeving and killing.

It seemed that Rory was of the same mind. Yet, while she wanted to improve clan relations because she was a healer, Rory wanted to repair clan relations as if he had something to prove.

Which hadn't made any sense at all until now. What did he, a born leader, have to prove? Once the shock of Hamish's deceit had sunk in, he'd risen to the challenge and worked tirelessly with her father. People naturally followed him.

Seeing how deep McCrieff deceit went, he could have just thrown it all aside. Left her and her clan to return to Lochmores. Being married to his enemy clan didn't mean he would be loyal and yet he had stayed. He had spent time with her father, with the McCrieffs. Spent time with Mary until she was certain of his forgiveness.

Spent time with her. Over the past fortnight, she'd shared with him her herbal plantings. She'd brought Rhona's journals up to their room to show him the beautiful illustrations. Her sisters were no longer kept away from him and, no matter what tricks were played, he still could tell them apart.

With Paiden recovering, his humour shining through, she saw a different side to Rory. He laughed more and sometimes seemed content with her family. Her father's good nature, her sisters' constant chatter, the fact she now willingly went in to his arms.

How could she not, when he revealed more every day? Which made her ask herself again, could she love him? And was it possible Rory cared for her?

Too soon to ask such questions, not with her secret still being kept. Yet, as much guilt as she felt for not telling him of Rhona's story she also felt that Rory, too, held something back, something she didn't quite understand, something dark that drove him.

She wondered what it was. Now following the two Lochmores through the sparse line of trees and seeing the village and Lochmore Castle loom over the next hill, she was beginning to understand. Beginning to know her husband and it broke her heart. His wasn't a cheerful home.

On and on they wove through the village; greetings were called out and sheep scattered. The village was immaculate. Not a roof needed thatching, the roads were

well gravelled and cobbled. Ditches ran along the side
for refuse and run off. She'd longed for such industry
and efficiency for McCrieff, but Hamish's greed and
missed opportunities depleted coffers that would have
been better spent on the Clan than on one bitter man
who was never satisfied.

Adjusting her skirts from the saddle, she gazed at
the dark flock of birds dotting the clear blue sky. Here
she was riding to her husband's home to visit with his
family and she was wishing a man on his death bed ill
will. If the Fates could hear her now, they'd heap more
mischief upon her. She carried enough grief and burden
without welcoming any more and she crossed herself to
ward off any ill omens heading their way.

Closer to the castle's gates and the roads narrowed.
Rory no longer rode side by side with his father, who
surged on ahead to visit with tenants who ran up to
greet him. It allowed her to move closer to Rory since
her own palfrey was so much smaller.

'Are you well?' Rory asked.

The ride across their lands had been brief; Rory
couldn't mean her physical health, but she wasn't prepared to tell him her turbulent thoughts and worries.
'Your home is very impressive, Rory.'

The gentle light in his gaze dimmed and he turned
his head to look at everything but his home. 'It's a…
fine roof and walls. My mother ensured it so.'

The immense stone castle and stronghold ahead was
more than stone and mortar. It had been built to impress and intimidate. She knew his parents' marriage
had been arranged for political and financial gain. Per-

haps those types of alliances were what created such lofty residences. Her own parents had married for love.

It was not lost on her that her own marriage had been arranged and, though she had done it from her heart, Rory had, in truth, done it for political gain. Seeing Lochmore's castle, she wondered if he would want his own home to intimidate and impress. Perhaps he envisaged no warmth between himself and the children she prayed they'd have.

After all this time, she had shared her past and they had addressed the present, but by some tacit agreement they had not talked of the future. Maybe she was cowardly; maybe they both knew how tenuous their future was.

Maybe he didn't imagine a future. She didn't know. Her husband was complex and intriguing, and just when she thought she understood him, she realised she didn't. 'You must have spent hours playing hide and seek in such rooms.'

Foolish remark. Rory was an only child. While no castle room could be truly empty, he didn't have what she had with her own siblings—

'Not so much hide and seek,' he said, his tone contemplative. 'Among us boys, it was more hide and hide some more. Paiden was a handful even then, forever stealing loaves of bread or, if it was available, dried fruit from the kitchens. You'd think on such lands, we'd easily get lost.'

'Except you were clever.'

'We had some good places. Behind the chapel, the crypt, the…passageway to the water. But I think he liked getting caught.'

'That's because he liked bragging of his prowess. Does no good to steal precious dessert when he can't take credit for it.'

A laugh burst through Rory's clenched lips 'So true! It all makes sense now why I couldn't talk him into any place else to hide.'

'So we know why he did it, but what did you do?'

Rory's easy smile fell. 'Oh, I stole, lied and cheated, but never something so innocent as dessert.'

This was different. Rory wasn't telling her of mischievous antics he pursued for fun. She was a healer and everything in her knew when someone hurt.

'What did you do to get caught?'

'I, unlike my faithful companion, wasn't so foolish as to get caught.' He snapped his reins once and his horse increased its pace. 'Come, we're holding up the men and my father has already made it through the gates.'

Without looking back, Rory urged his horse on ahead and she did the same. She'd let him go and she'd keep letting him go. He'd given her a glimpse of his past, at least one full of Paiden before he avoided further talking of the past.

There was more to settle between them, but some wounds didn't heal right away. Some injuries took time. She'd seen Rory avoid personal questions before. She knew he did it now to find the strength and drive he cloaked himself in before he went through the gates that surrounded Lochmore's castle, his home.

Though it made him more comfortable, letting him go was difficult for her. In fact, for one moment she wanted to call him back. To tell him she understood that as a child, he hadn't got caught because he was more intelligent than Paiden.

She knew by observing the cold nod to his father, by feeling the frigid air coming off Lochmore's stone. She was already guessing why he never was caught in that childhood game.

He hadn't got caught because no one had bothered to search for him.

Chapter Seventeen

It was not as if Rory had never intended to return to Lochmore land. The castles were not so far apart that he'd be excused from ever returning and, in truth, he meant to make Lochmore Castle his familial home.

He'd wanted to wait to make the journey, however, because of Paiden, because of the uneasiness of clan relations. More importantly, he'd wanted to wait until his marriage to Ailsa was on firmer ground. Over the last few days, he'd discovered more and more about his green-eyed wife. How tirelessly she worked at her craft, how caring and beloved she was among her people.

Beautiful. Intelligent. A woman whose father held influence in the clan. She could have married anyone. Someone worthy of her care, of her heart. Someone who didn't want to marry her for political gain or to prove his worth to his clan. Someone who wasn't lying to her.

Though his father acted as if he was his son, Rory had never felt as if he was. Ailsa had told him how the McCrieff story of the Great Feud was different from

Lochmore's. He knew, dead certain, that his past was different than what was told as well.

So they'd travelled here, partly because he wanted to search the Lochmore records for his namesake. He felt that if it was proven the Great Feud was as McCrieffs believed it to be, then maybe, just maybe, it was time to talk to his mother, to face the past.

He'd barely dismounted when he saw his mother descending the stairs to greet his father. By the time he'd helped Ailsa dismount, they were already walking arm in arm.

Face the past; he also needed to address the present.

His parents had not come to the wedding, they had not sent the familial brooches, or any missives of concern regarding Paiden's poisoning. They knew everything and they'd acknowledged none of it.

Rory might believe he was not worthy of her, but Ailsa was a wife to be revered. He'd be damned if they didn't acknowledge her.

As his parents walked towards him and Ailsa, Rory was all too aware that he stood in the middle of the courtyard. This was his home, where he was raised, but the similarities comparing this moment to standing in the middle of the McCrieff courtyard were there as well.

Many eyes were upon them, many ears were listening. The McCrieffs who travelled with them were meant to be loyal to Ailsa and her father, but there were no guarantees. There were no swords or arrows out, but he could not shake the feeling he was facing some adversary.

His mother, clasping the arm of his father close, nodded. 'Rory, you've arrived in good time.'

His mother's voice washed over him. Gentle, calm. As a child, he always knew to find her either in the solar with needlepoint in her hands or overseeing the gardens.

With Ailsa by his side, he was struck with the differences between these women. Growing up, trying to emulate his father, he had thought to seek a wife similar in temperament to his mother. He had thought he wanted soft spoken. He married blunt of tongue. He had thought he wanted gentle. He married a woman who threatened him with shears.

By Fate or by God, he'd married a woman he couldn't have conceived existed and was quickly becoming everything to him.

'I have more than arrived in a timely matter, Mother. I have brought you my wife.'

But his mother's eyes were not on him. Instead, her scrutiny of Ailsa was as precise as it was with her needlepoint. He felt that if Ailsa were to reflect any flaw, his mother would rip her out. Gentle voice, but harsh gaze.

His father had barely acknowledged Ailsa. If his mother insulted her as well, there would be words.

'You're not tall,' Helen said.

Ailsa's eyebrows rose. 'None of my family are. My father's…rather wide, truthfully.'

'Your mother's side?'

'Very short as well,' Ailsa said, her voice a bit clipped. 'But my mother's ancestors weren't of clan interest. There could have been someone of height, but we don't know.'

'Theirs was not an arranged marriage?'

'Quite the opposite.'

Helen pointed to Ailsa and looked to Rory. 'She's the Tanist's daughter. No relation to Hamish?'

'None,' Ailsa said, her voice once again at ease though his mother was uncivil in asking him. But for Ailsa, she acted as if an answer to an unasked question had been revealed, which completely confounded him.

'My father's lineage is extensive and well known throughout the clan,' Ailsa continued. 'It was why he was so easily chosen as Tanist when Hamish became ill. My mother's side is too common for Hamish's revered and proud family. Not a drop of my blood is of any relation to Chief McCrieff.'

His mother released a choppy breath. 'Not that it matters, of course, but we've had difficulties with the McCrieffs and particularly your Chief.'

'Of course,' Ailsa said.

A slight smile and his mother eyed Ailsa nervously. 'You must be tired from your journey. Why don't I show you to your chambers?'

He wouldn't be separated from his wife, not this soon. 'The journey is not far. Perhaps we could have a repast instead and converse on how everyone has been? You have not enquired about Paiden.'

'We received your missives,' Finley pointed out.

'But I received none from you. Paiden was sick, dying.'

'Your wife is a healer,' Finley said.

Was everything so easy before? Lochmores had been strategic in their attainment of power and there had also been some minor clashes with other clans. But true adversity, he realised, that is what Lochmores lacked.

Mere weeks away from his family, from Lochmores.

Barely any time at all and Rory knew it was more than enough to come to more conclusions.

As he stood facing his father, he realised his attempts to emulate Finley, Chief of Lochmore, wasn't his true path. He'd seen what Hamish's desire to gain power and control had done to his clan. He'd witnessed Frederick's attempts to make amends and wrench his own control to save it.

The kind of discord Frederick faced was nothing his father had ever had to face. Deception. Deceit. Murder. He was grateful it was Ailsa, with her shears and direct ways, who stood by his side.

'Ailsa can't perform miracles. We couldn't wake him. He's not here now because he's weak and couldn't make the journey even in the back of a cart.'

'Well, it's all over now,' Helen interjected. 'Let's not talk of McCrieff matters, shall we?'

His mother never wanted to argue or discuss any conflict, but her dismissal was out of character. He knew she cared for Paiden, so something else was going on here. And he felt he knew at least part of it. Ailsa hadn't acted insulted by the odd questioning about height and who her father was, but Rory was offended on her behalf.

'Ailsa is my wife, Mother. McCrieffs are her clan and so by our marriage am I part of hers. Talking of them should be accepted.'

'Son,' Finley said.

The rebuke might have meant something to him once. Discipline. Keeping his silence and never disappointing. This has been his life up until the fateful day he crossed to McCrieff lands. Not any more. He'd faced life threatening conflicts over the last fortnight and preferred directness over niceties now.

Helen tapped his father's arm. 'Rory, I apologise if there's been offence at my questions. I'm merely enquiring since we know so little about her.'

His mother was talking around Ailsa who for reasons he didn't understand was keeping her courtesy and her blunt tongue silent. 'You weren't asking about her, but asking of her ancestors. You were enquiring whether she was worthy of a Lochmore.'

'Rory,' Ailsa said.

Discourteous, but he'd risk sounding like a petulant child if it meant from this day forward his wife was treated with more respect.

His mother paled. 'That's not why I asked, I— You care for her.'

Ailsa stiffened at his side, but he wouldn't shirk the truth. 'Very much, so I won't have talk of McCrieffs versus Lochmores. Not in my presence.'

'There's something...' Helen said. 'You have to believe I wish only—'

Whatever it was she wanted to tell him, it wouldn't be here. Not in the courtyard, not before he talked to his wife. Once the truth was said, it couldn't be unsaid. He needed to prepare her. He needed to face his past.

All his life he'd felt like an outsider. Now that he was married, he refused for his wife to be made to feel the same way. For once, he'd face his past and see if he could find the truth, or at the very least, talk to his wife about his belief.

'I know what I believe, Mother, and it isn't here.'

Placing his hand on Ailsa's back, Rory turned them towards the chapel.

'Rory, wait!' Helen called.

Never again.

Rory didn't shorten his strides and Ailsa was almost running by his side. 'Where are we going?'

'I need to see a priest.'

Ailsa said nothing more. Rory's storm-ridden countenance didn't invite conversation, nor did she want any now. After Helen's questioning, and Rory's response, Ailsa had much to consider.

Helen's questions were very specific. She was concerned Rory might have married Hamish's family and then Rory defended her.

Soon, maybe now, she needed to tell Rory of Rhona's story. She shouldn't, couldn't lie to him any more. Especially now that Rory, in front of his parents, and Lochmore's Chief, confessed his feelings for her.

Ailsa kept her silence when they entered the chapel, kept it again as he talked to the well-intentioned priest. Agreed with him when he asked for privacy and so followed as he carried the chest full of cartularies to a quieter location.

Now they were here in Lochmore's crypt. Her family's burial tomb wasn't as fine as this. Cool and damp, but the stones were clean, the markers shining. Even dead, the Lochmores held more wealth than a McCrieff. For this crypt wasn't uncomfortable or unlit and the wooden benches, now covered with quilts, afforded a place to put the chest carrying the parchments and for them both to sit comfortably.

Only it wasn't the differences between McCrieffs and Lochmores she wanted to explore. It was Rory and his expressions as he…one by one…carefully opened the familial cartularies.

'What are you searching for?' she said.

A tightening of his jaw, a shake of his head. 'Ailsa, there is something I feel I need to tell you, but I—'

He read the document in his hand, his expression one of incredulity.

'You were right,' he said, looking back up at her. 'Lochmore's nephew who tried to stop the fight and was stabbed by the McCrieff was named John.' Rory handed her the journal. 'How could the story of the Great Feud possibly have been switched to my name?'

She read the inscription, the print so small it hurt her eyes. The entire document was written in this way. It was an effective way to preserve parchment and to keep secrets hidden.

'You keep forgetting that, according to McCrieffs, the baby who died was always named Rory.'

Rory picked up another journal, glanced at it and set it down. 'Ah, yes, so it's good I married a McCrieff to remind me.'

One mystery solved. Rory was named after the baby in the Great Feud. According to McCrieffs, Rory was named after a McCrieff baby. Ailsa was beginning to understand why.

Clever Helen. It was her way of telling Rory who he was without telling him.

All her life, Rhona carried the secret of the boy who was secretly born of Hamish and carried away from McCrieff land. She now knew Rory was that baby and that Helen knew it. So she had named him after a Mc-Crieff child.

Helen knew the secret, Ailsa also knew this secret. Of all the women Rory could have married, he had married her.

Was now the time to tell her husband? Her whole life, she spoke exactly how she felt. Now she wished she had gained other ways of conversing so that she could soften her words. Even as she clenched and unclenched her fingers, she suspected there would never be a way to soften these words.

'Rory, who named you?' she said.

'My mother.' Rory walked to a table, sat and within moments drummed his fingers against it. Each finger was deliberate as if he was counting points or facts in his head. 'I can't see my father... I would assume my mother. But my name isn't important and not the reason I came here.

'I want you to know, I'm not usually curt with my family, it's just...you can't help but notice my relationship isn't the same as yours with your family. My mother's recent questions aside, she's usually polite and kind. I need to talk to you about my father.'

She wanted to ask him so many questions regarding his relationship with his father, but now wasn't the time. 'I think we need to talk of your name,' she said firmly.

He opened his mouth to protest, but she pleaded with him. She needed to tell him the truth, or what she knew was the truth. He'd defended and announced he cared for her, she couldn't deceive him any more.

At his nod, she continued. 'With your name, do you

think…' Ailsa swallowed '…do you think your mother was telling you something?'

'I used to believe that she was telling me that she wanted me to be like the nephew who tried to stop the fight between the McCrieffs and Lochmores.' He stopped his drumming. 'You think she named me after the baby?'

She pointed to the journals. 'Look. Your records say the baby's name was Rory. Could she have read the journals?'

He'd always thought his mother would have been better placed in an Abbey than as a warrior's wife. Would she have read the old tomes? With certainty. 'Even if she did know the name of the nephew was John and not Rory, what could she possibly be telling me by naming me Rory?'

'How long have you known you were left-handed?' she said.

Rory closed his eyes on those soft, but precise words and ran his hand through his hair. His left hand. What his mother named him, he didn't care. He felt her affection for him, faint and removed though it was. It was his father for whom he feared he didn't belong. 'When I entered the lists with my father and held up my wooden sword to face him.'

'So you were a mere child. Five, six?' Ailsa said. 'I followed Rhona the moment I could walk without assistance. She always smelled so good to me. The lavender and mint, the rosemary and smoke.

'I watched what she did and listened to the many questions she asked. She was very observant so I learned to be as well. The McCrieff clan is large, but with healing you notice family traits and patterns. How red hair crops up in one family and deafness in another. How most families use their right hands and a few, a rare few, use their left.

'Your mother or father don't use their left hands, do they?'

'Ailsa,' he choked out. He hadn't been this vulnerable, this exposed, this weak since he was a babe. He'd trained and fought and educated himself so it would never come to pass and this woman, his wife, felled him. He'd always thought his height was the reason he didn't match his father—was it his left hand as well? If so, did Ailsa know Finley wasn't his father? 'You're as direct as ever, lass.'

'At what point will you admit you like my directness?'

He'd never get used to it, but he was realising he'd always want her words. Even now when she was hammering her point until he couldn't avoid the truth. He had no defence against it since he wasn't all that sure he wanted to hide the truth from her any more.

Still, he couldn't lie to her. Since childhood he'd been kept at a distance and all he could do was study his father. The way he walked, talked, ate, trained. His mannerisms as he ordered his edicts, the way he turned his back if Rory entered the room. His father used his right hand for everything, so Rory taught himself to use his right hand as well.

'Neither my father nor my mother used their left hands,' he said.

'You force yourself to use your right. It's amazing what you can do with your right hand, Rory, but I can't help but think how much greater you'd be with your left.'

'I'm better,' he said. Since the time he was a child, with a wooden sword in his hand, he'd known he was different. 'I fight Paiden with my left. Ever up for a challenge, he asks me to. He asked me to train him with his left as well, thinking it was something I taught myself, but…he was terrible at it. *Is* terrible at it.

'So terrible at it, I did some observing myself and tried to find someone else in my clan with a strong left hand.'

'There was no one?'

He shook his head.

'It's rare.'

He glanced over at his very direct wife, who looked mired in indecision and doubt. 'What are you not telling me?'

She fingered the straps of her healing pouch.

'You won't like what I have to say.'

'Ailsa, we're already talking about me not being the legitimate son of Finley, Chief of Lochmore. That I have no political right to marry you.'

'Now who is blunt?' She smiled, but it was weak, her gaze softening at every moment.

'You want more? I married you falsely. I'm not the man you were meant to marry. I'm a liar and a thief, and I've known it from the moment my father stared at that blunt sword in my left hand and demanded I change it. You deserve an honest man. Your clan deserves a true leader.'

'They deserve you.'

'Did you know I wasn't Finley's son when you married me?'

'I was guessing.'

He was glad he was sitting. 'You married me anyway. Here all this time… I came here not to find out my name, I came here to see if the records held who my true father was. Do you realise, I've been guessing all these years? I wanted you to know my fears.

'My mother is kind, but I don't think she knows what to do with me. My father, however, never approved of me. When I was young, I thought it was because of trivial things like using my left hand. As I got older, taller, broader, I began to believe my mother wasn't faithful. That I wasn't my father's son and that is why he never approved of me.

'Do you know what a relief it is, that you guessed as well? It shows I'm not unfounded in my wonderings. Do you know what that—? You've gone pale. Is this too much?'

She shook her head, her eyes pleading with him, and any relief he felt was gone. 'What aren't you telling me?'

'Left-handedness is rare, Rory,' she said slowly, almost quietly. 'But I know one person in McCrieff clan with it.'

'McCrieff clan! You're saying the man my mother laid with wasn't a Lochmore?' The drumming of his fingers wasn't enough to centre him. Instead, he slapped the table with his entire hand. 'And so that is why I was named after a McCrieff baby?'

McCrieffs and Lochmores tightly bordered each other. They also reeved and fought and squabbled for years. If he had another father, the likelihood he came from McCrieffs was the most possible. 'So I'm partially a McCrieff, that might be good fortune. Unless my father is yours?'

'No.'

Something alarming flooded through him. Ailsa looked ready to flee, fight, or be sick. She'd hadn't looked like that when he held a sword point to her neck. Her pale expression and the pain in those wide eyes were enough for him to stand before she said the rest.

'You know who my father is,' he said. 'Who my mother laid with that wasn't Finley, Chief of Lochmore?'

'Rory, there's more to this—'

'Tell me!'

'It's Hamish,' she whispered.

One moment, two, until staying and standing wasn't an option any more. Before he'd even thought he was halfway up the stairs and out the door.

Chapter Eighteen

How did he get to this point? Rory asked himself. He'd stormed out of the crypt, hatred and betrayal roaring through him, and hadn't seen his mother until she'd grabbed his arm.

His mother was quiet and reserved, but her fingers had gripped and yanked him out of his thoughts of the past and into the present.

When he'd registered who it was, he'd waited for her to speak. He was more than ready to hear her. Hamish his father, if true, meant he didn't know this woman at all. Had she lain with him willingly or had he raped her?

But she gave a gentle smile and, once she'd held his attention, released his arm and requested he attend evening meal.

Of all the subjects to talk of, food wasn't one of them. Shock must have been his response for he'd agreed.

Before another was spoken, she'd left. For one terrible moment, he'd wanted to run after her, to demand answers. But out in the open wasn't the time.

Food. Evening meal. This was the first night the Lochmores could greet and congratulate him and his wife. For Ailsa's sake, regardless of what was disclosed and shared in that crypt, he'd be there.

So that's how he got here, sitting at the High Table, wondering if leeks with rosemary would be served. But there were no leeks and nothing was garnished or flavoured with rosemary. A tiny detail that meant the missives he'd sent to home had been read.

And he sat next to his wife. She'd arrived in the Hall, stunning him with her beauty. Her hair was plaited and intricately bound and she wore a soft green gown, the fabric so fine it shone. To show respect both for Lochmores and McCrieffs she had taken pains with her appearance.

He wished he had done the same, but he hadn't returned to his rooms. Needing to gain control of his thoughts, he couldn't go where he would be found. Instead, he'd wandered the village outskirts. A few tenants greeted him, but most stayed away.

Hamish was his father? He was a hated man, who'd decided to poison his own clansmen. Finley had met with him many times and never trusted him.

Did Finley know that Hamish was his father? That would explain why he was so hard on him. It also explained that, no matter how hard he endeavoured, he would never be what Finley wanted.

However, Finley must truly love his mother. For the life of him, and all the secrets kept, he could not see her being unfaithful to Finley. It fit that Hamish would have raped her. At that thought, a blinding rage swept through Rory. He already hated Hamish for what he'd done to Paiden, what he'd attempted to do to Frederick.

Rory wanted to confront him, kill him. He wanted to rail against himself for having Hamish's tainted blood running through his veins. And yet, Finley acknowledged Rory as his son. Whether she was unfaithful or raped, the babe she carried—him—had been acknowledged as a Lochmore.

Well, somewhat acknowledged. The Lochmore brooches had not been presented at their wedding. But was that because Hamish was his father, or because of Ailsa?

Ailsa, who talked to his clansmen and was kind to the servants who congratulated them on their nuptials. His wife, who gave furtive glances his way to see how he fared.

Another bite of food he didn't taste, another drink of ale that didn't quench his thirst.

His wife knew he was Hamish's son and had married him. How had she known and what had she meant by saying there was more? What more could there be? It had been foolish of him to run out of that room. But he'd been avoiding the past for so long, it'd become habit.

He wasn't angry at her for not telling him. They barely knew each other and, worse, she'd told him of her guesses before he'd told his. No, he wasn't angry, but so much more had to be said.

Right now, he couldn't talk, couldn't demonstrate his affection and care for her. But he wanted to. Very much. And something of his desire must have shown in his eyes because the worried wariness faded from her expression and she gifted him with a true smile. One he wanted to echo back.

His eyes on Ailsa, and all that she meant to him, Rory caught the glimpse of his mother motioning a servant to gather her chair so she could stand. His father stayed seated. An unnatural quiet fell upon the Hall as it became clear his mother was about to address the clan. Not once in all his history had his mother done so. He didn't think her soft voice could even carry across the long expanse.

Except it did as she gave her thanks and greetings to the clan. Then, with another nod, a flat clasped box was placed on the table in front of his mother. Rory knew that box, recognised it. Out of all the revelations today, this box's appearance might have stunned him the most.

'I wanted to wait until you arrived to give these to you,' his mother whispered to him. 'I want to say so much more and will soon. But for now, I hope this will be a start.' Turning to the clan, his mother said further words and the clansmen grew quieter to hear every one of them. He grew quiet and he knew Ailsa heard every word as well.

His mother was addressing the clan, but also addressing Ailsa and him. As a married couple. As husband and wife. She hadn't made it to the wedding and wanted to give them a token of her love and appreciation for their marriage. She even teased that it took him long enough. By doing so, his mother was honouring him in a way that went beyond the vows he and Ailsa shared.

Raped by Hamish, that was the only conclusion he could come to. Did his mother see Hamish every time she looked at him? Was that why she cloistered herself away with needlepoint and flowers?

Whatever had occurred, his mother, in front of family and clan, demonstrated with words and now deed the affection she had for him.

A click of the box clasp and a slow measured opening of the lid. Inside, cushioned by velvet were two silver brooches of two varied sizes with an intricate pattern: A thrift flower surrounded by a solid circle and a pair of swords that crossed over the centre. Eternal. For ever. Scotland's strength, his clan's endurance. They were as beautiful and awe inspiring as he remembered.

'This day we celebrate the joining of Rory to Ailsa.' His mother took the smaller brooch out of the box and turned to Ailsa, who stood.

Rory stood as well. When he gently clasped Ailsa's hand, he felt her trembling and knew she was as affected as he was. Her face was part wonder and wistfulness. His mother's expression was one of tearful joy. Never could he have known that this was waiting for him upon returning home.

'With this brooch, Clan Lochmore celebrates the joining of Rory and Ailsa. Celebrates the joining of families.' His mother's hands were firm and sure as she pinned the brooch on his wife's gown just above her heart. 'As a mother, I celebrate and welcome my new daughter.'

When his mother turned to him, his father stood, passed her the second brooch and placed his hand on her shoulder. The significance wasn't lost on Rory. The brooch was the same that his father had worn on his wedding day and his father before him.

'With this brooch, your father and I celebrate your marriage. May it endure through the storms ahead and flourish underneath Scotland's brilliant sunshine.' The brooch stuck within his thicker tunic and she gave a quick exasperated sigh.

The sound was incongruous for his mother, as was his father's quick quip. 'It always did that,' his father whispered and her mother's slight frown turned grateful.

'With this brooch,' she continued in a louder voice, 'once I get it pinned, I, as a mother, welcome my son's wife and my son's children. Which, if he knows what's good for him, will be here very soon.'

Laughter ringing in the hall, his heart filling with familial love, Rory could not fully comprehend the fortuitous turn in his life. When the brooch was finally secured, his mother gave a hard pat on the brooch, then she rubbed and patted over his heart…a gesture she'd made since he was a babe.

When he'd opened the box at McCrieff Castle and seen only the necklace and ring, he'd never thought to be honoured with these brooches. Ailsa seemed to understand the significance for she clasped his hand that much tighter. The way he felt, he was one beating heart away from sweeping his wife into his arms and carrying her off to their room, to their future.

For now, he would keep holding his wife's hand.

Chapter Nineteen

'Do you want more to drink? There's wine,' Finley said.

Rory didn't want any wine. What he wanted was to spend time with his wife, to ask questions of his mother, but his father had requested a meeting with him. So with a look to his wife and mother who were engaged in conversation, he closed the door to Chief Lochmore's private chamber.

'I am full of food and ale and couldn't possibly imbibe further,' Rory said. He still couldn't believe his mother had presented the family brooches in front of the clan. It would be many years, if more than that, where he wouldn't feel this choking of emotions as she'd pinned it to Ailsa's gown.

Ailsa. His mother. He wanted to be anywhere else but here in his father's chambers. No, not his father. The few times Finley had discussed any matters with him had ended in Rory storming away or raising his sword. When he was younger, he'd picked fights with Paiden just to release the anger and frustration. The unending feeling of unworthiness.

Now he knew Finley wasn't his father. Hamish was. The irony of it all was if Hamish's blood ran through his veins, he truly was unworthy.

'Why am I here?' Rory asked. 'You have never invited me before.'

Finley walked further into the room, to the table laden with drink and even more food. 'You've changed much in the days you've been away.'

'There was much to change me.'

Finley lifted the flagon, smelled it, set it down. 'I didn't expect it, your marrying a McCrieff.'

He didn't want to talk of his marriage with this man who had always found fault. Ailsa didn't deserve his scrutiny. 'I was talking more of the fact that Paiden was poisoned.'

'Did you ever discover by whom?'

Since he had full expectation that he and Frederick would address the division in McCrieff clan, Rory intended to keep his silence regarding Mary and Hamish. 'There is still time.'

Finley lifted the other flagon and poured it. 'I would never have sent you there if I'd known. It caused your mother much worry.'

If Hamish was his father…ah, and that was why his mother questioned Ailsa regarding her height. 'There was no need for her concern.'

Finley shot him a sharp look. 'Then why marry? Did they hold a sword to your back? Your missive was without detail.'

'You've met Ailsa and the McCrieff clansmen who travelled with us—do you think them so vile as to force a marriage?' To various degrees, McCrieff hatred ran through every vein of a true Lochmore. His father, however, had remained diplomatic, despite his hatred of them. He tended to administer justice when necessary or negotiate with King Edward when the opportunity presented itself.

Finley held his goblet in both hands and peered into its depths. 'I sent you there to secure Lochmore's claim to the borderlands. You were there to fight, win, subdue.'

His father wasn't looking at him, and he sounded almost…concerned. 'What would it matter if I married her instead of raising my sword? In the end, I did secure the lands for the Clan.'

Finley's head whipped up at that. 'I wouldn't want it at the expense of my son.'

Rory took a step back and another. His father had been acting differently all through the evening. Nothing untoward and nothing he could say with certainty, but Finley wasn't as he had been before Rory had left that fateful day.

Or maybe he was acquiring his wife's observational skills and this was how his father had always been. A little worn, his shoulders stooping, his face carrying deep grooves and his eyes a little less clear. It wasn't only his physical appearance, but his mannerisms, too, that were softened.

Flummoxed at these observations, Rory couldn't make sense of the invitation or his father's statement. So he listened to the tone of the words; he watched Finley's almost imploring look. Then he answered the truth. 'I would not have married her if there wasn't some possibility of compatibility.'

Finley's wondering gaze fixed then and he took a swift drink. Rory had seen this expression on his father many times when he faced a merchant, a representative of the King…when clansmen lied at court.

It didn't affect Rory. He had quaked before his father since he was a child and, after facing the McCrieffs and almost losing his friend, he was past attempting to gain this man's approval.

'There is something you're not telling me,' Finley asked.

There was much he wasn't telling this man, but the tone of Finley's voice still wasn't one of command. So he answered another truth. 'There were no swords, but Ailsa did have shears.'

Finley let out a startled laugh and swept his arm to indicate the laden table behind him. 'Come now, then, a drink for celebration!'

His mother pinning the brooches, now this. His father never celebrated anything. Not a birth or a death. In turn, he didn't know how to celebrate with this man. First because of the conflict of the past and now with the discovery of his true parentage.

'I'll wait on that drink.'

'Still?' Finley said. 'Even after today spent in the crypt and then in the outer village?'

Long used to people and their gossip regarding the Chief's son, Rory didn't question his father's knowledge of his whereabouts.

Finley took another drink, then lowered the goblet only to become quiet. For once, Rory didn't say anything to fill that silence. Instead, he merely observed. He might not be this man's son, but he recognised that he took most of his mannerisms from him, including the quirk to his lips, the tilting of his head. The direct look.

Finley looked away first. 'I want you to know, I've had a good marriage. Arranged, like your own, but out of everything in this life, I never regretted being wedded to your mother.'

Experience told him Finley spoke as a chief, not as a father. 'If you want to know if I regret marrying Ailsa, I don't.'

Finley nodded. 'Your wife is nothing like your mother, though I never suspected you'd end with a gentle soul. I didn't know one such as she existed for you.'

At the truth of Finley's words, Rory let out the breath he'd been holding since the door closed. 'She's surprising.'

His father made some sound like a chuckle or agreement and Rory felt the need to sit. This was the most he'd ever talked to his father. The times before that, when they had conversed, it had usually been about how he'd failed at matters of politics and training. But his wife…he didn't intend to fail her.

'I am well wed.'

'Marriage isn't easy,' Finley said, flourishing the goblet at him, 'and you have no training.'

'She'll teach me soon enough…just as Mother has taught you.'

Definitely a laugh from his father now. Rory pulled out a too-small chair from the even smaller table and rejected both. It was probably better to stand on unsteady legs.

Finley tipped back his cup. 'Marriage often requires unexpected sacrifices. Compromises that you can't conceive of ever making, but are the right decision for your wife. For you. Yet, sometimes I've wondered if the decisions we made were the right decisions for everyone else.'

'Maybe I will have that drink.' Striding to the side table, Rory swiped the flagon of ale and poured it. He understood sacrifice and compromise. He'd negotiated everything the moment he met Ailsa. What he didn't understand was this conversation with Finley. Once the goblet was clasped tight in his fist, he leaned against the nearest wall.

Finley pointed at him. 'You always did that as a child.'

'Did what?'

'Lean or slouch against walls. Never could understand if you were simply trying to intimidate your friends who weren't as tall as you or—'

'The furniture in this house never fit me.'

Finley's brows suddenly dropped and Rory wanted to take back the words.

If he desired to announce that he didn't belong here, he couldn't have said it any clearer. The chairs didn't fit him here because his body wasn't like the other Lochmores. It was the truth, but why at a time of truce like this, did he have to reveal it? He couldn't even blame the extra ale since he hadn't taken a sip.

'You never said,' Finley said.

He still wasn't saying. At least not what he truly meant because he hadn't gained the benefit of his wife's blunt tongue. However, he had gained his wife's company and was beginning to understand a different way of looking at the things around him.

Maybe that was why after he'd come through the gates of Lochmore Castle, he'd forced himself to see his home differently, or maybe it was because his mother presented the family brooches. Maybe…just maybe… he'd listened enough to Ailsa's healing words and deeds.

Because instead of his first reaction, that of blame or of pointing out all the times he'd wished Finley had given him guidance, he found himself wanting to ease his father's frowns.

'It never seemed important,' Rory said. 'For the most part it suited me fine.' Relaxing against the wall, Rory realised the truth of those words. Growing up, he'd known no different than small chairs and smaller beds. It was only now he thought of changing things, of making his life different.

'When you get to my age, you realise what's important.' Finley set down his goblet. 'I was gone for many months during the time you were born. Such a surprise upon my return. Such…joy upon your mother's face. From that moment on, I wanted life here at Lochmore to be more than fine. I wanted everything for you and so I made you my own. Do you understand me?'

Rory shook his head, knowing he couldn't be hearing this conversation correctly.

'Truly? Even after you gathered the family cartularies and read them in the crypt? Even though you've been to McCrieff land, met McCrieffs?'

Shock had Rory bracing hard against the wall. His father, Finley, was telling him he knew he wasn't his father. That sacrifices and compromises were made.

'You need to know that your mother and I only ever wanted what was best for you,' Finley continued. 'One of my favourite memories was when you refused that vile green broth your mother kept trying to get you to drink. No matter what she did, every time she held the cup to you, you knocked it out of her hands. You were stubborn and fierce from the very beginning, just like us.

'From your expression, you're probably wondering how I noticed these things since I was never around.'

Rory cleared his throat. 'You are Lochmore's Chief and have many responsibilities.'

Finley made some non-committal sound. 'I raised you as my father did me. His…harshness suited *me* fine. Made me strong enough to support and care for this clan and your mother. So when I became a father, I did the same to you.'

All those years ignored with no praise and only criticism. 'I thought—'

'That I didn't care for you? How could I not? You're my son.'

Locking his knees, Rory wanted to sit now and damn the chairs if they didn't fit him.

'I called you my son the moment I saw you. When I gazed at my wife's adoring face as she held you, I claimed you. I was fiercely proud of you then and am even more so now.'

His father's words brought more questions to Rory's mind, but he did hold one absolute certainty. 'I'm proud to be your son.'

Chapter Twenty

'It's dark in here,' Ailsa's voice drifted around the cold stones. 'How did you find your way down the stairs without breaking your leg?'

'I lit a torch,' Rory answered.

'I can see that, but it's hardly enough to read by if that's what you're intending to do in the crypt in the middle of the night.' She turned the corner and he could see her. Her arms crossed over her body against the cool night air. 'Ah, you're not reading. No journals, just a flagon of ale.'

Rory slid over on the bench. 'With no goblet because I couldn't drink any more. But my father insisted on celebrating, so I couldn't leave the room without it in my hand.'

Carefully, she sat next to him. 'Celebrating?'

Ailsa was dressed in a simple gown with loose laces and plain slippers on her feet. But nothing was plain or simple about her red hair which was unbound and waving about her shoulders and down her back. Aside from the ceremonial brooch she'd pinned on her gown, she looked ready for bed and utterly beautiful. Especially when she curled her feet under her as she sat.

'Would you believe, as large as I am, my father can drink more than me? So he celebrated, while I became unsteady on my feet. How did you know I'd be here?'

'You didn't come to bed and the Hall is still full.' She played with the blanket that was on the bench. 'I thought you may have wanted quiet again. But it's an odd place...being in a crypt.'

He had no defence to that.

'Why didn't you come to bed?' she asked.

'I thought maybe to read the journals, but they had been put away and I didn't want to disturb anyone this late at night.'

'Then you stayed?'

He nodded.

'Because you're angry with me?'

Rory grabbed a corner of the blanket and pulled it over them. 'I feel many things, but anger isn't one of them. Neither is blame, accusations nor betrayal.'

'You—you stormed out of here when I tried to talk to you.' She seemed surprised by the blanket, so he tucked it under her legs, the movements bringing them closer, his body already responding despite the location, his exhaustion and conflicting thoughts. He knew it would always be thus with his wife, and he looked forward to it.

'Since then I walked around until we ate. Did you not see the mud on my shoes?'

'I see the mud on them now, as well as the splatters up your breeches.'

He looked like a beggar next to his wife. 'I should

have taken care with my appearance. You are very beautiful tonight.'

She shifted against him as if his compliment affected her. 'A significant walk, then. I informed you your entire existence is a lie and that I've known it from the beginning and now you're sharing a blanket.'

'It was quite a walk. There was even an unexpected rut or two I stepped into which put all matters into perspective.' He adjusted his arm so she could rest her head more comfortably. 'I wasn't angry that you told me. I was angry that my father was—is—Hamish. You need to know I already suspected I wasn't Finley's child. After all, I'm much larger than Finley and there was always a matter of…aloofness with my parents. I never felt as though I was a Lochmore. I knew this when I married you.'

Ailsa didn't want to be right that Rory had spent his childhood alone. How could a child ever feel as though he didn't belong? 'Did you think I'd be angry that you didn't tell me?'

'You have every right to be. This matter is grave. I am McCrieff's child. An illegitimate baby, but all the same his only issue. What's more, I wished Hamish dead. For what he did to Paiden, for what he tried to do to the rest of my clan, to *you*. If he wasn't on his deathbed, I would demand an honour match with my own father. What kind of child wants to kill his own father?'

Ailsa couldn't bear the pain in his voice. 'Don't. Don't torture yourself. Hamish is not a man anyone could tolerate. He was a harsh ruler and the older he became the more punishing his edicts. My father and myself were often his favourites to exact some petty revenge upon. If I hadn't wanted to preserve life or my soul…'

'And this man's my father.'

Curse her choice of words. 'Please don't grant him another thought!'

'I can't talk to Hamish, even if I wanted to,' he continued as if he didn't hear her. 'Anything I say won't erase the past, and if I said anything at all he'd know I was his son. And that can never be.' A drumming of his fingers as if, despite his words, he wondered what that conversation would be. 'Useless to even think about these matters, he's already passing.'

'Blame me. If I had told you earlier—'

'When I arrived? That's an impossible circumstance. I'll need to talk to my mother,' Rory whispered.

'What will that solve?' She started to pull away, but Rory held her fast and she let him. 'Even if you do know with certainty, it changes nothing.'

'Changes nothing? Hamish, my father, must have raped her. She must feel some resentment for me. I came down here to read the journals, to see if there's any evidence of my lineage. If we are to go forward, this is something that must not be known.'

She closed her eyes for two breaths. Closed them a bit more before she said, 'Rory, I have to tell you something.'

'There's more?' he said quietly. 'I may not like these crypt talks with you, my wife.'

She was the bearer of too great a truth not to tell him, though she feared she would hurt him even more. With every bit of her body and soul, she didn't want to hurt him more.

'A clan has secrets and as the healer and midwife Rhona knew of them. When she was ill, she wasn't lucid. She'd beg me to cool her fever with fire. She'd talked nonsense, and mumble details of clan members. Sometimes she'd look right through me and tell me such matters of healing import, I'd get cross with her for not telling me sooner.

'I'd call them ramblings, but they weren't. They were more gasps of memory between the pain. Everything she said was audibly clear, I just didn't understand the context of what she said. Not until I met you.'

'Me?' Rory asked. 'There's more to tell about my birth, isn't there.'

'There's more,' she said. Curse her small stature for her body didn't feel substantial enough to hold this man. Still, she wrapped herself as tightly about him as she could. Pressed every bit of who she was against him so he'd know she was there.

'It can't be worse than my mother raped and my father... Hamish.'

At the sounds of his hesitancy, Ailsa would have ripped her heart out and pressed that directly to his if she could have. Even so, the way she felt, the hammering of her heart and the feel of his... There was no easy way to speak of this.

'You mother wasn't raped,' she said. 'Because Helen isn't your mother.'

She felt Rory's heart stop for one beat, his breath stop for two more before he suddenly released both with force. It shook her as well as him. Then he slowly extricated himself from her. It was his fingers first, each lift bringing the fresh chilly air to her skin. Then one limb before another. His legs next before he shifted his body.

Until the only thing that held them together was the blanket he had over their laps. It was still tucked around her, but was slowly unravelling from him and slipping to the floor. She watched it slide down his leg, watched how he didn't grab to secure it to him. She hoped, wished, whatever happened next that what they'd found with each other wouldn't be so easily lost.

'Finley is not my father,' he said. 'And now Helen is not my mother.'

Free from his hold, Ailsa carefully adjusted herself so that she could face him. What she saw were shadows and light flickering against his dark hair and darker eyes, and she silently cursed the lone torch he'd lit. What needed to be said next was very important and she wanted to see him! 'You're not questioning me.'

'After everything, the one certainty I have is that *nothing* is certain.'

Was that true for them as well? She took courage from the fact that he was still in the room with her, that he hadn't left the bench and was instead turned towards her so they could face each other.

'If Helen is not my mother,' he said after another moment. 'what are you trying to tell me? Am I to assume the McCrieff healer knew that Helen wasn't my mother? That she talked of this? Did she…?' He swallowed. 'Did others hear her?'

'*No one*. I was the only one to care for her. Sometimes she'd look at me, grip my arm as if demanding I know things I hadn't before. Sometimes she told me matters she didn't mean to tell me. When it started, I never left the room. I didn't want her burned or tortured in her old age if her words were heard by the wrong ears. She was hurting enough as it was and I made sure no one was there when she was awake. Others took the linens and the waste pots and came and brought me food.'

'It was just you,' he whispered as if he couldn't believe it to be true.

'She wasn't ill long, death came fast. It was just me.' Why were they having these conversations in a crypt? No one had died, but Rory was as pale as a ghost and she knew, in a way, she was killing his childhood.

'You knew,' he said and repeated, 'You—knew. How did she?'

'Hamish is a callous man, who used everyone around him. And he liked young girls the most. As far as I know, none of them consented. Rhona helped one of these girls, Marion, a girl from the McNeill clan, with the pregnancy and the birthing. Rhona, who must have been very young herself, said Marion's body barely recovered from his use and the birthing was too much.'

'Marion was my mother…and she died.'

There was no reason to repeat the truth, especially when it was cruel. 'Rhona said her hatred kept her alive until the baby was birthed. Rhona admired hatred and especially anyone that hated Hamish. Because she was weak or maybe because Hamish didn't care enough to know, Rhona was able to keep the pregnancy hidden.'

'Rhona gave the baby, me, to my parents? How did they know?'

'Rhona only told me that the baby was given away to a woman who couldn't conceive, who was desperate.

There was no husband there. But I always dreamed the baby went to a cheerful home.'

'That baby's name was…is… Rory.' He grabbed the blanket and returned it to his lap. 'That's why you say my name the way you do.'

'Though I suspected, I didn't know the baby was you. What are the chances?' She pulled a corner of the blanket, grateful when she felt the tug as he firmly held on to the bit that was half across his lap. 'My entire life has been formed by the Lochmores. From the tales of the Great Feud and how I felt about the baby who died, how I felt when Magnus died. Both of those led me to become a healer, something I am blessed to be.

'But learning of Rhona's story and Hamish's baby given away, and then you, Rory, arriving in the Mc-Crieff courtyard. When I married you, I couldn't be sure whether I did it for the clan, for myself, or because of the stories that were told to me.'

'For yourself?'

'I was…attracted to you.'

'I see,' he said, a quirk to his mouth that she loved. 'That is good.'

She more than lifted her lips, she smiled. She could feel it from ear to ear. It *was* good. They were good. Flickering torchlight, cold crypt in the middle of spring, dead of night, but they were good. She'd make certain it would happen despite the doubt in his eyes. It would be up to her to erase that doubt, though it would be far more difficult than simply pouring a tincture. Rory's past and present would require time and healing. For now, she'd show him she cared, that she loved. 'In the end, right now, I know it doesn't matter why I married you, I'm simply glad I did.'

Rory had no happy answer to Ailsa's bright smile or sweet words. 'I as well, my wife, but it is not as simple as that.'

But he wanted it to be simple. He wanted it to be easy, because if it was, he'd be able to take the woman who sat next him into his arms. Hold her, comfort her, love her. Not stare helplessly into her wide green eyes shimmering with tears in the flickering light of the torch. Not tell her she shouldn't, couldn't, be glad they married.

'I'm a McCrieff!' he said. 'With many people not wanting me ruling McCrieffs. Except, even if I am a McCrieff, I don't deserve to rule. Who would want Hamish's issue ruling the McCrieffs when he has done such harm?'

'I want you to. My father most certainly does. There isn't anyone worthier than you.'

Her words were no balm. 'My blood's a McCrieff, and not just anyone's, but a man hated by many. And you were wrong. My mother *was* raped. He raped Marion.'

She tightened her lips. 'Do you think you're capable of that?'

He wanted to say no, but that would be a lie. 'On our wedding night, I demanded you to undress so that I could consummate a marriage I had no intention of honouring.'

'That's not proof. In fact, I remember I made demands of my own.'

'Because you're fierce and intelligent. If you had been any other woman—'

'You think if I had been weak, I would have just laid there on the bed for you? You can't know women then. Remember, I wanted you before we were married, I wanted you that night.'

'I seduced you and instead of honouring our marriage, I left. I left so that if there was a chance I needed to annul the marriage, I could take it.'

Wide green eyes no longer reflecting love or warmth. Just resignation on the truth of his words. 'You were hurting; Paiden had just collapsed. You're *not* Hamish.'

'You can't prove to me otherwise. Even before Paiden, I married you so that I'd make my own future. I married you because I wanted my own power and control. I didn't care about the consequences or saving lives. I didn't care.'

'You wanted to talk to me alone. There was no reason for you to do so unless you wanted to see if we were compatible. If you didn't care, you would have simply agreed to my father's proposal.' Her expression resolute, she continued, 'It doesn't matter. I wouldn't have married you if I didn't see the man you truly are and, since we're confessing it all, I wouldn't have let you control me.'

So true. So fortunate he married this woman. Fortunate for him, but maybe not so for her. 'I held a sword to your neck. I know your strength and it far outstrips mine. But still, I'm not worthy of it.' He felt restless. In the past, when he found himself in these confrontations, he'd storm off, lean against a wall, pick a fight with Paiden. But here he sat near Ailsa and he was loath to move from her side. 'My family isn't worthy.'

'Your family are the Lochmores. You have a mother and a father here.'

There wasn't enough air to fill his lungs, and not enough words for him to convey the connections he shared with his wife. He felt as if they were as tangled as her gown's laces. Impossible to unravel and still so very necessary.

'Finley knows that I'm not his son,' he said. 'Whether he knows I'm Hamish's or whether he's talked to Helen about my birth, I don't know. What I do know is that he loves my mother so very deeply that when she presented me to him, he claimed me.'

'And that is why you're worthy.'

'Because a woman hated the man who raped her, so she denied him an heir by agreeing to give me away? Because I was stolen away in the middle of the night and given to a family who didn't know quite what to do with me once they had me?

'Helen, my mother, if you so insist, presented me to her own husband and pretended I was his. What does that make me? A lie.'

'They love you. Your mother gave you the brooches. They're significant, aren't they? They were what you were expecting back at McCrieff Castle, not the necklace and the ring.'

'They are very significant. When they weren't in the chest sent to us after our wedding, I was certain our marriage would fail. These brooches that we wear now have been handed down for generations. They're symbolic.'

'And sentimental,' she said reaching across their laps to take his hand. 'I watched your parents and the love they had for them. So Helen waited to give them to you and me in front of all the clan. Your father didn't stop her. They love you, they've claimed you. Your mother gave you to this clan. You're a Lochmore.'

In that truth, and with Ailsa's touch, he was defeated. Though deceit and lies surrounded them, there was still this connection with Ailsa, still this future that showed some hope. This marriage, and wife, he desperately wanted. The brooches they wore shouted to all the world their love and devotion for each other. There was hope.

Turning his hand so he now held hers, he gently pulled her across the bench to hold her that much tighter in his arms.

Ailsa welcomed her husband's warmth and for a long time she simply welcomed this one moment between them. She told him everything in his life was something else and yet he appeared to be accepting it. Accepting her.

'You believe me,' she said quietly.

'You asked me that before,' he answered and she felt his words through his chest. 'I believed *in* you even when I didn't know you. You have too much honesty and truth about you, Ailsa, it's startling and wondrous. I can't understand it all. I do believe if you weren't holding me right now, I'd spout words and feelings about my lack of deservedness. But I don't think you'll let me talk of that much longer.'

'You do deserve it,' she said. 'You have my heart, Rory.'

She felt him shake his head. 'You married me thinking I was the legitimate Lochmore heir. You gave your heart to a different man.'

'I gave it to a man I barely knew, but I knew enough

before I married you. Remember how observant I am. Merely a few hours in your company revealed to me your noble and honest heart. So it was very easy to give you mine.'

Slow steady heartbeats and breaths, she concentrated on that instead of the tension threading through him and, after a time, it eased. 'You give me words of love when everything between us has fallen apart.'

'Nothing is falling apart. I wouldn't love a man who wasn't deserving of it.' She hesitated to talk more now there was peace between them, but it had to be said. 'Now that a Lochmore and a McCrieff are wed, when our fathers die there is a chance for the clans to unite.'

He stiffened underneath her. 'I won't make promises I can't keep.'

She tilted her head and he bowed his. 'We're married, you won't talk of it?'

'We shouldn't. It's treason with the Chiefs still living and, with the Great Feud, though we know other facts now, our clans won't put much merit on our marriage.' A muscle in his jaw tightened, released. 'Has this been your purpose all along, Ailsa, to have the clans unite?'

'I told you why I married you. I simply want to stop bloodshed. I will never forget Magnus or all the other injuries I and Rhona have healed over the years.'

'Uniting our clans isn't possible. After everything we've been through, you know that.'

She did, but something in her held on to that bright future. 'And you? If you're Chief you gain—'

'No,' he interrupted. 'I've given up on control and power a long time ago, lass. Around the time you brandished your shears at me. Perhaps earlier than that, when I spied that hair of yours in the doorway.'

That moment was like that for her as well. 'I like that doorway, I like our courtyard, but if we're to stay together, I have accepted it won't be at McCrieff Castle.'

'Clever wife. You may be smarter than me as well.'

'Now you admit it.' She laughed softly.

'I have thought on this, too. I know we need to return to your clan, but your clan is divided and, as long as I am a Lochmore, our children will be considered Lochmores. It wouldn't be safe there. Even here, I am thinking of building tunnels to safeguard ourselves.'

She couldn't think of their homes as not being safe, but since she met Rory it was the truth.

'You wouldn't mind living here, Ailsa? My father and Mother are older, Lochmore Castle is large. There are plenty of storerooms to hang herbs.'

She liked the image of that. 'I think my father would expect me to be with you.'

'Yes, but you're not just a daughter of a Tanist, you're also the McCrieff healer.'

'I have trained Hannah and to some degree Mary. With more training, they will be enough when I am not there.'

Rory took her hand and placed it on the brooch still attached to his tunic. The longer he did so, the more she felt the weight of the smaller, but identical one that was pinned to her breast. These pins were significant. Indicating they were both of the Lochmore clan, that they were married, that they were a pair never to be separated. For the rest of her life, she knew she'd wear that brooch.

'We're married, we're…united. I can't help, but…'
She just couldn't say it.

'Hope,' he said. 'I do, too, but outside this crypt, we
can't talk of it. It's too dangerous.'

'What do we do, then?'

'In the meantime, we support both Lochmores and
McCrieffs. When their purposes collide, we can inter-
vene or remain silent. We can't choose loyalties no matter how much we may agree or disagree.'

Else they'd tear their own marriage apart. 'They
won't make us choose loyalties.'

'There are many uncertainties ahead and I won't
make promises,' Rory continued. 'Yet I can promise
you I'll try to mend the divide between our families.'

That was what she saw that day in the courtyard.
A man defying his enemies, his past, demanding a
brighter future. That was who she fell in love with as
he walked the village with her father, greeted and gave
advice when needed.

Tears spiked her eyes, she swallowed hard and
gripped her hand over his. 'Even if this is only the beginning between us and even if it only *stays* the beginning
between our clans, I'm humbled it's us. I'm overjoyed
to be here now, with you, at this beginning of the clans
uniting no matter how long it will take. I'm beside myself that by Fates or God, I was fortunate enough to
share this time with you.' She drew in a breath. 'I love
you, Rory. I have for a very long time.'

'Though I've known you for mere weeks?'

'I knew the story of your birth,' she said. 'All these
last years since Rhona's death and being subjected to
Hamish's taunts, you were my glimmer of hope. Late

at night, I liked knowing there was a boy out there who survived that man's bitterness. In my dreams, I dreamed of you, Rory, and how grateful I was that you, by your very birth, spited him. That you, a mere babe, were a victory against him and all men like him.

'In my dreams, Rory, I loved you even then. I think this is how it was meant to be.'

'What is?'

'Our wedding night, when you touched me, you said for me to let go. Because that was how it was meant to be.'

'I didn't mean those words the way—'

'I know how you meant them, but I will interpret them differently now.'

'You are clever, but to bring up that wedding night now? I still haven't recovered from not touching you.'

He exhaled roughly and adjusted his body on the narrow bench. She made sure they didn't lose the blanket or his hold on her. 'You wanted me?'

'Very much. But not as much as I do now. My love for you is too large for this body, Ailsa,' he said. 'Too considerable for this room, for this country, for the stars above us. And far, far too encompassing to merely be chained to my short life. I'm bursting with it and it only keeps expanding. I can only believe it's larger than me and us. That it always existed across clans and time. It was here in the past and will be far beyond us in the future.'

She rested her head on his chest again and enjoyed that for every breath he took she felt it, too. Felt the strength of his body and of his heart. This man fought and won against his past. With her by his side, she was determined with the battles ahead he wouldn't fight alone again.

'You've gone quiet,' he said. 'Do you know what I'm saying? Am I saying enough?'

'I didn't know you could talk so directly,' she said. He rubbed her back with his left hand. She felt his fingers as they started their drumming caress that she never wanted to end. 'I rather like it. Are you seeing the benefits of my bluntness?'

'Don't be giving me a difficult time now. Not when I'm telling you I love you. If I could have known you existed like you did me, I would have loved you always, too.'

There wasn't enough wonder in all the world. It was impossible that such fortune existed to bring this man into her life. How could she have guessed that this man would one day be hers? However, if he said one more word of love, she'd cry and wouldn't stop. His love might be bursting out of him, but hers was as well and she had more words to say.

'I like that you didn't know I existed,' she said. 'I like that you know me now.'

'Why?'

'So I can keep surprising you.' He huffed and she felt that laughter and surprise through her body as well. She loved the way he filled her world, her heart, simply by being alive.

'You're unexpected, my wife.'

'That I am. Can we retire to our chambers now? I don't mind our discussions, my husband, but I do mind where we keep having them.'

Another soft chuckle before he stood and she took

his hand to help her rise. Slowly, he wrapped the blanket around her shoulders before tucking her within the cradle of his arm. As they ascended the stairs, he grabbed the lone torch which shone like a beacon.

'Ailsa? I intend for us to keep surprising each other.'

'Always,' she promised.

Epilogue
by Janice Preston

Lochmore Castle—October 1849

Lady Flora McNeill stood on the front step of Lochmore Castle, her thoughts anchored in the past. The weather was mild for the time of year, warm enough for her to wear a simple shawl over her black gown. A soft breeze whispered across the inner bailey and she could hear the gentle shushing of the waves on the rocks below the castle, which was built on a high, rocky promontory.

She did not hear her husband of one year, Lachlan, come outside until two strong arms wrapped around her from behind. She leaned back into his hard body, glanced down and smiled as his hands caressed her swollen belly. Their first baby was due in January and they could not wait to be parents.

'Well, Flora.' Lachlan's breath tickled her ear. 'Today is the day you've been waiting for.'

Flora's gaze flicked across the inner bailey to the old chapel, visible above the perimeter wall. In there,

Ailsa Lochmore, née McCrieff, lay waiting to be reunited with her beloved husband, Rory. Dead for over five hundred years, they had been entombed together in the stone crypt under the old chapel until their double tomb had been desecrated during a raid on Lochmore Castle in the sixteenth century and Rory Lochmore's remains had been spirited away. But the secret of why that particular body had been taken, and by whom, had gradually been lost in the mists of time until almost nobody knew what had happened, let alone remembered details of whose body was missing and, more importantly, why.

Flora would never forget the day when—aged twelve and in a fit of pique at her father for constantly dismissing her ideas because she was a mere girl—she had gone exploring in the forbidden Great Tower at her childhood home, Castle McCrieff. She could still feel the wave of grief, anger and aloneness that had battered her when she found the skeleton she now knew belonged to Rory Lochmore. She'd had a similar experience, just last year, when she discovered the empty tomb next to Ailsa's, down in that cold, lonely crypt.

The desolation. The isolation. The *longing*.

'I still cannot believe that Benneit finally managed to persuade Father to allow Rory to come home.' Flora turned within the circle of Lachlan's arms and smiled up into his dark eyes. 'Or that the McCrieff lairds kept that secret all these years.'

The story had been passed down through generations of McCrieff Chiefs—mortal enemies of the Lochmore clan through most of those centuries—to the present incumbent, Flora's father, Lord Aberwyld. It was only three months ago that Flora had finally summoned the courage to challenge her father about the identity of the skeleton hidden at the top of the Great Tower and the link between that and the empty tomb in the old chapel at Lochmore Castle, now her marital home. Father had admitted the skeleton was that of Rory Lochmore and that it had been stolen by members of the McCrieff clan during a raid but, true to character, he had stubbornly insisted Rory—sired by a McCrieff and not a Lochmore—must remain at Castle McCrieff.

'Well, none of us would be any the wiser had you not found Rory in the first place, and then refused to take "no" for an answer.' Lachlan dropped a kiss on Flora's nose. 'So it's all thanks to you. I am proud of you for challenging your father...and continuing to challenge him.'

'I could not ignore it—I knew when I first found Rory that I must do something to put things right, but I had no idea what that might be. It was only once I knew their story that I understood—Rory and Ailsa *need* to be together.'

Flora trusted her instincts. They had never let her down and that same sixth sense had driven her to keep insisting to her father that the lovers—for she knew instinctively that theirs had been a great passion—must be reunited.

It had taken the current Chief of the Lochmores— Benneit, Duke of Lochmore—to finally bring Father to his senses.

'If what you tell us of Rory Lochmore's paternity is true, Aberwyld,' he had said, 'then there is no justification for keeping his remains at Castle McCrieff. Think about it—is there not as much McCrieff blood running through the Lochmores as through the McCrieffs? We are, like it or not, one clan. And do not forget that Ailsa, too, was a McCrieff. You must do right by them.'

Father had huffed and puffed but, in the end, he'd had to concede that there was no reason to keep Rory and Ailsa apart in this modern day and age, not now that the centuries-old feud was firmly behind the two clans.

The distinctive rumble of wheels along the track that led up through ancient woodland to the castle alerted Flora to the approach of a vehicle.

'They're coming!'

Their friends and neighbours, Benneit and Joane—former owners of Lochmore Castle—were joining them for the reunion of Rory and Ailsa.

'Drummond.' Lachlan turned to summon their butler. 'Would you please ask our guests to join us? It's time.'

Flora's father and brother had arrived last night, escorting Rory's newly enshrouded remains, and the former Lochmore Clan Chief now lay on a trestle table set up in the new chapel, awaiting Ailsa. The 'new' chapel adjoined the castle itself. It had been built in the sixteenth century by Ewan Lochmore, the Lochmore Chief at the time, who had decreed the old chapel in the outer bailey too vulnerable to attack after the raid on Rory's tomb.

Ewan Lochmore and his lady, Marguerite, had been the first occupants of the new chapel and were buried in a double tomb in the chapel itself, whereas subsequent Lochmores had been buried in the crypt below. It seemed fitting that Rory and Ailsa would now be reinterred in a double tomb constructed next to that of Ewan and Marguerite.

Flora fingered the disc-shaped silver brooch pinned to her shawl: Rory's brooch. Every curve and indent was achingly familiar—she had worn it and cared for it from the day she found Rory until the day she discovered the empty tomb in the old stone crypt and recognised the matching, smaller brooch on Ailsa's tomb.

The Lochmores' carriage drew to a halt and Benneit— tall, broad-shouldered and still straight-backed, despite being in his sixties—climbed from the carriage and turned to assist his Duchess, Joane—as petite and elegant as ever—to the ground. Flora and Joane had forged a strong friendship, despite the gap in their ages, and Flora eagerly greeted the couple.

'So,' said Joane, once they had all exchanged greetings. 'Is Rory home at last?'

'Yes. He is in the new chapel. But Ailsa is still in the crypt. I—I know it is silly, but I felt it was important for you and Benneit to be here when they are reunited.'

'We have come to trust those feelings of yours, Flora.' Benneit's voice held no hint of mockery, unlike Father, who made no secret of his scorn for Flora's intuitive streak. 'Besides…' Benneit paused as Father and Donald joined them at the bottom of the steps. The greetings over, he continued, 'Besides, there are four men here and I think it fitting that *we* escort Ailsa to her final resting place. Not servants, but Lochmores and McCrieffs. It's a shame Jamie is away, but Lachlan is an honorary member of both clans, is he not? So he will be a more-than-fitting substitute.'

Jamie was Benneit's son and heir by his first marriage. Lachlan smiled his appreciation of the Duke's words and Flora knew they would mean the world to him. All he had ever wanted was to belong. As the four men headed for the old chapel, Joane's large grey eyes settled on the brooch Flora wore. A frown creased her forehead.

'Is that Rory's brooch? I thought you left it with Ailsa's brooch on her tomb?'

Flora fingered its familiar surface again. 'I did. But we opened the tomb yesterday to prepare Ailsa and I... well, I pinned her own brooch to her shroud but...but...'

Sympathy and understanding shimmered in Joane's large grey eyes. 'You wanted to take care of it for Rory?'

'Yes. And, if I'm honest, I wanted to wear it one last time. I will pin it to his shroud before the new tomb is closed. But...last night...' She shrugged. 'I can't explain it. I could have pinned it on him last night, but it feels almost as though that should be the final act. When they are back together.'

Joane smiled. 'And that will be very soon.'

Lachlan, Benneit, Father and Donald, each holding one corner of a wooden board upon which Ailsa lay, now entered the inner bailey. Emotion constricted Flora's throat as she and Joane walked side by side to wait by the chapel door, ready to follow Ailsa inside.

'I am so pleased,' Joane said in a whisper, 'that we could all agree not to involve Pastor Collins in this. It feels right, somehow, to keep this informal and private.'

'I agree. It does feel right.'

Flora had dreaded their officious local pastor taking charge of what, to her, felt intensely personal. As it was, both Father and Benneit would speak a few words before Rory and Ailsa were covered and left in peace, together for eternity.

The chapel interior was dim and cool, lit by flickering torches set into old-fashioned wall sconces. A pair of trestles had been set ready for Ailsa and, for the first time, they could all see the couple side by side— Rory had been a big man, tall and broad, whereas Ailsa had been petite. A little like both Lachlan and Flora and Benneit and Joane, Flora realised. That observation made the couple feel even more real to her and she only half-listened as first Father, then Benneit, spoke of reuniting the couple and of laying them to rest.

Her memories were again in the past and she relived that swell of anguish and pain she had experienced when she first ventured into the crypt under the old chapel.

Always—the whisper had seemed to come from both within her and without, at the same time.

She blocked the men's voices, holding her conscious thoughts at bay…listening, seeking…

She heard nothing. But she felt…contentment. Peace. Deep and satisfying.

And she relaxed.

It was time.

Father and Benneit lifted Rory and placed him in the waiting tomb. Lachlan and Donald moved Ailsa. Flora stepped forward, fumbling to unpin Rory's brooch from her shawl. She stared down at the two shrouded bodies, lying side by side in the double tomb. Flora pressed her lips to the brooch, blessing the comfort it—and Rory—had afforded her over the years, then she bent over to fasten it to Rory's linen shroud. As ever, the stiff catch made it tricky to fasten, but she managed and then straightened with a sigh, placing her hand to the small of her back. Lachlan's arm slipped round her waist, supporting her.

'Are you all right?'

'Yes. It was merely the discomfort of stooping.'

The stone lid waited to be lifted in place. To cover Rory and Ailsa. The four men positioned themselves at each corner and bent to grasp it.

'Wait!'

They paused. Flora smiled self-consciously. 'Just one moment…one last thing…' She reached out one hand and placed it on Ailsa's brooch, pinned in the position of her heart. A gentle pat of reassurance? A farewell? And then she did the same for Rory, quickly, before stepping back and allowing the men to heave the stone lid into the air and settle it gently over the tomb. Flora read the carved inscription through blurred vision.

Here lie Rory Lochmore,
Chief of the Lochmore Clan,
and his lady, Ailsa.
Rest in Peace.

Rory and Ailsa—together again. Always.

There were no effigies on this tomb lid, but merely carvings depicting the two brooches. Flora blinked back her tears, for it made no sense to mourn two people who were long dead. They were happy tears, she decided, as she fetched the bundle of greenery she had deposited in the chapel earlier that morning—rosemary, for remembrance, and heather, the scent of home—and placed it on the tomb.

And, come the spring, she would bring thrift, for as long as it bloomed along the Lochmore cliffs.

That evening, after their guests had departed, Flora and Lachlan strolled arm in arm around the castle grounds as was their custom whenever the weather permitted. Tonight, Flora's head was full of Rory and Ailsa, hoping they were content now they were together again. She gazed up at the night sky above them, at the myriad stars that spangled the heavens, and she prayed that Rory and Ailsa were up there, somewhere, together. She prayed that their love truly was—as she believed—eternal.

A breeze picked up and it teased a few tresses out of Flora's coiffure. Lachlan caught them, sifting her hair through his fingers, before raising them to breathe in her scent.

'Have I ever told you,' he said, his voice husky, 'that I adore your hair?'

Flora smiled. Yes, he had. Often…especially when it was unbound for the night, waving about her shoulders and down her back in fiery red waves. She leaned closer to her beloved husband and raised her face for his kiss, but then tensed, her hand to her belly, as the babe made its presence felt.

'Are you all right?' Anxiety laced Lachlan's tone.

'Yes, of course. He just rolled over. And kicked me, for good measure.'

'Or *she*,' said Lachlan pointedly, always quick to re-assure Flora that he would be happy for his firstborn to be a girl. He knew her father's disappointment that his firstborn was a girl had marred Flora's childhood.

'Or she.' Flora stroked her swollen stomach lightly, her mind racing. 'Lachlan...when we discussed names...' They still had not decided on what they might call their baby. 'What would you think of—?'

One finger pressed against her lips, silencing her. Startled, she gazed wordlessly into Lachlan's smiling eyes.

'Rory if it's a boy; Ailsa if it's a girl?' His smile broadened. 'I love the names—they are perfect.'

Flora kissed his fingertip. 'They will never be forgotten again and we will make sure our children and our children's children remember them.'

'Always.'

* * * * *

If you enjoyed this story
be sure to read the other books in
The Lochmore Legacy miniseries

His Convenient Highland Bride
by Janice Preston

Unlaced by the Highland Duke
by Lara Temple

A Runaway Bride for the Highlander
by Elisabeth Hobbes